More praise for Lynda S. Robinson and *Murder at the Feast of Rejoicing*

"Good scholarship authenticates the historical setting; imagination provides the sense of danger and romance to make it come alive."
—*The New York Times Book Review*

"A triumphant blend of fact, fiction, and suspense . . . Brimming with authentic historical detail illuminating the intricacies of ancient Egyptian culture, this fascinating tale of court intrigue and familial squabbling will delight both history and mystery buffs."
—*Booklist*

"Robinson makes ancient Thebes come alive as she describes the personalities, clothing, golden jewelry, the intrigue, and the smells of the desert."
—*San Francisco Examiner*

"A typically trenchant backdating of the English country-house mystery, with all the mod cons of politics and psychology."
—*Kirkus Reviews*

By Lynda S. Robinson
Published by Ballantine Books:

MURDER IN THE PLACE OF ANUBIS
MURDER AT THE GOD'S GATE
MURDER AT THE FEAST OF REJOICING

MURDER
AT THE
FEAST OF
REJOICING

Lynda S. Robinson

Maxine Dozier

301 - 262 - 4277

BALLANTINE BOOKS • NEW YORK

This book contains an excerpt from the hardcover edition of *Eater of Souls* by Lynda S. Robinson. This excerpt has been set for this edition only and may not reflect the final content of the hardcover edition.

Copyright © 1996 by Lynda S. Robinson

Excerpt from *Eater of Souls* copyright © 1997 by Lynda S. Robinson

All rights reserved under International and Pan-American Copyright Conventions. Published in the United States of America by Ballantine Books, a division of Random House, Inc., New York, and distributed in Canada by Random House of Canada Limited, Toronto.

All the characters and events portrayed in this work are fictitious.

http://www.randomhouse.com

Library of Congress Catalog Card Number: 96-97154

ISBN: 0-345-39532-8

This edition published by arrangement with Walker and Company.

Manufactured in the United States of America

First Ballantine Books Edition: March 1997

10   9   8   7   6   5   4   3   2   1

A simple list of adjectives—kind, spiritual, selfless—fall short of describing a man I admire and who inspires my faith in people when it seems that inhumanity will prevail in this troubled world. This book is dedicated to Bill Pieper—who has brought love and brightness of spirit into my family—with my love and thanks.

Acknowledgments

▽

I would like to thank Dr. Charles van Siclen for reviewing this manuscript and for the wonderful discussions on such arcane topics as ancient Egyptian beards and chariot stability. His professionalism, kindness, and patience were much appreciated. Any errors remaining are mine.

In writing a novel set in ancient Egypt, there are many problems a writer must solve. For example, there are those long, incomprehensible proper names. Names of historical figures such as Tutankhamun or Ankhesenamun can't be changed, but for fictional characters I try to select shorter ones or use nicknames in order to facilitate readability. In addition, a writer can't use too many names beginning with the same letter without risking confusion. Such requirements reduce the pool of usable names from which I can choose. Also, many times scholars disagree about how information should be interpreted. Often on disputed points I select the interpretation that seems the most logical, the most probable, or the one that fits with the fictional world I've created in the Lord Meren series. This is where literary license comes in, and this is where the ex-anthropologist in me struggles with the writer.

Whatever the difficulties, the quality and the sheer amount of published information on ancient Egypt are overwhelming. I would like to express my gratitude to the many scholars whose works have helped me re-create ancient Egypt. They are too numerous to list here. Without them I couldn't make the world of Tutankhamun accessible to readers and tell the story of an amazing people who were, despite being separated from us by thousands of years, not so very different from us.

1

▽

Year Five of the Reign of the Pharaoh Tutankhamun

Kysen hadn't wanted to come to the ghost-ridden and deserted city of heretics. But what son of Egypt would dare refuse the wish of the living god, the Son of the Sun, Tutankhamun? He walked to the railing of the barge that had brought him to Horizon of Aten, leaned over the water, and listened to the slap of waves against the side of the vessel. The scribe who was taking down his letter stopped writing and waited patiently, rush pen twirling in his fingers. When Kysen failed to return, he shifted uneasily.

"Is something wrong, lord?"

"No . . . no, I don't think so. Did you hear anything?"

"No, lord."

"I thought I heard . . . I'm sure it's nothing." Since coming here he'd been on edge, certain that renegades, outlaws, or some chance intruder would penetrate the isolation so vital to their task.

Before him along the east bank of the Nile stretched a city once filled with courtiers, government officials, servants, and royalty. Its carefully planned avenues, so different from the snarled and twisted streets of older cities, were now empty—empty and silent. Even the men on the five barges moored in a line beside them were quiet.

Kysen brushed his hand over his brow. "It was nothing."

The scribe remained seated, awaiting orders. He was

one of Meren's. He would wait all night if Kysen ordered it.

The sun was setting, but there was still enough light to see the tiny figures of infantrymen standing guard on the cliffs to the east. Kysen glanced over his shoulder, and movement caught his eye. A charioteer drove over the rocky surface of the western desert, the first of a long, widely spaced line of vehicles that patrolled the environs of the city.

Inhabitants of nearby villages had been evicted, as had the royal mortuary priests and necropolis guards. Akhenaten's capital city was truly abandoned now, except for pharaoh's soldiers and the fleet of barges, freighters, and service ships. The whole of it had been Meren's idea.

The ships' crews were in fact royal sailors, the passengers royal agents assigned by the king and his advisers. Traveling in a group designed to look like a flotilla on an expedition to the south, Kysen and his companions affected to be traders of the temple estates of Ra. Traders of the temples, royal institutions, and great households plied the waters of the Nile and markets of Egypt, dealing in commodities both rare and abundant; Kysen's cargo was rare indeed.

After criminals had desecrated the tomb of Tutankhamun's heretic brother, the Pharaoh Akhenaten, the king had asked him to witness the secret removal of the bodies of Akhenaten and his queen, mother, and daughters from their houses of eternity. He was to aid in the execution of a plan to keep their bodies safe until new tombs could be provided, a task better suited to great generals and priests. Yet pharaoh had chosen him, and a few others whose faces weren't well known, for this sacred effort. It was almost finished.

Some of the grain and fine limestone on board had been put ashore to make way for the intended cargo. Kysen watched a pair of sailors carry a load of grain suspended from a pole on their shoulders. Timing their steps, they crossed the gangplank and stepped onto the bank.

Others on deck rearranged bags on top of a long, tarp-covered mound. The outer layer of this mound consisted of grain, precious Tura limestone, and natron. Had this expedition been real, the ships would have returned from the south carrying gold, incense trees, leopard skins, and, sitting on the mast, baboons. Catching his lower lip between his teeth, Kysen tried not to think of what lay beneath the tarps and ropes.

He would never forget his first sight of the most precious of all their cargo, lying in the royal tomb, bereft of outer shrines and draperies. Urged on by the commander of the expedition, he had stepped into the wavering torchlight as master craftsmen strained and grunted to lift a heavy weight. Into his vision emerged a wall of gold. Then Kysen realized why the craftsmen were straining so hard. The heretic's innermost coffin wasn't of wood overlaid with gold foil like the outer ones—it was of solid gold. He hadn't slept through a night since.

He was only the son of an artisan, of such humble origin that he would never have dared look into the eyes of pharaoh. It didn't matter that Lord Meren, pharaoh's most trusted confidential inquiry agent, had adopted him. Deep in his bones, to the innermost recesses of his ka, his soul, he was still a carpenter's unwanted son. And to look upon the body of a pharaoh in a coffin of gold made him want to sink to the dirt and hide his face in fear. He hadn't, though, for that would have disgraced his adopted father and his new, noble lineage.

So now he awaited the arrival of that golden coffin in the form of a man. A special place had been reserved for it inside the hollow mounds lined with the dismantled outer coffins of the king and the Great Royal Wife, Nefertiti. The queen had already been gently shoved into place. Other family members would be concealed on the accompanying barges, to be hidden in out-of-the-way places assigned by the vizier Ay. There they would await the preparation of eternal houses in the royal burying grounds at Thebes. At the moment Kysen was waiting for Nentowaref, called Nento.

Nento posed as the chief overseer of the expedition, head of the so-called traders of Ra. His real titles were numerous, as Kysen had discovered to his regret. Nento was most proud of the simple appellation Royal Scribe, but he also loved to be called Scribe of the Royal Treasury, Overseer of the Seal, Overseer of the Magazines of the Temple of Amunhotep III, and Bearer of Floral Offerings to Ra. His most important duty on this expedition was to serve as a makeshift priestly guardian to their royal charges.

Kysen couldn't remember any more of the honors Nento kept repeating to him. When they'd first set out, Kysen had thought Nento officious and suspected him of condescending to a youth of common blood. Then he realized that Nento was trying to impress him—because of Meren. Nento had many titles, but none of them included that of Friend of the King.

Leaning on the railing of the barge, Kysen gazed down the road that led from the quay to the city. He heard a low rumbling sound before he saw them. Slowly, their paces matching the beat of a drum, a line of men and oxen rolled a sledge over logs toward the barge. The cargo was padded with linen to protect it and disguise its true shape. It was covered by tarps lashed with ropes. Ahead of the sledge, glancing back every third step, rode Nento in a chariot manned by a driver. Nento couldn't drive a chariot without tripping both horses. Charioteers rode on all sides of the group around the sledge.

His eyes darting to the cliffs that formed an arched backdrop around the city, Kysen checked once more for a soldier out of place, a suspicious movement. He swept his gaze over the rooftops of the city, then across the river and over fields and the encroaching desert. Nothing but charioteers and infantry. What was he doing? More experienced men than he manned strategic posts and scanned the horizon for just such clues. All at once it seemed as if a stone slab lifted from his chest. He sucked in a long, deep breath.

He could envision the scene in the eastern desert now taking place, the disguised priests of the royal Theban necropolis huddled around the restored blockage of the royal tomb shaft, the application of thick plaster, an arm moving in wide, swirling circles. Then at last, and forever, a seal pressed into white dampness, the seal of the heretic royal cemetery. It would never be used again.

Soon the mortuary priests and guards would return to Horizon of Aten. Sacred rituals would resume. Patrols would sweep the desert, watching ceaselessly for intruders. Kysen wondered how long they would keep vigil over empty tombs.

Sighing, he walked back to the scribe and lowered himself to a camp stool beside the man. "Very well, we can begin."

He'd already accomplished the frightening task of actually addressing a letter to pharaoh. Writing to Meren would be easy. That is, it would be easy if he didn't have to disguise the real contents of the message.

"The usual salutation," Kysen said.

He paused while the scribe wrote "Tjerkerma," the name Kysen had adopted for this journey, Meren's name and titles, then "year five" followed by the month and the day in the waning season of Drought.

He cleared his throat. "Tjerkerma greets his lord, Meren, in life, prosperity, and health, in the favor of Amun, King of the Gods, of Ptah, of Toth, and all the gods and goddesses. May they bestow upon you love, cleverness, and favor." It had taken him years to master the formal letter-writing style.

"See! I am about to embark from the place, Refuge of Maat, upon the morn with good speed. All is in readiness. The cargo is disposed as you ordered. The traders sail to their appointed destinations."

In this prearranged phraseology, he let his father know that the royal family and their burial furniture would embark in the morning. With raised sails they would float south from Horizon of Aten in the direction of Thebes, and the journey would be a slow one. On this journey they would have to pass Thinis, ancient seat of his father's family, and Abydos, sacred city of the god Osiris. As he continued to dictate the letter, his guts began to twist like cobras in a basket.

He hated Meren's plan. Oh, not all of it. Only the part that risked his father's life, for that was what the effect of this design would be. Not three weeks earlier Meren had almost been killed. He wasn't fully recovered either from wounds received while thwarting the rebellion of one of his closest friends or grief at the friend's death. Yet in a few days he was going to do something that might place him in as great a danger as any he'd faced while tracking down that traitor.

His father was supposed to be resting in the country. Upon hearing of Meren's plan to go to the family seat, the estate of Baht, Kysen had tried to dissuade him. He knew Meren's family; visiting them wasn't the way to gain peace and solace, especially while dealing with this new, added burden. It exasperated Kysen that Meren still thought he would be able to rest when his plans came to fruition. No doubt he would continue to think so until the demons of chaos struck, as they were sure to do when he was dealing with the secrets of god kings.

* * *

Dawn had long given way to the furnace of early morning by the time Meren finished his correspondence. He left the cool shelter of the palace at the royal way station to brave the sun and the west wind that scoured its way across the valley. There were many such mooring places along the Nile, kept in readiness for times when pharaoh, his family, or favored friends might need to seek refuge during the long journey up- or downriver. This one was half a day's sail from his country home.

Followed by a pair of charioteers, Meren walked up the long ramp beside the palace. It led to a high brick platform on which his traveling household had set up their tents. A flight of stairs brought him to the walk on top of the defensive wall. Few sentries stood guard. He was going home to rest and wasn't on official duty. The walls had swarmed with guards a few days ago, when pharaoh passed on his way to Memphis.

As he gazed out at his ship, *Wings of Horus,* Meren furrowed his brow and rubbed the sun-disk scar on his inner wrist. Pharaoh had promised to confine himself to military exercises in the practice grounds near the Sphinx. Meren could only pray to the gods that no bandits chose to raid any nearby villages while the king was in the capital. If only the golden one hadn't asked Kysen to be his unofficial witness to the arrangements at Horizon of Aten. Meren had counted on his son's presence among the king's war band to distract Tutankhamun from his obsession with acquiring real battle experience.

Shaking his head, he drew his gaze back to the long, sleek lines of his ship. Painted black, with lines of red and gold, it outsailed every other craft on the river. Only a few ships in the king's fleet could match it. Not long ago, *Wings of Horus* had sped him on his way in pursuit of a traitor. Soon it would take him home. Already most of his household had removed there, including Nebamun, his physician, and Remi, Kysen's son. His aide, Abu, was in charge at his house in Thebes. As Meren indulged in a moment's admiration of his ship, another slid past it going north with the current, in the direction of Memphis.

Meren squinted at the vessel and motioned to the charioteers behind him. "Reia, Iry, isn't that Lord Paser's yacht?"

The two young charioteers joined him in peering at the slow-moving craft.

"Yellow with a green deck," Reia said.

Iry nodded. "Aye, lord, it's the same one we saw yesterday."

"And the day before," Meren said. He folded his arms over his chest. "Hmmm."

Paser was one of a faction at court that was growing around Prince Hunefer. Hunefer fancied himself better fit to advise pharaoh than the vizier Ay, who was the craftiest of statesmen. Although Hunefer's heart was far from clever, dissatisfied place-seekers had flocked to him in hopes of using the prince to topple Ay.

The question was, why would Paser follow Meren? He was only going home to rest and give the shoulder wounds Tanefer had given him a chance to heal. Everyone knew that. Everyone should know that.

Meren was considering the unlikely possibility that either Paser or Hunefer was more clever than he'd thought when Reia gave a startled exclamation and pointed to the canal that ran beside the royal mooring place.

"Look, lord!"

A skiff floated up to the bank and unloaded three figures, a man and two girls. The girls hopped ashore and started running. They vanished inside the way-station gates before their companion could tie off the skiff.

"What—why—?" Meren glanced at Reia, then at Iry.

Both men appeared expressionless, but he could see the corners of Reia's eyes crinkle in amusement.

Pressing his lips together, Meren composed himself. He would remain where he was and let his two youngest daughters find him. He wanted an explanation. They were supposed to be at home, waiting for him, not sailing on their own with but one servant to accompany them. He hadn't long to wait before the two came racing toward him across the platform, long tresses flying behind them.

The older girl, Bener, slowed as she approached, but Isis flew past her and flung herself into his arms.

"Father, Father, I knew we'd find you! Aren't I clever? I said you'd be delayed, and here you are. Bener thinks she's the chosen one of Toth, with her writing and her ciphering, but I'm the one who found you. It was my idea, and she thinks she's so quick-witted."

Meren hugged his youngest child, and as her words streamed over him, he forgot his resolution to be stern. He'd spent months maneuvering through vicious intrigues, guarding his every word for fear of betraying his king, keeping his senses alert for danger. Until now he hadn't known how great the strain had been.

Kysen and Tutankhamun had both warned him of his weariness. He hadn't listened. But as Isis babbled to him in her golden voice, the muscles in his neck and shoulders loosened. He'd lived with them twisted as tight as the rope of a wine press. The demons that jabbed spikes in his temples vanished.

Isis squeezed his neck. "I missed you, Father."

"And I you, my little goddess." He loosened his grip on Isis and looked over the top of her head at Bener, who had walked up to them sedately. She was standing with her arms at her sides, radiating composure. Was this his little girl, the one who climbed palms and stole pomegranates from the kitchen? She was almost as tall as Kysen.

He held out his arms. "Bener, my sweet."

To his consternation, she met his eyes, then glanced at Reia and Iry as if asking for their dismissal. Hoping his jaw hadn't fallen open, Meren waved the young men away. Once their backs were turned, Bener chuckled and floated into his arms.

Laying her head on his shoulder, she murmured, "I've missed you, Father, and I know you're angry at finding us here, but we had to warn you."

"It was my idea," Isis said as she tugged on his kilt.

Bener drifted out of his arms too soon, leaving him disturbed by her composure. She glanced down at her sister.

"I told you not to throw yourself at Father like a monkey. You're never dignified."

An argument erupted, but Meren was too busy studying his daughters to interfere. They had changed in the few months he'd left them in his sister's charge. Idut had warned him, but he hadn't taken her seriously. He should have. Bener was a woman now, tall and slender as a papyrus reed, but her arms and legs bore the elongated muscles of a leopard. Her face still held some of the plumpness of childhood, but she moved with the stateliness of a priestess and seemed to cultivate the demeanor of a woman three times her age. She reminded him of her great-grandmother.

And Isis. Isis frightened him, for she was beautiful, and he knew the dangers the world held for beautiful women. She had always been pretty, but she had matured into a double of her mother, who had always startled people by her resemblance to the fabulous Nefertiti. Once she left behind the immaturity of childhood, Isis would make men step on their tongues when she passed.

He was imagining trouble before it arose. He'd drive himself mad.

"Enough quarreling," he said quietly. His daughters

immediately broke off their exchange, which aroused his suspicions. "How did you get here, and why are you here? No, Isis, let Bener speak."

Bener exchanged a quick, apprehensive glance with her sister, wet her lips, and began. "It's not our fault."

"What isn't your fault?"

Again that quick glance.

"Remember your letter to Aunt announcing that you were coming home?" Bener asked. "Um, you see . . . That is, Aunt didn't pay attention to the part about how you wished your return to be private, just for us."

Isis burst in with an aggrieved tone. "I knew she'd ruin everything. We haven't seen you in months, and she's ruined everything."

"Father," Bener said, "Aunt has arranged a great feast of rejoicing in honor of your homecoming."

Meren leaned against the defensive wall at his back and scowled. "I made myself plain. I sent instructions."

"Aunt says she forgot," Bener said with a lift of her arched brows.

Isis kicked the wall with one sandaled foot. "My ass, she forgot."

"Isis!"

His youngest daughter lifted her delicate face to him, and he noted the way her fragile jaw set in place as if mortared there.

"She's ruined everything. How can we go sailing and fowling or even talk to you at all with all of *them* coming?"

Rubbing the back of his neck, Meren asked, "Who? Who has she invited?"

"Everyone," Isis said.

"Don't be a goose-wit," Bener replied. Isis ruined the elegance of her features by sticking out her tongue.

Meren fixed her with a stern glance. "Out with it."

Twirling a lock of hair around her fingers, Bener hesitated, then began a list that included Idut's son Imset, who was supposed to be studying in Memphis, Meren's cousin Sennefer and his wife Anhai, three of his uncles and their wives, and over a dozen of the local nobility. She didn't include the family retainers and supporters, tenants, and servants who would flock to this grand celebration.

"Oh, and I almost forgot, Great-Aunt Nebetta and Great-Uncle Hepu."

He kept his expression blank as she spoke the two names he least wanted to hear. Surprise made him vulnerable to the burn of old, festering hate. How could Idut have invited Nebetta and Hepu? She knew he never wanted to meet them this side of the netherworld. She knew what they'd done to their own son. His beloved cousin Djet was dead, and they had killed him as surely as if they had stuck a dagger in his heart.

No, don't think about it. Your anger will grow until it swallows you. This isn't the time. Old grief compounded new—the loss of his companion in war and in celebration, the bright, merry, traitorous Tanefer. Djet and Tanefer, both gone. He might forget Tanefer one day. He would never stop grieving for Djet. He used to tease Djet that they were each other's twin soul. They had learned to shoot the bow together, to hunt, to fish, to sail. He and Djet had shared those early discoveries of the body that every boy experiences. They had even spent the night in the haunted temple near Baht on a dare. Together they had braved that isolated valley, slept within the crumbling walls of the temple, and screamed when, in the blackest part of the night, the desert fiends howled down the valley on the wind.

"Father, is something wrong?" Bener asked.

He shook his head and smiled. "Naught is wrong, my

little geese. Now tell me how you got to the mooring place of pharaoh."

"That was my idea too," Isis said. "Uncle Ra was going home, and I begged him to take us this far."

"Ah," Meren said faintly.

He turned his back and gazed out over the river. Fishing boats, skiffs, barges, and pleasure craft sailed with and against the current. One of the yachts that floated past with its elongated rectangular sail unfurled to catch the north breeze had been his brother's. Ra hadn't even stopped. The reason was obvious to Meren, who knew his brother well, so well that from childhood he'd called the younger boy Ra after the powerful sun god. Ra didn't want to be there for Meren's grand return. He didn't want to see crowds rushing to the dock to greet Meren, didn't want to hear the cheers, hear Meren's name called, see countless backs bent in homage. And Ra knew how much his absence would hurt his older brother.

Meren's thoughts veered away from that idea. He had a more immediate problem. His private homecoming had been transformed into a grand celebration. Privacy was necessary, and not just for him and his daughters; quiet and calm, a sedate, unremarkable visit, these were conditions upon which he'd counted. If the feast interfered too much with his plans, he would have to leave his country house far sooner than he wished.

He hoped Isis wasn't right. He hoped his sister hadn't ruined everything. If she had, Meren was the one who was going to pay.

2

Late that afternoon Meren left the deckhouse at Bener's call and joined his daughters at the bow of *Wings of Horus*. He'd been contemplating the prospect of doing anything in secret with a house full of curious relatives. The elders still thought of him as barely old enough to leave off the sidelock of youth. Just as worrying was the certainty that the house would turn into a teeming anthill in which he would find no place to carry on private conversations with his daughters.

The ship sliced through the water, angling toward the east bank, and he caught sight of Baht, the country home of his family for countless generations. It lay between the narrow strip of cultivated fields and the desert that forever threatened to invade. Baht, like the houses of most noblemen, was a continually growing collection of family dwellings, servant's quarters, granaries, stables, cattle pens, and outbuildings surrounded by whitewashed walls and refuse heaps.

From this distance all he could see were the carefully tended trees his ancestors had planted, and through them, blank walls and roofs. Within, in the main house, lay a paradise. At least, that was the way he imagined it. In truth, he'd spent little time there since his father had sent him, as a boy of eight, to court to become a Child of the Nursery, one of the favored few privileged to share the training of royal princes.

He remembered being very small and living here with
his mother. He remembered days of quiet, of peace, listening to his mother's gentle voice directing the servants,
listening to the rhythmic shushing sound of the winnowers as they bent, scooped grain into winnowing fans,
and tossed it in the air. He still dreamed of hot, silent
days like today, in the season of Drought, when the harvested fields baked into dust and there was nothing to
fear but the bite of the desert wind.

A cry jolted him out of his reverie. A fisherman had
recognized *Wings of Horus*. His call was taken up by
laborers making mud bricks on the east bank and passed
on to farmers and servants. From all directions he could
see scurrying figures. Isis danced on her toes and waved
until Bener scolded her. She maintained her dignity for a
moment, then tugged on Meren's hand.

"There's Tetiky, Father. He's even more prosperous
than when you left." She pointed at a farmer trotting
alongside a canal toward them.

"Yes," said Bener, "and you mustn't speak to him, for
he has brought a complaint against Pemu, and he'll have
you sitting in judgment on the dock."

Meren grinned as he nodded to the fast-growing
crowd. "Old Pemu, lazy as a male lion and still moving
boundary stones when he thinks no one's looking."

Isis began chattering again, and she was still talking
when they stepped onto the dock. But the moment he
lifted a hand for silence, she closed her mouth. She and
Bener dropped behind him, suddenly acquiring the dignity of princesses. The wind caught the diaphanous folds
of his overrobe and swirled it around his legs. Zar, his
body servant, had insisted he wear court dress for the
arrival, when all he wanted to do was hop off the ship
and run all the way to the house. He hadn't had the
freedom to do that in many years.

Instead he stood receiving the obeisance of laborers,

fishermen, servants, and farmers while his golden wristbands, rings, and broad collar captured the sun's heat and
burned his skin. He fingered the hilt of the dagger in his
belt as he listened to humble greetings from men who
remembered him as a naked child. He tried to conceal his
impatience and make a gracious reply. These were the
people whose labor was his to command, but he'd
learned long ago that their industry depended much upon
their contentment. Still, he was glad when his steward,
Kasa, arrived with a chariot and a band of servants to
assist in transferring his belongings to the house.

He left Kasa to handle the arrangements with Zar and
drove with the girls down the road beside the main canal.
It soon turned into a graded path that left the fields and
ended up at the white-plastered and painted gates of
Baht. The tree-shrouded house was an oasis of cool
shade in the blistering heat. A group of naked toddlers
and children shrieked at them from the protection of a
palm near the entrance. Bener waved, and the young ones
burst into a run behind the chariot. Porters had already
swung the heavy gates open and were bending low as
they drove inside.

Meren walked the horses down an avenue of sycamores. To either side lay twin reflection pools shaded by
trees older than he was. Geese swam in the pools while
herons stalked across them. He breathed in warm, water-
sweetened air. Bener slipped her arm around his waist,
and he looked down at her. In her eyes he saw his own
pleasure reflected. Abruptly he realized that she shared
his love of simple pleasures of the senses—the smell of
freshly harvested grain, the sound of water lapping
against the side of a reflection pool.

Her expression changed as she glanced toward the
loggia that sheltered the entrance to the main house. The
corners of her mouth drew down, and her eyes widened.
Then the frown was gone behind a mask of pleasant wel-

come, and Meren was left to wonder just how much more he had in common with this daughter who had transformed herself into a woman without his permission. Bener knew when to conceal her thoughts to suit her own needs. Of this he was certain. But then, she'd always been quick of wit.

Vowing to solve this small mystery, he pulled up to the loggia and descended from the chariot. This was the moment he'd been dreading since the girls had broken the news of the feast to him. He'd expected all three of his uncles and their families, their children—except for his enemy-cousin Ebana—and his aunt Nebetta and her husband. None of them stood on the steps waiting for him. Was it too much to hope they hadn't come? Only Idut, her son, and his great-aunt in her carrying chair waited for him, along with a half-dozen servants.

He handed the chariot reins to a groom and received a welcoming kiss from his great-aunt. The old woman laid a dry hand grooved with crevicelike wrinkles on his cheek and studied him with mottled, nearsighted eyes. Cheritwebeshet was ancient, older even than his grandmother. Her shift hung around her frail body like a slack sail, and her hands shook as she touched him. But her voice was sharp.

"So, they haven't killed you yet. You're smarter than your father was."

"May the gods protect you too, Aunt Cherit."

"And still too pretty for your own good. Not married, adopted a plain-blooded son of a butcher, consorting with that fool Ay."

"Kysen wasn't a butcher's son, Aunt." He bent down and kissed her wrinkled cheek. "I've missed you."

"Why couldn't you marry again and produce a son, that's what I'd like to know? It's not as if you lack for women in your bed. Ah! You didn't think I knew, did you? These old ears hear like a hyena, and I have lots of friends at court. Now don't put on your offended prince's face. I'll be quiet. For now." Cherit tapped one of her bearers on the shoulder. "Carry me back to my chamber. It's too hot out here. Welcome home, boy."

Bener was still standing beside him.

"I remember promising myself not to harangue my children that way," he whispered to her. All he got in response was an eloquent lift of her brows.

"Meren, Meren, you're a day late," Idut said.

He hugged his sister and ignored her complaint. Idut was a head shorter than he and several years younger. His gaze took in her grave countenance without surprise. Idut had always been something of a mystery to him. She seldom smiled, except when entertaining, and was given to long silences that disturbed him. She always seemed to be brooding about something, but he could never figure out what she was brooding about.

Like Isis, Idut had the fragile facial structure that so reminded him of Nefertiti, but her chin came to a decided point. When they were children he used to tease her that she could poke holes in a copper target with her chin. He noticed a fan of tiny lines radiating from the corners of her eyes, and she still had the habit of curling her toes under when she stood for any length of time.

"Idut, I want to talk to you about this feast."

"Imset, come here and greet your uncle."

He frowned at his sister, but accepted Imset's speech of welcome. Idut was proud of her son, and Meren had to admit that he was brilliant of wit. He had managed to acquire the skills of a scribe twice his age at the school in the temple of Osiris in nearby Abydos. But Idut confused intellect with maturity.

The youth stood goggling at him with the heavy-lidded stare of a frog. Bener ignored her cousin, and Isis had disappeared. He tried to engage Imset in conversation as they all walked inside, but the youth had exhausted his social talents with the completion of his memorized speech. Idut saved him.

"I know what you're thinking, Meren, and you're wrong."

"What am I thinking?"

"You're thinking I'm going to pester you about an appointment for Imset, but I'm not." Idut lifted her chin and gave him a triumphant look. "My suitor, Wah, has found a post for Imset with the viceroy of Kush. That's something you, his own uncle, should have been able to do, but wouldn't. He's leaving at once and only stayed to give you greeting."

"I rejoice in your good fortune, sister." To Imset he said, "May the gods bless your journey."

All he got in response was another toadlike stare. Meren was still trying to think of something to say to Imset when two figures stepped into the cool darkness of the entry hall. He blinked rapidly to adjust his vision to the lack of sunlight, recognized the newcomers, and felt blood rush to his head. The voice of his heart, the pulse, pounded in his ears. Nebetta and Hepu. The only sister of his father, and her husband.

Time stopped; then the years flowed backward in less than a heartbeat. He was hot and swimming in a lake of misery, lying in pain, trying to wake, trying to open his eyes. He was too weak to accomplish this one small act, and the weakness frightened him. He tried to cry out for help. His lips moved, but his voice wouldn't come out of his throat. He tried to speak again, and something cool and wet pressed against his mouth, bringing relief. The cold dampness brushed over his cheeks, forehead, eyes, and at last he could lift his lids.

Memory returned. His father was dead, and pharaoh had had him beaten into submission. Then Ay had saved him. Where was he? The damp cloth passed across his forehead again, and his blurry vision cleared.

His cousin Djet leaned over him and touched the cloth to his lips again. His cousin's great height made him seem to bend like an acacia tree. They were close in age and shared the sharp, angular jaw of their grandfather. Djet's eyes were more almond-shaped and glinted with biting humor. They had been close as boys, sharing the rough and raucous escapades of noble youths. Until the family had decreed that Meren take a wife. Soon after that Djet left, taking foreign posts that kept him out of Egypt. And yet, after all this time, there was no one Meren trusted more.

Djet set the damp cloth aside and sat back down on the ebony chair beside the bed. "You're awake at last. No, don't try to speak. I know what you want to say. Ay sent all the way to Babylon for me weeks ago. I know everything, damn you and your cursed uprightness and honesty. It's near gotten you killed. Why couldn't you have lied about believing in pharaoh's upstart god?"

"Father's d—dead."

"Because he was a stubborn fool."

Meren tried to get up. "My family!"

"Your wife and daughter are safe in the country." Djet shoved Meren back onto the cushions of his bed. He needed little strength to do it; Meren was shivering with the effects of his ordeal, starvation, and tortured thoughts. He was about to sink into another stupor when Djet lifted his head and pressed a cup to his lips. Meren drank in hot beef broth that steamed its way down his throat to his stomach.

Meren shoved the cup aside. "You shouldn't be here. You don't know the danger. The king is—"

"I know the danger. Now drink some water."

"Why did you have to come back now? I've begged you to come home for years, and you never would. But you come back now, when you could get yourself thrown into a crocodile pit for a misspoken word. You're mad. Go back to—uhhh!"

"You see. Babbling has cost you what little strength you have. Sleep, cousin. I'm here, and I'm staying until you're well and safe."

The words echoed through his weariness and pain, easing both, and giving him release from dread. No one would come upon him to do evil as long as Djet was there to keep watch. Djet was as formidable a young warrior as any in pharaoh's chariotry. He could rest. For the first time since pharaoh had killed his father, he could rest.

Someone was calling his name. Meren blinked and pulled himself out of the memory, only to come face-to-face with Djet's parents. He smiled coldly, hating the sight of them.

"Dear, dear Meren," Nebetta said in a voice that had always reminded him of spoiled honey—much too sweet, and sickening.

Walking with her into the reception room, where cool beer and bread awaited, Meren observed Nebetta's dead gray hair, faded eyes, and bulbous nose and cheeks. She had a lumpy body, and Meren was sure that its shape was caused by her having swallowed most of her character. For, like her husband, Nebetta was consumed with virtue. And all that tedious virtue and uprightness had collected inside her along with every unexpressed feeling of anger, every lie she never told, every fault she ever tried to squelch. She looked as if she was going to burst from swallowing all those sins. Meren was sure that when she came before the gods to give her confession, each denial of sin would be the truth, because Nebetta wasn't interesting enough to have transgressed.

What liveliness and beauty she'd inherited had been washed away in a continuous bath of bleaching morality. It was said that Nebetta had acquired her rectitude from

Hepu, and Meren had to admit that of the two, Hepu was the more obvious and overbearing. It was Hepu who respected his own excellence so much that he wrote books of instruction to be passed down to succeeding generations. He produced these tomes continually, and donated them to various schools and libraries in every major temple, whether asked to or not.

For most of his life Meren had ignored their pomposity and belief in their own worth—until the day Nebetta and her husband disowned Djet, when he was thirteen. Without warning and with no explanation Djet was cast out, banished from the favor of his parents. He had sought refuge with Meren's family, his face drawn with grief. Blue shadows highlighted Djet's dark eyes, and he lost weight. His sarcastic humor vanished. And no matter how much Meren coaxed him, he refused to speak of the thing that had cost him the love of his father and mother.

Years passed, but the rift only grew worse, until one day, soon after Meren had recovered from being tortured, Djet drank poison sweeter than the sweetness of his mother's voice. What kind of woman so reviled her son that she would drive him to kill himself? What kind of father would do the same? And what insane reasoning allowed his sister to think Meren would enjoy being welcomed home by these two?

Idut was talking to him. "Meren, you're not drinking your beer. Don't you like it?"

They were sitting in the reception chamber amidst carved and gilded chairs and beer jars festooned with wreaths of water lotuses, cooled by maids waving ostrich-feather fans. Nebetta was talking with Bener while old Hepu was speaking to—lecturing—Isis. Hepu didn't carry on conversations; he discoursed.

"Meren, I asked if you liked your beer," Idut said.

"I want to talk to you," he replied. "Now. Alone."

"Good, because I want to speak to you as well."

Surprised, he followed his sister back outside to the shaded walk that bordered one of the twin reflection pools. The sun was dropping below the front west wall, but the heat of its rays seemed as strong as at midday. Idut waved away two maids who had followed with fans, and they were alone.

Before the maids were out of sight, Meren burst out, "Did I not write you to say I wanted privacy? Did I not say I wanted to spend time with the girls? Don't you ever read what I write? No, of course you don't. You only read what you wish to read. And you invited Nebetta and Hepu. You know I don't like them. *You* don't like them. This house will be stuffed full of interfering, squabbling relatives."

"Families should be together," Idut said airily. "Relatives should continue in harmony."

"You sound like one of Hepu's books of instruction. The fool fancies he's written another *Instruction of Ptahhotep*."

"That's not respectful, Meren."

"You have to make them go away. All of them."

Idut touched his arm. "I must speak to you of something far more important."

"Don't avoid the subject—"

"Bener has a lover."

A goose honked. It spread its wings, flapped them at a rival, and hissed. Meren strove to comprehend what his sister had just said.

"Explain."

"You know how much she loves writing and ciphering. She spends too much time with the steward and his scribes."

His steward, Kasa, managed the fields of Baht, its tenants and laborers, and the production of commodities upon which the manor survived. He'd been in charge since before their father died. His two sons had been trained to follow him.

"One of Kasa's sons?"

Idut shook her head. "An apprentice scribe, Nu."

"I don't remember this Nu." His head was beginning to ache.

"He's the grandson of your old nurse."

"Are you sure, Idut?"

"They spend hours together every day in the steward's office."

"But that's all?" he asked.

"You know what it's like to be in love fever, Meren. Who knows if that's all?"

He gazed out over the blue surface of the water. Fish shimmered beneath its surface. A cloak of calm settled over him. He dared not examine what lay beneath. Meren nodded to his sister.

"Very well. Now you listen to me, Idut. Get rid of all these—these guests."

"I can't . . . the feast!"

"After the feast. Lie, Idut. Tell them the servants have a plague."

"Oh, Meren."

"Do it, or I will, and I know you won't like how I manage the task."

"I don't know why you have to be so discourteous."

"And I don't know why you insist upon ignoring the evilmindedness of most of the people you've invited. Now where is this Nu?"

"He's probably still in the steward's office."

He went quietly. Passing out of the gate, he walked quickly to the modest house that lay a few yards to the south. Commanding silence from the porter and servants, he slipped into the room that served as Kasa's office. Neither the steward nor his sons were there.

He was about to leave when he heard the scrape of a rush pen. Through an open door lay a porch on which were stacked sheets of papyrus anchored by smoothing stones. Meren walked outside. Leaning against a column, head bent over a sheet of papyrus stretched across his crossed legs, a youth dipped his pen in black ink and resumed writing.

"You're Nu."

The pen jerked. A wide slash of black disfigured the neat script. The boy looked up, eyes on fire with rage. Then he realized who was standing there. He dropped the pen and paper and scrambled to his feet to bow deeply with raised hands.

Ignoring the boy's discomfort, Meren asked, "Are you?"

"Aye, lord. I am Nu, grandson of Herya, apprentice to master Kasa."

Meren turned his back on the youth. He hadn't thought about what Nu would look like. He wasn't pleased. A scrawny student with a squint, that's what he would have preferred. Nu wasn't scrawny; his eyes were large and sad, and he looked as if he belonged in a chariot facing a Hittite army. This menace needed curbing without delay.

Meren turned around and walked toward the boy. "Nu, you're a fortunate lad."

"My lord?"

Nu backed up and hit the column with the back of his head. Meren stopped within arm's reach, studying his quarry in silence until Nu swallowed and lowered his gaze to the floor.

"Look at me."

Nu lifted his eyes to meet Meren's, and they widened as Meren smiled at him.

"Yes, you're a fortunate lad, Nu. Most men would have killed you for interfering with their daughters." He paused upon hearing a choking sound from Nu. "I, however, am not a hot-bellied man. I ask for explanations before I kill. Explain, Nu."

Nu's mouth worked, but nothing came out of it.

"I can't hear you, boy."

"I, I, I . . ."

The slap of sandals on the packed-earth floor saved Nu for the moment. Meren turned to find Bener rushing out of the house, breathless and wild-eyed.

"What are you doing here?" Meren snapped.

"A message, Father." She thrust a folded and sealed packet at him.

Meren snatched it from her, glaring. He was about to order her home when his eye caught the inscription on the letter: Kysen. He opened it and read swiftly.

"Everlasting damnation. Fiends of the netherworld!"

Nu scuttled behind the column while Bener gawked at him.

Meren rounded on her and pointed. "Go home, daughter."

"But Father, Nu is only an apprentice. Aunt has imagined things. And she's only trying to distract you because you're angry with her."

"Go, at once!"

Bener vanished, and he turned on Nu. "Come out of there, you worthless little sneak."

Nu stumbled from behind the column and sank to his knees. Touching his forehead to the floor, he waited in silence. Meren touched the sheath that housed his dagger, but the cold metal didn't spur him to action. It brought him back from the brink of violence. Reason returned. He knew his daughter, and she'd been telling him the truth. Most of it.

"As I said, you're a fortunate lad. My daughter's word is as the word of the goddess Maat, lighter than the feather of truth. You may go."

Nu rose and slunk past him, only to start when Meren lifted a hand.

"This isn't the end of our conversation."

"Yes, my lord."

Nu scurried away, leaving Meren alone on the porch staring into the distance. Worry over his daughter warred with a new concern. Kysen was coming. No doubt he'd arrive before Meren could rid himself of this infestation of relatives. Nento would be with him. Both were ostensibly traveling with the trading flotilla for convenience. No one would think it odd that Kysen had invited Nento to break his journey at his father's house.

But curiosity had always been a family trait. All Meren could do was pray to all the gods of Egypt that his unique preparations would be enough protection against the invasion his sister had arranged for the feast of rejoicing. But prayers wouldn't be sufficient.

He would send Reia and his men out to patrol the countryside. Lord Paser's ship had sailed past him this afternoon again. Paser could have moored farther south and even now be lurking about, spying. But he was more worried about others. The powerful priests of Amun had vowed a truce in their relentless and secret warfare against the boy king Tutankhamun.

Meren wasn't sure their promise extended to the heretic king who tried to banish Amun and the other gods from Egypt. Akhenaten, Tutankhamun's brother, had denuded the fabulous temple of Amun, wiped out his name, beggared his priests. These acts had made Akhenaten's very name anathema. And there were those among the restored priesthood who would give their lives if they could destroy Akhenaten's body and thus deprive him of the afterlife. Ultimate vengeance. A vengeance that Meren had sworn to the king he would prevent.

Unfortunately, he'd experienced the cruelty of which Akhenaten had been capable. His own cousin Ebana had suffered a far worse fate. Determined to wipe out any potentially powerful enemies of his heresy, Akhenaten had ordered Ebana assassinated. Ebana had escaped, but his wife and son hadn't. To Meren's dismay, his cousin had blamed him for not preventing the attack, and nothing he said had ever changed Ebana's attitude. Ebana currently served the high priest of Amun in opposition to pharaoh, while an incongruous twist of Meren's fate had put him in the position of protecting the body of the man who had killed his father and nearly brought about his own death.

He folded Kysen's letter and smiled. If he didn't love the king as a son, would he be fighting so hard for Akhenaten's life in the netherworld? A difficult question, and one to which he wasn't sure he wanted the answer.

3
▽

Before dawn on the third morning after confronting the apprentice scribe, Meren slipped out of the house with a tray bearing food, wine, and an alabaster lamp. He walked swiftly down the avenue between the reflection pools to the small chapel where lay shrines to the gods and to his ancestors. A flight of steps took him to the entrance, which was flanked by two painted columns. Shoving open the carved doors with one hand, he entered.

The yellow glow from the lamp illuminated the painted murals on the walls, pictures of his family, his parents, his grandparents, and those who had gone before them. Deep in the heart of the chapel lay golden shrines housing images of Amun; of Osiris, god of Abydos; of Montu, god of war; and others. But it wasn't these Meren intended to visit. Instead, he turned to his right and went to a narrow niche in the wall.

There stood a double statue of his parents, together in death as they had been in life. The sculptor had carved them in their finest clothing, sheer linen draping their bodies. Ornate wigs covered unruly hair; gold hung from their necks, wrists, and ears. Meren whispered prayers for the dead and offered food and wine. When he was done, he stared at the images, wondering why he never felt like they heard his invocations. Yesterday before dark, he'd visited Sit-Hathor's eternal house. He always felt that his wife listened to him. He'd told her all the things he could tell no one else, and he never worried that she might disapprove. She'd always been on his side—after she'd learned to love him, that is. When they first married, Sit-Hathor had thought him a nuisance. But she'd changed her opinion, unlike his father.

In life he had rarely pleased his father, whose quick temper and demands for perfection had made Meren want to fight him rather than comply. And his mother? What he remembered most about her was her constant pleading. *Do as your father says. Don't make trouble. Why must you disagree with your father?*

One of his earliest memories was of playing in the garden and being called inside by his nurse, Herya. The woman was washing his face when, with sudden violence, his father burst into the room carrying his toy hippopotamus. Appearing like a giant demon from the underworld, Amosis hurled the wooden miniature to the floor. It hit with a loud crack, making Meren scream and burst into tears while Amosis railed at him for cluttering up the garden.

Of course, Meren hadn't understood what Amosis was saying. The sudden terror wiped out all else from his heart. And when his mother came to comfort him, all she said was that Father didn't like him to leave his toys lying around. *Don't make trouble, don't provoke Father's temper.*

What was it in his makeup that made Meren refuse to placate tyranny? Even so young, he had resented unreasonable abuse. And as the years went by, resentment grew until one day—he couldn't have been more than twelve—Meren realized that he didn't respect his parents. He resented the deference the world demanded he pay to them, disbelieved his father's glamorous reputation as a courtier, governor, and warrior. The gods had proved Meren right. The day came when Amosis's temper pitted him against a heretic pharaoh and cost him his life.

Useless to be proven right at such a cost. Meren glanced down the line of figures arrayed beside his parents until he came to one standing apart on a pedestal in the corner. Djet stood as he had in life, wide of shoulder, long, striding legs, that sad, brooding expression. After Djet had died it was Meren, not Djet's parents, who had provided for his cousin's afterlife. He'd commissioned the statue from the royal sculptor who had carved so many hauntingly beautiful images of the royal family at Horizon of Aten.

"Greetings, Djet," Meren whispered. "I've brought your favorite spice bread, and some good Delta wine. And I've come to ask you a favor. Could you intercede with the gods to make my relatives vanish? Your cursed mother and father are here, and Idut has invited your brother. You know what an ass Sennefer is, trying to mount every pretty serving woman on the manor, bragging, expecting me to play witness to his prowess."

Tearing off a piece of bread, Meren took a bite and sighed. "Fortunately Uncle Thay, Uncle Bakenkhons, and their families couldn't come. I've managed to avoid the others by taking the girls sailing two days in a row. But tonight there's a feast. That's Idut's fault. You know how she is. She ignores how everyone quarrels and just proceeds as if the family were loving and cooperative."

Taking a sip of wine from the glazed pottery cup, Meren sank to the floor and gazed up at Djet's unmoving features.

"I thought I had everything arranged. I would come home to quiet and peace. No great crowds, no danger, away from the spies at court and in the temples. Now the house is stuffed with prying relatives. I made Idut promise to get rid of them after tonight's feast, but if she doesn't, I'm going to have to send them away myself, which will get me into even more trouble. I might as well throw myself to the Devourer right now."

He stood and put the bread back on the altar in front of Djet's image. "I miss you, Djet. Ebana hates me now, you know. Why did I have to lose the two of you? Both of you were more brother to me than Ra. Of all the family, he's the only one who hasn't promised to come. He left so he wouldn't have to see me. And on top of everything, Great-Aunt Cherit says Grandmother Wa'bet has decided I should marry again." He sighed. "I think I prefer court intrigue, royal machinations, and murder. I can't think clearly when I'm surrounded by relatives."

Drawing closer to Djet, Meren lowered his voice so that it was barely audible.

"If you have any answers, send them to me in a dream." Shoulders slumped, Meren turned away. He couldn't remember how many times he'd asked Djet to answer one imperative question—why he'd killed himself. In the last few years, he'd stopped asking. What did it matter? Djet was gone.

"Stop brooding, you fool," Meren said to himself. Kysen would be here soon, and he would have to be alert. Heading for the door, Meren stepped in a patch of light coming into the chapel from one of the windows set high in the walls. Bright sunlight. How long had he been in here?

Leaving his offerings, he stepped outside into a world already bereft of what little coolness the night offered. Before him lay the entry gate, to his left, the sprawling white facade of the main house. The loggia was supported by papyriform columns, while the doorway was decorated with a frieze of red-and-green palmetto leaves.

Inside lay the family quarters, the great central hall, and his office. To either side of the house, in courts separated by gated walls, lay giant granaries, cattle pens, and a well court. To the rear were the kitchen, storage rooms, servants' quarters, and stables.

Baht wasn't so much a house as a small village. The smaller houses used by his uncles, cousins, and other relatives clustered beside the main one, just outside its walls. Already a train of donkeys bearing grain baskets was plodding through a side gate on its way to the granary court. As Meren walked back to the house, he saw the steward Kasa marching around the corner of the house on his way to the cattle pens. He was at the head of a line of assistants—his two sons, three cattle herders, and the unfortunate Nu.

Seeing the youth reminded Meren of another problem. Bener had tried to persuade him that she spent so much time with Kasa because of her interest in writing. Meren wasn't convinced. But he'd reserved judgment because he feared he'd been hasty. Perhaps he'd spent too much time steeped in intrigue and deception not to look for it where it didn't exist. Bener wasn't a deceitful girl. She wasn't a fool. He shouldn't assume she would succumb to Nu's pretty face.

He was pondering this dilemma on the front steps when the clatter of hooves signaled the approach of a chariot. Turning, he saw his cousin Sennefer clatter down the avenue toward him. Too fast.

"Sennefer, pull up!"

His cousin hauled on the reins. Meren backpedaled as a wall of horseflesh thundered down on him. A hoof pounded the stone step he'd been standing on. Meren cursed and jumped farther back. Grooms rushed down the avenue from their post beside the gate. Sennefer hopped to the ground and threw his reins at the men.

"Ha! Meren, you jackal, I haven't seen you in months and months."

Sennefer clapped him on the back. Meren suppressed another sigh and tried not to sound too morose. "Greetings, Sennefer."

"Give me beer, cousin. It's a hot sail and a dusty drive from my place to yours."

"You can go back."

Laughing, Sennefer hit him on the back again. "And miss one of Idut's feasts? Besides, the daughter of the mayor of Abydos has become importunate. Why do they always try to suffocate you, Meren? They demand that you spend time with them, suck you dry, and then want more."

"Someday you're going to get a dagger in your heart for interfering with married women, Sennefer."

"It's not my fault," Sennefer said as they reached the reception hall. He broke off to smile at a serving maid who offered a bowl of water for his refreshment. "What do you expect? There are so many, and they want me, they beg. I can see it in their eyes."

Meren waved the serving maid away, and when she was gone, Sennefer continued.

"You see. That one was ready to jump behind the nearest bush with me."

"She didn't even look at you, Sennefer."

Shaking his head, Sennefer led the way into the central hall and collapsed on a couch with his beer. "You always were jealous."

"Oh, certainly."

He didn't care what Sennefer thought. Sennefer had always been an impoverished version of his younger brother Djet. Sennefer bragged of his exploits; Djet kept quiet and drew into thrall countless admirers of both sexes. Sennefer boasted incessantly of his courage in battle when it was known he never participated in anything more dangerous than a skirmish with unarmed thieves; Djet had received the gold of bravery from pharaoh. Meren stopped listening when Sennefer began to lecture him on how to seduce his serving maid. Then his guest said something that caught his attention.

"Did you say your wife wants a divorce?"

Sennefer waved a hand. "She says she wants children. I can't help it if she's barren. And she thinks she's going to get my estates in the Hare nome. What an imagination, eh?"

"You can't make her stay if she wants to leave."

"She won't leave without the riches she wants, believe me. Anhai's first love is wealth. I swear, Meren, she's counted every piece of food, every pot, every grain of barley and wheat we ever produced since the day we married. If there was gain in it, she'd market the sands of the desert and the dung in the cattle pens."

"You shouldn't criticize your wife to me," Meren said. He was going to kill Idut. He was trying to think of an excuse to leave before Sennefer could recall more misery to impart when Isis burst into the hall, obviously aggrieved.

"Father, Remi says he's going to jump into the garden pool."

Meren looked at her in surprise. His household did not come to him with the small misbehaviors of a three-year-old grandson. "Where is the nurse?"

"Aunt Idut sent her to help in the kitchen because of the feast tonight, and I'm watching him."

Waving his daughter away, Meren said, "Then simply tell Remi not to jump in the pool."

"I have, but he said he's going to do it anyway, to retrieve his toy chariot. You know he'll do it, Father."

"By the gods, Isis, if he does, haul him out."

His charioteers would have recognized the irritation in his voice and decamped. Not his daughter. She smoothed the pleats of her spotless robe and tossed a thick lock of hair from her wig over her shoulder.

"I can't," she said. "I would ruin my costume."

Meren narrowed his eyes and studied Isis. Why hadn't he noticed that she was arrayed in elaborate dress? There were more pleats in her robe than feathers on a duck. Her eyes were painted with kohl and green paint, her arms and shoulders laden with electrum and carnelian. He should have noticed, but he thought of Isis as a babe. Yet dressed as she was, she looked older than Bener.

Frowning, he glanced at Sennefer, who had been snickering during the exchange. He intercepted a predatory stare at his daughter. Jolted into awareness, he stood up so that his body blocked Sennefer's view. His cousin smoothly drew his gaze back to Meren, only to falter at the image of death he found there.

Lowering his voice so that only Sennefer could hear him, he said, "Attempt it, and I'll cut your cock off and make you eat it." Sennefer gave him a look of outraged innocence that was ruined by the way he swallowed hard as though nauseated. Turning to Isis, he said, "Come, I'll attend to Remi. If you don't intend to take care of him, don't say you will. Find a maid to do it."

As he followed Isis, with Sennefer in tow, he passed servants busy cleaning the chambers and hall in preparation for the feast. The garden lay in a walled enclosure behind the house. Its pool was deeper than the reflection pools in front and large enough to support one or two pleasure craft of the type designed to hold several people. In contrast to the barren fields and desert, the garden at Baht was lush with carefully tended greenery.

Generations of his family had cultivated willows, sycamores, pomegranates, and fig trees here. Incense trees graced painted earthenware pots. Arbors of grapevines provided secluded alcoves in which to rest. Flowers bordered the pool in thick beds. Meren scanned the court for the small figure of his grandson and found him bending precariously over the edge of the pool.

Raising his voice, he called, "Remi, stay back."

Like Meren's pet hounds and his thoroughbreds, Remi only heard what he wanted to hear. Meren's second call was drowned by the splash Remi made as he dove into the water. Cursing, Meren raced across the garden, leaped over a flower bed, and dove in after the boy. The exertion caused the newly healed skin over his shoulder wound to pull. He'd jumped in an area thick with water lilies that could bind him underwater.

Fish slithered against his body as he sliced through the water. Shadows from the water lilies obscured his vision. Searching the dappled haze, he spotted the gleam of bronze and a little hand reaching for it. Meren darted for the bottom, snatched Remi and the toy chariot, and thrust himself up and out of the water. Bursting into the open, he winced as the child's weight stressed his shoulder. Remi sputtered, then laughed and grabbed the toy. Swimming one-handed, Meren reached the side of the pool and handed Remi to Isis.

His hair was plastered to his forehead and hung down over his eyes. Gripping the edge of the pool, he hoisted himself out of the water and stood dripping beside Sennefer and Isis. All at once he noticed there were more people in the garden than he'd realized. Nebetta and Hepu huddled beside a grape arbor and gave him disapproving looks. No doubt they were scandalized at his departure from the demeanor of a great lord. Hepu probably had written a whole Instruction on the subject. He glared back at them, and they scurried out of the garden, muttering to themselves.

Then he heard a soft laugh. Lungs heaving, blinking back the water that dripped from his hair to his eyes, he turned to behold two elegantly dressed women standing beside a flower bed. One was Sennefer's wife, Anhai. The other was Bentanta, one of the few people alive who could make him blush. Anhai was chuckling at him. Thank the gods, Bentanta wasn't smiling at all.

"What are you doing, Meren?" Anhai asked. "I thought you were one of the Eyes and Ears of Pharaoh, not a nurse."

"I was—"

He stopped in midsentence as Anhai suddenly laughed, stepped toward him, and patted his cheek. She had a laugh like the chimes of a sistrum, one that evoked good humor in everyone. Meren forgot his embarrassment as she smiled at him.

"You're an amazement," she said. "You're one of the few who can call himself Friend of the King, you're entrusted with pharaoh's secrets, well-being, and defense, you're quite pleasing to look at, and you love your family."

"I thank you, Anhai, but—"

She went on as if he hadn't spoken. "While I am cursed with a man who not only can't keep his place at court but also hasn't the seed to give me even one child in the dozen years we've been married."

Meren felt his jaw come unhinged. He'd forgotten for a moment what Anhai was like—a ka filled with putrescence and surrounded by a fine layer of jeweled charm. He stared at her while she appeared to reflect upon her words with pleasure. Bentanta had the diplomacy to appear engrossed in an examination of the water lilies. He didn't return Anhai's smile, and stared as she left the garden with an air of having gained some great victory.

Isis, who was holding Remi's wet hand, also stared at Anhai's retreating back. "I don't like her. Come, Remi, you're going back to your nurse before you get my gown wet."

Meren regained his composure and glanced at Sennefer. His cousin was one of those men who make up for a lack of stature by cultivating an abundance of muscle. At the moment every one of those visible was flushed, as was his face. He had a short, sharp nose that reddened almost to the color of wine. He muttered something Meren didn't catch, then excused himself and rushed after his wife.

Meren was left alone, wet and uncomfortable, with Bentanta. She didn't seem to be in a hurry to leave, and he was slow to recover his composure. Bentanta was a childhood friend grown into a woman of grace. Once he'd swum naked in the Nile with her, Djet, and Ebana, but their lives had taken them along different paths. She was a widow with children the age of his own. Once she'd served the great queen Tiye, mother of Tutankhamun, and Nefertiti, wife of Akhenaten and daughter of Ay. She was as well versed in court intrigue and imperial diplomacy as he, but of late she'd retired from service to Tutankhamun's queen, Ankhesenamun, to live quietly.

But whether a private person or a royal attendant, Bentanta was a formidable woman. And the last woman in Egypt before whom he wished to appear in nothing but a clinging, wet kilt.

He cleared his throat. "Blessings of Amun be upon you, lady. I didn't know you were coming to the feast of rejoicing."

Bentanta left off her examination of the water lilies and gave him a stare that seemed to slice through his body and probe his ka.

"There's no need for foolish courtesy, Meren. I know you weren't expecting me. Neither was your sister. I'm here because I was visiting Anhai, and she insisted that I come with her."

"You sound as if you don't want to be here."

Her lashes fluttered, and she gave him a smile as false as the gilt on a coffin lid. "Of course I want to be here. I came to see you."

Wary, he gave her a skeptical look. "Oh?"

"I've much leisure time now that I'm no longer at court, time to reflect on the happy memories of childhood. This reflection has given me a desire to renew old friendships, like ours." She turned her back on him and walked away. Glancing over her shoulder, she said, "You can stop looking like a trapped gazelle, Meren. I only mentioned friendship, not marriage. My view of husbands isn't much more cheerful than Anhai's."

She left him standing by the pool, dripping, his kilt clinging to his hips. He shoved damp hair from his forehead, looked down at himself, and cursed. This morning he hadn't bothered to don anything other than a kilt. He might as well have been wearing a loincloth.

Sputtering curses at his own lack of judgment, he stalked back into the house to his private apartments. Zar was already there, instructing bathing attendants. The man seemed to know what he would need before Meren did. A convenient and at the same time unsettling habit. Meren glared at the servant, went into the bathing chamber, and stepped into the limestone bathing stall. As a bathing attendant poured water over him, he wondered that his skin didn't steam from the irritation that boiled within him.

He consoled himself with the thought that he only had to survive the rest of this day and the evening's feast. Then everyone would be gone, those slugs Nebetta and Hepu, Great-Aunt Cherit, the lecherous Sennefer, Anhai,

Bentanta, all of them. Then he'd have peace, and the freedom to do what he'd promised pharaoh he would do. And if Idut didn't get rid of his relatives, he was going to throw them out himself.

4

▽

Lord Paser was a man of unique appearance; of this he was quite certain. He prided himself on his closely cropped hair and perfectly barbered goatee and mustache. He felt that his missing right canine tooth lent him an air of battle-hardened experience. No one had ever mentioned to him that his forehead shined as if he oiled it, or that when agitated, he flapped his arms like the wings of a pelican coming in for a water landing.

At the moment Paser was quite pleased with himself. Yesterday afternoon he'd given up following Count Meren, depressed that his strategy of spying on the Friend of the King had yielded nothing but boring days of watching the man sail that evil black ship of his. Meren hadn't, as Paser suspected, gone to some secret meeting of allies. He'd gone home, just as he'd said he would—and stayed there. Paser had watched for two days and then given up. After insisting to Prince Hunefer that Meren never simply went home to rest, Paser had been faced with the prospect of returning to court with nothing to report for his trouble.

He'd directed his ship toward the capital and was drifting slowly northward with the current when he passed a south-going flotilla of trading ships of Ra laden with cargo. He'd been lounging beneath the awning in front of the deckhouse in his favorite gilded cedar chair, his face lifted to the north breeze, when he happened to glance at one of the barges.

The two vessels passed within a few skiff-lengths of each other. As they did, a man walked around the giant mount of grain sacks stacked on the deck, and Paser jumped out of his chair. Hurrying to the railing, he shaded his eyes and peered more closely.

Kysen! Had his yacht been going faster, he might not have had time to make out that wide jaw, the rounded youthful chin shadowed with a man's stubble, and those half-moon eyes. But he'd gotten a good enough look, long enough to see the grave expression on the youth's face. Unguarded, not so well versed in masking emotions as his father, Kysen's expression revealed what Lord Meren's never did—misgiving, apprehension, uneasiness.

That look was enough to make Paser order his ship to come about once out of sight of the flotilla. Now he was trailing after the slow-moving fleet, biding his time, watching. As he plied his fly whisk in the shade of the canopy that stretched before the deckhouse, a hail signaled the arrival of a visitor. While the last ship in the trading fleet disappeared around one of the bends in the river, the visitor climbed from a skiff up a rope ladder on the side of the yacht.

The newcomer hoisted a leg over the railing, then the other, and stalked over to Paser. Retreating to his chair, Paser flapped his whisk, already annoyed without having spoken to his visitor. The intruder started talking before reaching the awning.

"What are you doing? I'm on my way to Count Meren's feast of rejoicing, and I see you skulking down the river."

Paser turned in his chair to scowl at his guest. "I said I was going to follow Meren to see what he was really up to."

"But you're not following him, you fool."

"Don't you call me a fool. I'm not the only one scrambling for a place at court."

"And who told you to do your stalking in a yellow-and-green yacht, of all things? Do you think Meren's blind?"

"There are many craft on the river—mine's no more noticeable than most."

The guest lunged at Paser, pulled him out of his chair, and hurried him to the railing. Pointing, the newcomer hissed into Paser's ear.

"See! See those fishermen? They've been with you for hours, and their nets are empty. Why do you think that is, Paser? I'll tell you why—because they're not fishermen. They're charioteers. Meren's charioteers, you worm-witted son of a dung beetle."

Paser jerked his arm free, gave the fishermen a derisive sniff, and returned to his chair with his guest dogging his footsteps. "I care nothing for those spies. My diligence has been rewarded. I saw Kysen on that trading flotilla, and I've been following him instead of Meren."

"You're following Kysen? Why?"

Tapping his guest with the fly whisk, Paser asked, "The question is, why is he traveling on a trading ship? He was going with the king to Memphis."

"He's going to Meren's feast of rejoicing, you fool."

"Who is a fool? Would you abandon a place at the side of the living god to attend a paltry feast?"

"Kysen isn't like those of us with noble blood. He knows nothing of what is proper for the son of a Hereditary Prince and Sole Beloved Friend of the King."

"But that's it," Paser replied. "What if he's learned? What if he's pursuing the duties of a Sole Beloved Friend of the King? What if he's doing that right now?"

There was a long silence in which his guest stared at Paser. Having put this rude interloper in his place, Paser settled back in his chair with a smirk.

"If what you suspect is true, then I have to ask again why you would follow Meren's son in a bright yellow boat in full daylight."

"I know what I'm doing. Say!" Paser gasped as a knee landed on his stomach and the tip of a dagger pricked the linen of his robe over his heart.

"Now you listen to me. I know Meren far better than you do, and I know Kysen. Neither will be fooled by your clumsy machinations. I'm going to the feast of rejoicing, which is where Kysen is going. You, conversely, are going to turn this green-and-yellow gourd of yours around and sail back to Memphis, or I'll dump you in the mouth of the next hippo we pass."

Paser slapped the dagger away. "I'm not your minion. I'll do as I wish."

"You'll do as I say." The guest stepped back, releasing Paser. "I've lost much because of Ay and Meren and the changes that came with the new pharaoh. But Meren is going to alter his opinion of me, and I'm not going to let you ruin my chance for gain. Go back and report to the prince. I'll follow when I've finished with Meren."

The guest sheathed the dagger. "Do what I say, Paser. Any other choice would be unhealthy."

Meren felt better after bathing and having Zar rub his skin with oil. At least in his apartments he was safe from annoying relatives and unexpected guests. And he enjoyed his rooms at Baht. They had once been his father's, but Sit-Hathor had had them refurbished.

Patterned friezes decorated the tops of the walls, long series of lotus blossoms in blue, white, and green. Brilliant blue faience tiles bordered the bottom of the walls. In his bedchamber there was a mural of a papyrus marsh depicting ducks, geese, and herons in flight. The remaining walls were plastered and bore a wash of pale blue.

He and Sit-Hathor had shared a love of simple, cool

beauty. He remembered feeling so grateful to her for this gift when Djet brought him home after the nightmare of Horizon of Aten. To these rooms he would retreat if he began to lose his temper at the feast tonight.

Meantime he would slip out of the house and go spearfishing. That way he wouldn't have to play host when the trickle of arriving guests became an invasion. He was particularly anxious to avoid his neighbors in the district, most of whom—knowing that he had the trust of pharaoh—tried to ingratiate themselves. He hated unctuous sycophants. Once he was on the river, he'd send for the girls. And he'd take the opportunity to explore further Bener's relationship with Nu, for it now seemed likely he wouldn't have the chance to see the boy before the feast.

"The lord's robe is ready."

Meren glanced at the long garment with its waterfall of pleats. Zar had laid it on the gilded bed, along with a broad collar, belt, and bracelets consisting of thousands of tiny lapis, gold, and turquoise beads.

Meren frowned at the servant. The years had eroded away his hair in two scoops on either side of his head, leaving a sparse fan of gray hair like a tongue in the middle of his forehead. In contrast, the hair of his eyebrows grew in abundance, as if to make up for its laziness elsewhere. His body was short and compact, his stomach slightly rounded from excesses at the table. He was giving Meren one of the disapproving looks that made him look as if he'd just smelled a chamber pot.

Since Zar and his family had served Meren's for generations, he considered himself an authority on noble demeanor and appropriateness. No one knew more about court ceremony, proper address and manners, appropriate dress and protocol. And he cared about these things, for Meren's distinction and importance added to his. When Meren succeeded his father, Zar's life became a series of trials, for Meren would rather avoid the luxury, ceremony, and formality that Zar considered the embodiment of a happy life.

"Zar, I'm going spearfishing."

The body servant rocked back and forth on his heels while studying the heavy, luxurious wig he'd just removed from its box. "Noble hosts do not vanish upon the hour of their guests' arrival."

Meren waved a hand at the servant, walked to the door of the bedchamber, and cracked it open, listening.

"His honored visitors will expect the gracious hospitality and manners of a Friend of the King, a Sole Beloved Companion, a Fan-bearer at the Right of the King, one who should not disgrace his heritage, one who—"

"I don't hear anything. Zar, go out to the hall and also to the front porch and see who's about."

Zar replaced the wig in its box and left with an aggrieved expression. He returned while Meren was shoving a dagger in his belt.

"The noble Hepu and Nebetta are taking their leisure beside the garden pool, along with the noble Sennefer, Lady Anhai, and Lady Cheritwebeshet, my lord. Mistress Idut is giving instructions in the kitchen, and your noble daughters attend her. There is no one in the forecourt or at the gate."

"Good. Send word to the overseer of fowling and fishing, then send Reia to me at the riverbank, and bring my daughters to me without letting the entire household know where they're going." With great care, Meren pushed the door open and slithered into the corridor. Hugging the wall and walking swiftly, he reached the central hall, which was filled with servants lugging in great jars of wine and beer and maids bearing flower garlands. He sped through the reception room and, without stopping, rushed out onto the columned front porch.

He should have been more careful, for he dashed into

the open in full sight of a group coming up the steps. Meren almost ran into a lanky figure draped in a fine Upper Egyptian linen robe.

"Ah, Lord Meren, how good of you to come before the lady, your sister, to greet me."

Meren backed up, glanced to either side for an escape, then realized he was trapped. "May the favor of Amun be with you, Wah."

While Wah began a long-winded inquiry into the health of his family, Meren cursed his ill luck. Had he been a bit quicker, he'd have been out of the house before Wah arrived. Now he would have to play the host, because Wah was Idut's new suitor.

A glance at the guest left Meren wondering for the hundredth time how Idut could contemplate marrying one who had the reputation of being the kingdom's premier toady. When Meren had been a youth at Horizon of Aten, Wah had been one of the new men who rose to preeminence through their espousal of the Aten heresy. He still remembered the day he'd walked into the office of pharaoh's accounts to find Wah poring over a vast papyrus roll on the floor.

Wah had looked up from the document and said, "Ah, young Lord Meren, come see what I've done."

He shoved the papyrus, causing it to unroll across the room. An assistant stopped it and placed a weight on the end. With a sweep of his arm, Wah indicated the endless lines of cursive hieroglyphs.

"It's nearly finished, the accounting of the estates of the old gods. I'm working on the decree of transfer."

Meren said nothing, but Wah took no notice.

"Think of it. The whole of the vast estates of Amun will soon be transferred to the service of the one god, the Aten. Think of it." Now Wah seemed to have forgotten Meren and began speaking to himself. "I'll be overseer of the cattle of the Aten."

"All of them?" Meren asked. "You're taking the estates of all the gods? What will the priests do? And the artisans, the laborers, their families? They can't all work in the temples of the Aten. How will they live?"

"I'm busy, Lord Meren."

Yes, Wah had been one of the busy officials of the new order. He had prospered, receiving estates and offices for his labors. Uncle Hepu had also prospered. Unlike his brother Amosis, Hepu had measured the ruthlessness of the heretic pharaoh accurately and conformed, eschewing all other gods but the Aten. Meren remembered Hepu's devotion. It had seemed as convincing as his current devotion to the old gods. But then Akhenaten had died, and the wrath of the kingdom fell upon those most directly connected with the disestablishment of the old gods. Self-serving as ever, Hepu had retired from court before the storm of retribution broke. Wah hadn't been as clever. He'd been trying to get his place at court back for five years.

Meren was one of those Wah had importuned in his efforts to regain favor. Having few good memories of his time at Horizon of Aten, he wasn't anxious to further the career of a man so closely allied with the heretic king. Akhenaten had killed his father, nearly killed him. Meren still had nightmares in which Akhenaten's black eyes appeared, staring at him with that eerie look of obsidian fire. And always there was that secret burden of guilt over Akhenaten's death. He had allowed Ay to send him away from court when he suspected a movement to rid the kingdom of Akhenaten. When he returned, pharaoh was already dead. Ever since, Meren had wondered if he could have prevented the king's death if he'd stayed. Would he have tried to save Akhenaten, or let him die? Did he really want to know?

As Meren replied to Wah's inquiries about his family's health, he was conscious of renewed annoyance at the way Idut had ambushed him with this feast. Of all the guests, this one made him the most uncomfortable by inciting haunted memories. But even if Wah hadn't reminded him of old wounds, he was still tiresome.

He didn't like Wah. He didn't even like the way the man looked. His ears looked like a pair of dates. His cheeks had pronounced folds that deepened into caverns when he smiled, and there were folds over his eyes that made his deep-sunk eyes almost vanish when he smiled. He was so long and thin he had to fold himself into chairs, and his knees stuck up high when he sat on a stool.

Worst of all, Wah had a nasal voice and eyes that watered so that the kohl around them was always streaked. However, the habit Meren couldn't forgive was the way the man kept a pouch or basket filled with dates about his person and continually popped the fruits into his mouth. He was constantly chewing, so that conversing with him was like talking to a cow.

Meren's luck improved when Idut appeared just as Wah finished his long list of inquiries.

"Ah! Here's Idut." He was already leaving the porch as his sister joined Wah. "My apologies, Wah, but I just remembered I have some royal correspondence to attend to. Idut will give you a proper welcome."

Ignoring his sister's warning looks and Wah's open mouth, Meren scurried through the reception room and the central hall and back to his rooms. He darted around a slave carrying a tray of used dishes. Shoving open the door, he was about to close it when a thick-fingered hand planted itself on the portal and shoved it back open.

"There you are," said Hepu. He called over his shoulder, "You were right, my dear, he's in his rooms."

Meren pushed at the door. "I'm busy, Hepu."

Hepu pushed back, catching Meren off balance. "Not too busy for your old uncle and aunt."

Meren tried to shove the door and Hepu without success. Nebetta crowded in behind her husband, and the battle was lost. Retreating into his bedchamber, Meren summoned Zar and requested his scribe and the cases that contained his correspondence.

"You have to forgive me, uncle, but I've much work to do. I've just received letters from pharaoh, may he have life, health, and prosperity. They must be answered at once."

Nebetta waddled over to Meren's favorite chair, one of those Sit-Hathor had designed for him, and settled herself in it. The woven seat creaked, making him wince.

Hepu, who had an armful of papyri, handed a few rolls to his wife and said, "You're being most negligent in your duties as a host, nephew."

"I told you I have correspondence."

"Dear, dear Meren, we're worried about you," said Nebetta in her breathy, too-sweet voice.

"Yes, my boy," Hepu said. "I see you're still favoring your shoulder. No doubt it's those wounds that make you so discourteous to your elders. Aunt Cherit complains that she hasn't seen you since you arrived." Meren tried to speak, but Hepu held up his hand and plunged on. "No, no, no, don't beg my forgiveness. In a way, your conduct has benefited me and soon many others, because I'm going to write an Instruction on the proper behavior of a noble host."

"But that's not what we want to speak to you about," Nebetta said. "I think you suspect our little plot already. Come, you can't pretend you didn't know we want you to marry again."

Meren stared from Nebetta's lumpy face to Hepu's self-satisfied one. Nebetta was one of the few people he knew who might undergo the judgment of the gods in the Hall of the Two Truths and utter the negative confession without protective spells. As far as he knew, she had never done crimes against anyone, blasphemed a god or robbed the poor, killed or damaged offerings in the temples, or committed any of the other sins that could get one fed to the Devourer.

. But if she or Hepu passed the weighing of the heart against the feather of truth and were admitted into the netherworld, he would throw himself to the Devourer. He'd rather be eaten by that monster, part lion, part crocodile, than spend eternity with these two.

Nebetta left her chair to stand beside him, touched his arm with a cold, damp hand, and regarded him with faded eyes. "Dear, dear Meren, it's been a long time since Sit-Hathor went to the West. And you're still alone. It's time you married again. End this lonely existence."

"Yes," Hepu said as he set his bundle of papyri down on a table. "I've made a list of suitable alliances. It's in here somewhere. Of course, we were hoping you'd think of Bentanta. After all, her family is connected to Treasurer Maya's and contains royal blood as well. Distant royal blood, but royal nevertheless."

What little tolerance he possessed was obliterated under this tide of muck. Meren turned his back on Nebetta, went to stand on the dais that contained his bed, and gripped one of the gilded poles that supported the canopy around it. "We had this conversation years ago. I'm surprised the memory of it faded so quickly. Do you recall what I said to you about interfering in my affairs?"

"Now—now don't curse the cool north breeze, dear Meren," Nebetta began.

Hepu was scowling at him. "We're only thinking of your welfare."

"And think of the strong sons Bentanta could give you," Nebetta said. "Why, hers are healthy and handsome, and—"

"By Hathor's tits!" Meren gripped the hilt of his dagger and left the dais to swoop down on the two. "I

knew you weren't trying to plan my life for my benefit.
You care naught if I'm happy or not. You want me to
marry again so that I'll spawn noble-blooded sons and
get rid of Kysen." He ended with a string of soldier's
curses.

Hepu drew himself up, squaring his shoulders, while
Nebetta retreated behind him.

"Watch your tongue, my boy," Hepu said. "Everyone
in the family thinks the same. I've been delegated to
speak for them."

Meren's voice quieted and took on a smooth, even
tone that should have warned Hepu. "I see. Tell me, just
who are these family members?"

"Oh, your uncles, Aunt Cherit, your grandmother."

Turning away from them, Meren walked to a table and
poured himself a cup of wine. Taking a sip, he glanced
back at the two. They were watching him, Nebetta with
apprehension that made her bulbous cheeks twitch, Hepu
with righteous determination.

Running a fingertip around the rim of his faience cup,
Meren spoke in a musing tone. "Do you know what made
me notice Kysen? I was in Thebes at a market when his
bastard father put him up for sale. He was a scrawny little
thing, covered in white dust, sweat, and blood from his
latest beating. But as I passed him, he looked at me with
Sit-Hathor's eyes. Two half-moons of obsidian, lakes of
fire just as defiant as hers, set in a face of suffering."

"Oh!" Nebetta waddled over to him, wringing her
hands. "You mean he's Sit-Hathor's bastard?"

Meren's hand squeezed the hilt of his dagger, almost
drew it from his belt. Dragging his gaze from Nebetta, he
looked up at Hepu. "She can't be that stupid. Get out,
now, before I—just get out."

"We're leaving," Hepu said, "but you should think
about what we've said. You should have forgotten your
grief by now. The family thought this nonsense with

Kysen would pass. You can endow him with estates and get rid of him. The family needs an heir it can be proud of, Meren."

"By all the gods, no wonder Djet killed himself."

Hepu flushed as he ushered Nebetta to the door. She scurried out, with her husband close behind, then stuck her head back over the threshold like a belligerent sow.

"I know what you think about us and Djet. Just you reflect upon this, dear Meren. Djet's death was your fault, not ours."

Gaping at her, Meren swore. "What do you mean?"

A slammed door was all the answer he received.

5

He had little time before the feast of rejoicing began, and already the house was full of tension. He didn't know what Nebetta had meant by his having been responsible for Djet's death, but after he'd accomplished his most urgent tasks, he was going to find out.

Meren stood on the roof and gazed out over the countryside that was his hereditary domain. North and south, for many hours' sail it stretched along the river, a land now baked under the force of Ra's heat. After Inundation the fields would burst into green life, defying the threat of the deserts that menaced the valley.

He turned to face the setting sun across the river. There lay the family tombs and those of preceding generations who had gone to the Land of Eternity to dwell in peace and luxury. There also lay the haunted temple of the old ones that so frightened the villagers of the region.

As the north breeze caused the palm trees to flutter their leaves, Meren thanked the gods for one blessing in this disaster arranged for him by his sister—Nebetta, Hepu, Sennefer, and Anhai weren't staying in the main house. They and Bentanta had taken up residence in a smaller building that huddled next to the walls of the larger compound; at least they weren't ensconced in chambers near him.

His glance dropped to the front gate, where musicians were entering. They carried harps, flutes, castanets, drums, and cymbals. Behind them came a chattering group of dancers and acrobats.

The young women reminded him of Bener. He had never escaped to the river with his daughters. His steward had cornered him, and he'd been forced to deal with accounts, disputes among farmers, and decisions in criminal cases. Bener had appeared at the steward's house, where he'd gone to administer his judgments. She had watched him work for several hours, a vision of injured sadness. When he finished, they walked back to the house together.

"Father," she had said, "you shamed me."

"What?"

"You threatened poor Nu, who has done nothing."

"If he's done nothing, he shouldn't be afraid, and you shouldn't be ashamed."

Bener rolled her eyes. "Please, Father. Remember how you felt about Great-Aunt Cherit."

"Hmm."

Bener was too clever. That conversation had convinced him to make a decision over which he'd been hesitating for months. He needed to have Bener and Isis where he could keep a vigilant watch over them. He was trying to think of a diplomatic way to inform Idut of his decision when he noticed a chariot with two men coming down the avenue toward the house. It passed through the gate, and as it came nearer, he recognized the driver: Kysen. And Nento.

He hadn't seen Nento in a while, but he would always recognize that ostrich-egg head and watermelon-shaped body. From here Meren could even see his neatly combed and oiled mustache. Nento was one of the few men who annoyed Meren because of his smell. It wasn't that he reeked; Nento was the kind of man who rarely exerted himself and took care to use deodorants and scent. So he always smelled like cinnamon.

Meren studied his son for signs that all was well. Kysen appeared unconcerned, but he was still some distance away. He turned to descend the stairs and meet Kysen but whipped around to face the gate again when something caught his eye. Across the river, the sun had disappeared. But there was still a soft, diffuse glow that cast vague shadows in the groves of trees to either side of the road that led from the river to the house. There was a lull in the traffic along this path.

A tall palm sat next to the road, its trunk a dark shadow. The shadow was too dark, and it moved, separating from the tree. A man stepped onto the road for a moment and raised his eyes to the roof of the house. Meren took in his great height, the ebony hue of his skin, the athletic grace of his movements—and cursed. Raising his hand, he gestured toward the rear of the house. The black figure vanished.

"Demons and fiends," Meren hissed to himself. "Son of a dung-eater, damnation." He raced across the roof, around an awning beneath which lay cushions for lounging, and to the back outer stair.

Taking the steps two at a time, he landed at their base to surprise a group of kitchen helpers bearing feast cakes into the house. Waving them aside, he gathered his composure and walked swiftly down the path that ran between the garden wall and the kitchen and well court. He stopped at a long, single-story building and stuck his head inside.

"Reia, Iry, come with me to the back gate."

He led them to the door that pierced the back wall, turned, and spoke in a low voice. "Let no one come this way."

They took up sentry positions while Meren unbolted the door and slipped outside. He was immediately assaulted by the smell of a refuse pile that grew just beyond the wall. Hurrying around it, he searched his surroundings. Beyond the house sparse grassland soon gave way to the desert. Pens for goats, cattle, and other animals dotted the landscape. A herder was driving several cattle toward a nearby village, but everyone else seemed to be busy inside the compound. The herder was soon gone.

A few thorny acacia trees clung to the edge of the barren pasture a few paces from the refuse pile. Meren walked toward them. As he reached their sparse shelter, a giant Nubian stepped into view. Meren cursed again and stepped behind the largest trees.

"Come back here," he said angrily. "Stay behind the trunks, or someone may see you."

The visitor loomed half a cubit taller than Meren, who looked up to meet his eyes. For a moment neither man spoke. The Nubian contented himself with folding his arms over his chest so that the muscles bulged as large as those in Meren's thighs. Undisturbed, Meren scowled at him.

"Please tell me you've brought a letter."

He got a head shake in reply.

"A spoken message?"

No reply. Meren felt his body grow cold, and scorpions seemed to sting a path down his spine.

"Then I'm right?"

A low rumble signaled the Nubian's first words. "Yes, lord."

"By all the fiends of the desert." Meren shut his mouth and thought furiously for a few moments. "I cannot believe you've done this. Leave. Before someone sees you. Meet me at the dock tonight. I'll come as soon as this cursed feast is over. You know about the feast, I assume."

"Aye, noble one."

"Very well. Go, and pray to all the gods you don't pay for this with your life."

"I already have, lord."

Meren hastened back inside the gate, instructed Reia and Iry to have the charioteers ready, and headed for his rooms. By now Kysen would be there. At least he'd be able to share this terrible new fear. Unfortunately, neither of them could control its source.

Kysen was waiting for him, but they weren't able to talk privately until Zar had been allowed to dress Meren for the feast. With his patience strained near to breaking, Meren hastily garbed himself in a transparent, pleated robe of the finest Egyptian linen. He slipped into gilded leather sandals and tried to stand still while Zar loaded him down with a gold necklace, heavy bracelets of gold and lapis, and the thick tresses of a court wig. He waved the servant away when the man approached with a garland for his head.

"I've got gold hanging from my arms, legs, shoulders, and ears, Zar. That's enough. Now go away."

Once the servant was gone, Kysen said, "I couldn't believe it when you wrote about Idut's feast."

"Forget the feast. You're late."

"Lord Paser was following me. I almost had to sail to Abydos, but he broke off his pursuit. He never did have much patience."

"Curse it. I thought he'd gone."

"You saw him too? I sent men after him to make sure he keeps sailing north."

"Good, because we've another difficulty—no, not a difficulty, a disaster." Meren threw up his hands. The gold and jewels on his body glittered in the lamplight. "Just now I found—"

His chamber door banged open. Meren shut his mouth as his sister swept into the room along with Bener and Isis.

"I knew you'd be here instead of in the reception hall

where you're supposed to be. Come along, because I'm not leaving without you."

"I'll be there in a moment," Meren said, but Idut snatched his arm and dragged him along in her wake. Bener grabbed his other arm, while Isis grasped Kysen's hand and started chattering.

Idut pulled him out of the room. "Now, Meren."

He soon found himself standing amidst his family in the reception room, performing the ceremony of greeting for an unending procession of guests. The soothing strains of a harp filtered in from the central hall. Servants decked each guest in garlands. Others offered scent cones, those coveted unguents that, when placed on the head, melted and spread soothing oil over the guest. In this season of unremitting and desiccating heat, the unguent provided relief and soothed the skin.

Meren breathed in the scent of myrrh, lilies, and frankincense as Great-Aunt Cherit hobbled over to him on the arm of a slave.

"I want to talk to you, boy."

"Blessings of the gods, Aunt. May you feast well this night."

"Nebetta told me what you said to her. It's time someone took you in hand."

Meren glared at the slave. The woman tugged on her mistress's arm, and Idut intervened by draping a garland around Cherit's neck.

Kysen slipped away from Isis to stand beside him and stare at the group coming toward them. "By the gods, she's invited the Antefokers. Isn't that the family that's brought suit against Anhai?"

"Smile, my son. Yes. She cheated them on the weighing of the final payment for some land. Used false weights to make the copper *deben* seem more then they actually were. Unfortunately for Anhai, Antefoker has Syrian merchant's blood and can smell a false weight like a crocodile scents prey, and he'd rather lose his sons than one-tenth of a deben of copper. He almost attacked our cousin's dear wife. Ah, Antefoker, Mistress Nofru, how good of you to bring all three of your sons and your daughter."

Antefoker, a robust man with the square build of a block statue, hardly bowed to Meren. "I want to talk to you."

"Of course, my friend, talk, eat, drink, dance. We'll make merry the whole night. Have an unguent cone. Kysen, our good friend Antefoker and his family are here."

"Where is that woman Anhai?" Antefoker demanded.

Meren didn't answer. Turning to greet the next arrival, he was taken by surprise. Bentanta walked over to him with her graceful stride that always reminded him of the long-legged pace of a Nubian warrior. But something about her was different. Richly dressed for the feast, she wore gold ring beads threaded through her hair and an elaborate pleated robe. No, it wasn't her dress that seemed different. Usually she disturbed him with her air of calm amusement, but as they spoke, he realized that her salutation was carried out in a distracted manner. She hardly looked at him or at Kysen when his son addressed her. Then Sennefer came in with Anhai, and he forgot his curiosity.

"Don't look so disgusted, Meren," Sennefer said. "I don't see how you can when you're surrounded with such beauty."

Anhai gave her chimelike laugh. "He means his own wife. Do you not, Sennefer?"

Sennefer's smile became fixed.

"Pay her no heed. I mean all these ladies with smooth skin and, and . . ."

Sennefer's words faded as he encountered Meren's

gaze. Bentanta had been talking to Kysen, but both broke off at the abrupt silence.

"I'm sure your compliments are intended for your wife," Meren said at last.

He would have continued, but Wah bustled into the room and swooped down on them. He was forced to introduce the man to the others.

"I know Wah," Anhai said. "He was Queen Nefertiti's steward at the North Palace when I attended her."

"Yes," Sennefer said. "My wife has spoken to me of you often."

The mention of Akhenaten's queen brought a glance from Kysen. Wah opened his mouth, but snapped it closed as Anhai praised the dead woman. Nefertiti had been a woman with the beauty of Hathor and a wisdom blessed by Toth. The delicacy of her face had masked the power she wielded through her influence over Akhenaten.

For years she had advised moderation and caution when the king wished to embark upon some mad course demanded by his god. But finally Akhenaten's appetite for extremity devoured her. She lost favor and was banished to the North Palace at Horizon of Aten. There she lived for a while, until one of the plagues sweeping across the kingdom from Syria took her. And with her went any hope of curbing Akhenaten's excesses.

Wah shifted from one foot to another like a giraffe with sore hooves. "Good lady," he said, interrupting Anhai, "I'm sure Lord Meren doesn't wish to dwell on death tonight."

"Meren lives with murder and death," Anhai retorted. "He likes killers, plots, and blood. Our poor queen's illness isn't likely to disturb him." She continued with her account.

Left to his own thoughts again, Meren recalled his gratitude to the queen. He'd always suspected that

Nefertiti had spoken to the king on his behalf after his father's death, and that it was her influence as much as her father Ay's that had saved his life. He had mourned the day she died, and long after. So many at court had been taken by that plague, which had come to ravage Egypt.

"I hate to remember her like that," Anhai was saying. She had moved next to Wah and plucked a date from the basket he carried. "You remember, Wah. The plague turned her skin red and dry, like she'd been staked out in the desert. You could hear the voice of her heart, and she had visions from her fever."

"Let us not dwell on unhappy memories." Wah smiled at Anhai, revealing his slightly brown teeth and the tip of his tongue.

Anhai examined the date and went on unperturbed. "But we all have happy memories of the Great Royal Wife Nefertiti, don't we, Wah?"

"But we're here to rejoice at Lord Meren's homecoming," Wah replied.

"I agree," Meren said. "Come, my friends. I think it's time to go in and partake of that ox my sister had sacrificed. And I hear she's brought in wine from the vineyards at Buto."

Waving the whole group forward, he herded them toward the central hall and the other guests. Inside waited tables heaving with roasted quail, beef, heron, and duck, along with grapes, stewed figs, cakes, and melons. He paused just before entering the hall, sighing and wondering how he was going to avoid being ambushed by his various relatives and the importunate Wah.

All at once there was a great crash behind him. A crowd of young men beating hand drums, barking with laughter, and stumbling over their feet invaded the room. One had fallen over a water jar stand. Another tripped over the fallen man and landed in the water, unable to right himself because he was beset with giggles. More young men streamed toward Meren, uttering hoots and imitating the cry of a hawk. Several paraded around the room with garlands and streamers of flowers. Last of all, borne on the shoulders of his comrades, brandishing a golden goblet, and singing a hunting song, came the leader of this band of drunks.

"Carry me to my host!" the leader shouted.

Meren glanced over his shoulder to find that half his guests had crowded out of the hall to witness the drunken arrival. The newcomer slid off the shoulders of his bearers to land on his feet, but his knees buckled, and he sat down hard.

"Goat's dung! My ass will be sore for a month."

Eyes red and watery, mouth slack, hard body turned flaccid with drink, he leered up at Meren and stuck out his hand.

"Help me up, O great lord, O noble prince, O Sole Companion, O great one, Eyes and Ears of Pharaoh."

Meren grasped his hand, yanked the younger man to his feet, and said coolly, "I didn't think you were coming to my feast of rejoicing. Welcome, dearest brother. Can it be that you're drunk with the happiness of seeing me again?"

6

Meren stared at his brother while Ra's friends staggered past them to join the guests in the hall. The women returned to the cushions and chairs reserved for them on one side of the room, while the men went to the other side. This separation wouldn't last, and the more beer and wine were consumed, the more convivial the two sexes would become. Idut called for the acrobats, and the two men in the reception room were left to themselves.

Meren gestured to a servant who had been clearing away the broken fragments of the water jar. The man vanished. So did the porters at the front door. Folding his arms over his chest, he waited for his brother to speak. Ra gulped down the last of his wine, turned his back on Meren, and went to a stand upon which rested a round-bottomed wine jar. Lifting the pottery jar, he filled his goblet to the brim. When he brought the vessel to his lips, some of the wine spilled down his chest and onto the floor.

Still sipping, with the goblet obscuring his view, he swayed a few steps. He thrashed about with his free hand. It hit a column. Using it for support, he took another couple of steps and bumped into it. Frowning at the pillar, he put his back to it, bracing himself there as he slowly sank to the floor, drinking all the way down. Once he was seated, he held out the goblet to Meren.

"Get me some more, will you?"

Meren walked over to stare down at his brother. "I thought you weren't coming."

"I wasn't, but I heard that my favorite relative was going to be here, so I changed my mind."

"What favorite?"

"Anhai," Ra said, waving his goblet. "That lovely scorpion Anhai. Poor Sennefer. He never should have married a woman with more wit than he, and certainly not one more ruthless than a Hittite."

Ra pointed with his goblet to the scene in the hall. Through the open double doors the women's side of the room could be seen. Anhai was seated among the ladies on a chair carved of cedar and inlaid with ivory. From the wary glances she elicited from the other women, Meren could tell that she affected them like a hawk among pigeons. Meren could sympathize, for Anhai's character was disturbing.

Cool, humorous, articulate, she could hold an audience's attention with her stories and jests. Yet beneath her humor lurked viciousness that could lash out without warning. Once aroused, Anhai used her tongue like a scorpion's stinger. Once Meren had seen her reduce a princess to tears with an offhand remark of unexpected malevolence.

Her extraordinary character was matched with an ordinary appearance that belied her power to attract attention. Her hair was plain brown rather than glossy black, her eyes the same. Her nose was neither too long nor too short, but sharp, like a sparrow's beak. Of middle height, she never caught interest because of either long legs or diminutive stature. And yet despite her modest looks Anhai had attracted Meren's brother.

A maid placed an unguent cone on Anhai's gleaming black wig while the lady sniffed a lotus flower. She glanced up from the petals, her eyes meeting Ra's directly and without any pretense that the exchange was

an accident. Ra gave her a loose-lipped smile. Meren had
seen enough. He unfolded his arms and stepped in front
of his brother, blocking the link between the two.

"You're interfering with a married woman, your
cousin's wife?"

Ra gave him a resentful look. "She understands my
burdens and trials."

"What burdens?" Meren could feel exasperation
building inside him. Just receiving one of those I-have-
suffered-so-much looks from Ra was enough to make
him want to kick his brother. "What burdens, Ra? Having
to visit three taverns a night? Enduring the trials of
hunting and fowling instead of serving in government or
the army or the priesthood? Those burdens?"

"Unlike you—"

"I offered to sponsor you in any office you cared to
pursue. I did sponsor you, but when you entered the
charioteers, you refused to accept training. A charioteer
does have to train, you know. Otherwise he gets himself
and his fellows killed. You're not stupid; you could
achieve anything, if only you'd work."

"Why should I? You didn't. All you had to do was get
born first."

Meren dropped down beside Ra and stuck his face in
front of the younger man's. "How many times must I say
this? I worked; I work now. All the time. You may not
remember because you were so young, but I spent my
whole life studying and training, and Father noticed
every mistake I ever made. While you were playing with
your friends, he was screaming at me that I was worthless. I worked, Ra. I trained as a charioteer, apprenticed
myself to great warriors and ministers." Meren snatched
the goblet from Ra's hand, stood up, and glared down at
him. "My success isn't due to magic, dear brother, only
to ordinary, unending hard work."

Rising, Ra appeared abruptly sober. "And perhaps it

was also due to catching the eye of Nefertiti and Queen Tiye. Did you bed them to get what you wanted?"

Meren cursed, swooped at Ra, and hit him across the face. Ra stumbled backward against the column, laughing. "Someday that flapping tongue will get you killed," Meren said. "The gods will hear you and punish such obscenities."

Ra wiped blood from the corner of his mouth. As quickly as it had appeared, his humor vanished. "They won't punish me for speaking the truth, and the truth is that you won't share your power with me because you're afraid I might be better at serving pharaoh than you are. Just as I would have been a better heir to Father than you are."

"As long as we're speaking the truth," Meren said, "you should listen to a little of it yourself. Father and Mother provided well for you. I inherited so much for the reason anyone does; I'm the one who cares for our parents' kas. I see to it that their mortuary temples are attended by priests and supplied with food and drink. You see, dear brother, of the three of us, I'm the only one they trusted to do this duty forever."

Ra's mouth distorted with a sneer. "And you're so dutiful. The perfect son. But not such a perfect father, eh? Or the perfect husband. You let Sit-Hathor die, didn't you? And now you're too afraid of her ka's wrath to remarry, so you adopted a peasant."

"You know Sit-Hathor died in childbirth," Meren said after a long silence. "Speak of her again, and I'll give you the beating you've been inviting for years."

Ra lunged forward and jabbed a finger in Meren's chest, his words flying out like sparks of a fast-burning fire. "You'd rather spend time with your common son than play the dutiful father to your daughters. And what of your duty to the family? The rest of us might as well shut ourselves up in our tombs for all the care you show us. Gods, Meren, you make me want to puke."

Slapping Ra's hand aside, Meren suddenly realized he was gripping the hilt of his dagger as if preparing to draw it. Ra's mood changed again without warning, and he smiled.

"Take comfort, brother. You'll see even less of me than usual if I decide to marry."

"You're already married."

"Oh, I'll rid myself of my old wife if I take a new one. I'm not fool enough to try to make two women happy."

"Your wife's family is powerful at court. Don't make them angry. Who do you think you're going to marry?"

Without answering, Ra laughed in Meren's face. Turning his back, he sauntered into the central hall, stopped by Anhai's chair, and whispered something to her. Anhai chuckled, causing heads to turn in their direction. Meren swore silently. Ra had always enjoyed baiting him, but from the look in his brother's eye, it was obvious that Anhai appealed to him. Perhaps he admired a tongue even more cruel than his own.

Meren tore his gaze from the scene and unwrapped his fingers from their clench around the dagger. Then he forced himself to smile and entered the hall. At once he spotted Antefoker bearing down on him. He sidled behind a group of men watching the acrobats and plunged into another crowd gathered around a pair of jugglers. Taking a cup of wine from a servant, he slipped behind a column and took a long drink. When he lowered the cup it was too late to avoid the clawlike hand that descended to his arm.

"Ah, my dear host," said Wah. "What a beautiful feast this is. And what great fortune it is for me to be able to talk to you. I'll be Idut's husband soon, with your permission, and I'm sure you and I can agree on a suitable contract."

"But not tonight," Meren said.

"Of course," Wah said. He popped a date in his mouth and chewed while he talked. "But there's something I've been wanting to talk to you about. Much time has passed since the unfortunate—uh—heresy. I know you understand that I, like you, was only doing the bidding of pharaoh at Horizon of Aten. Much time has passed, much time."

"Wah, you personally took a chisel to the name of Amun in his great temple."

Wah glanced around before coming closer. The scent of his unguent cone nearly choked Meren as he whispered, "You know I couldn't refuse. Who among us would refuse the will of the living god? Others have been forgiven, and I have great skills."

"Silence!" Irritation caused Meren to speak so loudly that several men looked their way. He lowered his voice. "There is nothing I can do."

"Yes, there is."

Wah droned on, but Meren was too unhappy over his brother to heed him. He settled for smiling and nodding while Wah continued to make his case. Over the man's shoulder Meren could see Anhai fanning herself with her lotus flower and leering at Ra. Near them Bentanta seemed to be talking urgently to Sennefer, who was touching a fresh scent cone that was beginning to melt on his head.

Then Sennefer whirled around and stalked to his wife's side. Anhai ignored him and slipped away to join Bentanta, who was sitting on a couch. The two women began to speak. Bentanta threw up her hands. Meren couldn't hear what they were saying, but their speech was growing more and more agitated. Anhai leaned toward Bentanta and growled into her ear. Then Bentanta jumped up with an exclamation. Grasping Bentanta's robe, Anhai attempted to hold her in place.

Bentanta's voice rose above the music and chatter. "Let go, you foul bitch!" Her hand struck out, knocking Anhai's arm and freeing her robe. Heads turned as she fled, shouldering her way across the hall and vanishing into the reception room.

"So you will aid me?" Wah was saying.

"What? Oh, I'll think upon it."

"After all, I'm to be your brother."

"I said I'd think upon it, Wah. That's all I'll say."

He waved a hand in dismissal and threaded his way through the crowd toward the reception hall. Anhai was there before him. The two women stood in the shadows, toe to toe, breasts heaving. He heard Bentanta's voice, strained, quiet, menacing.

"I wish I had the courage to kill you."

Anhai's light laughter filled the room. "If my husband and his parents don't, why should you? Take heart, Bentanta, perhaps Antefoker will do the work for you."

"Stay away from me," Bentanta said. "Or you'll regret it."

Bentanta walked out of the shadows, saw Meren, and hesitated, her eyes wide with alarm. Meren approached her, but she hurried by him. He caught up with her as Ra passed them on his way to Anhai. Meren slipped around Bentanta and blocked her way.

"What's wrong?" he asked. "I thought you and Anhai were longtime friends."

"Anhai has no real friends," Bentanta said. "She has followers, worshipers, people who are enamored of her charm and haven't the wits to see beneath it and into her scorpion's soul."

"But what has she done to you?"

Uttering a little gasp of impatience, Bentanta said, "Don't you ever listen to your family, Meren? She wants to leave Sennefer and take his most valuable estate with her."

"I know, but what has that to do with you?"

"She wants me to help convince Sennefer to give in. Sennefer likes me and trusts my judgment, possibly because I'm one of the few people who know what Anhai is really like."

"But still, to ask you to interfere in such a matter—why would she demand such a thing of you?"

"I know not," Bentanta said, throwing up her hands. "If you want to know more, ask Anhai."

"You're not telling me everything. You're worried. I can see it in your eyes. If I didn't know you better, I might think you were afraid. Of what?"

Bentanta gave him an incredulous look and laughed. "I didn't know you had a storyteller's imagination, Meren."

Meren didn't return her smile.

"You're right about Anhai. Beneath that humor and charm lies the ka of a netherworld fiend. Don't anger her."

"Oh, go away, Meren. You make too much of a simple quarrel."

"Then you won't mind if I talk to Anhai and Sennefer."

"I care not, Meren, only leave me alone."

She brushed past him, but he caught her arm. She looked up at him with dark, startled eyes as he whispered to her.

"What is it that has you so disturbed, Bentanta?"

Bentanta looked away and shook her head. Meren released her, and she walked away. Not quickly, but calmly, with an unfaltering step that belied the fear he'd seen in her eyes. Meren stood frowning at her retreating figure and musing over the last few moments. Bentanta was a formidable woman, one capable of making him feel like a newly circumcised youth. But tonight she'd lost her composure as he'd never seen her do. And she'd threatened to kill Anhai. Anhai was malicious, but hardly worth killing.

What had Anhai done to anger Bentanta so? Meren drummed his fingers on the side of his wine cup. He was worried, and to his great surprise, he was worried about Bentanta. Her mysterious predicament had thrust the quarrel with Ra out of his thoughts. Astonishing.

Just as he began to ponder this development, Antefoker called his name. Too late he realized the man had planted himself in front of him and was waving a joint of beef as he launched into a litany of complaints about Anhai's grasping and cheating nature.

"Oh, Antefoker, not now," Meren said.

"Can't you make her pay me?" Antefoker asked.

Kysen walked up and saluted them with a wave of his wine goblet. "There you are, Antefoker. Sennefer was looking for you over there by the musicians. He wants to talk to you about some matter of a contract or something."

Antefoker rushed off, and Meren gave his son a grateful look.

"I'm in your debt, my son. Was Sennefer really looking for him?"

"No. Now let me speak to you before someone else comes near. Nento has left, complaining of an ague. By now he's at the barge. The poor man is frightened near to pissing with this unexpected feast. He was quite brave until he saw all the guests. Then he realized the risks. I had to find him a stool and pour two cups of wine down him."

"Then I'm glad he's already gone. We'll meet him as soon as the house quiets down for the night. Gods, I could strangle Idut for disobeying me."

"She's not thinking of you, or anyone else but herself. Look at her. She's enamored of Wah."

Meren glanced at his sister and her proposed husband and shook his head. "But why would she want to marry that snake?"

"I overheard him flattering her just now," Kysen said as they gazed at the couple in disbelieving curiosity. "He's as obsequious to her as he is to you, and with much more flattery in the mixture. Don't worry about it now, Father."

"Do you know how many things I have to worry about? There's our secret guest—enough to turn my hair white. There's Bener and her scribe. There's this warfare between Sennefer and his wife. There's Bentanta's fight with her too, and then there's Nebetta and Hepu. Did you know they tried to blame me for—never mind. Oh, and there's Ra, who is going to get himself killed if he doesn't keep away from Anhai. And all this has to happen on the one night I can least afford to have it happen."

"The family will fight whether you're here or not." Kysen handed Meren his wine cup. "Here, taste this. It's spiced pomegranate wine. Lady Bentanta brought it from her own vineyards."

Meren took a sip and gasped. It was like drinking liquid gold. He'd never tasted anything that so resembled the tales of wine in the perfect netherworld. Fruity, light, but not too sweet, it made him feel as if he were bathed in cool night waters in a pool in the north breeze.

"Ky, I think I hear the music of Hathor."

"I told you."

"I'm going to have more of this. But not tonight, nor should you."

"There you are!"

Meren jumped as his sister caught his arm and began dragging him toward the dais at one side of the hall.

"You're supposed to be in the host's seat, not skulking among the lesser guests. Great-Aunt Cherit was asking for you."

Idut herded Meren and Kysen to the dais, where they sat on either side of the aged lady. Thus ceremoniously ensconced, they watched a line of women dance to the accompaniment of harp, double pipes, flutes, and drums. Bener and Isis persuaded one of the women musicians to teach them to use sistra. A loop of metal attached to a handle, the instrument bore small wires suspended across the loop. The bars held small metal disks, and when the sistrum was shaken, it produced a light rattle. Meren was admiring his daughters' agility with the instruments when Cherit poked him with her elbow.

"Pay attention, boy."

To his disbelief, Hepu stood before him, a roll of papyrus in hand. He glared at Meren, cleared his throat, and began to read.

"Instruction of the Lord Hepu for his nephew, being the teachings for existence, instructions for well-being, every rule for conduct with *elders* . . ." Here Hepu paused to give Meren a significant glance. "For conduct with magistrates; knowing how to answer one who pleads, to reply to one who sends a message . . ."

Now Meren wished he'd drunk four or five glasses of Bentanta's wine. He fixed a pleased smile on his face, pretended to look at Hepu, and watched Isis instead. His thoughts strayed to the work ahead of him until he noticed that his daughter wasn't among the musicians anymore. He found her in the midst of a group of young men, some of those who had come with Ra. Jolted into alertness, Meren sat up straight and directed a severe glance at Kysen.

Kysen rose, left the dais, and strolled over to the group around his sister. The young men welcomed him with jokes and smiles. Kysen smiled in return as he spoke quietly to them. They turned as a group to cast apprehensive glances at Meren. Kysen was already making Isis laugh as he smoothly guided her away from them. In a moment he had deposited Isis on a cushion at Meren's feet.

Unaware of almost being the cause of her friends' near-demise, Isis began to listen to Hepu's endless recital.

Kysen rested his arm on the back of Meren's chair. "Harmless."

"Ra's friends aren't harmless, they're unwholesome, lazy, and in need of flaying. Where is he? He should be keeping watch on that bunch of drunken colts."

"You're not going to be pleased."

"Tell me anyway."

"He's gone to the village of Green Palm. At least he took Antefoker with him." The village lay between Baht and the haunted temple.

"Green Palm. Damnation, Green Palm."

"With more of his friends. They were going to a beer tavern, to visit the women. Now, Father, I know what you're thinking, but there is no chance Ra knows what we're doing. And he wouldn't dare interfere if he did."

"I'm not so sure anymore," Meren said. Gripping the arms of his chair, Meren pretended to be pleased with Hepu's reading. "He's worse than ever, Ky, and losing what little judgment he ever possessed. If he's heard something or suspects what we're about, he might try to ruin the plan just to thwart me."

"I don't think he knows."

"I pray to the gods he doesn't."

They lapsed into silence, each pretending to enjoy Hepu's speech. He noticed Sennefer propped against a column, yawning, his head drooping, causing his unmelted scent cone to hit the pillar. Stifling his own yawn, Meren almost smiled when Hepu let the papyrus roll close. Then a servant handed him another. Meren sat back, eyes wide.

"Section twenty-one," Hepu said.

"Uncle, how many of these wondrous sections are there?"

Hepu inflated his chest and beamed at Meren. "You're most fortunate, nephew. There are fifty-seven."

"Fifty-seven!" Isis exclaimed.

Meren gave her a surreptitious kick. He settled back in his chair and whispered to his son, "Ky, get me a cup of that pomegranate wine, a large cup, the largest you can find."

7

Meren walked along the riverbank, careful not to go too near the water, where crocodiles were likely to be lying in wait for the unwary. Kysen had gone ahead with most of the charioteers to assist Nento. Meren was following the giant Nubian, who was a darker shadow against the moon's silver illumination. As far as he could see up- and downriver, the fields were deserted. Baht wasn't even visible at the edge of the desert. A few boats had been beached for the night, their owners having gone home to the scattering of modest mud-brick houses overlooking the fields.

The Nubian stopped abruptly, glanced back at Meren, and pointed. Ahead, its long body running parallel to the bank, lay a modest yacht. They were approaching the mooring stake when several men rose up from concealment behind the tall reeds by the shore. The Nubian ignored them. They studied Meren, then returned to their hiding places. Before he walked across the plank connecting the ship to the bank, Meren spotted half a dozen other watchers disposed behind palms or huddled behind dropoffs and irregularities in the shoreline.

Once aboard the yacht, Meren hurried to the deckhouse. The Nubian vanished inside, then returned and lifted aside the hangings that covered the doorway. Without saying a word, he nodded at Meren, giving permission to enter. Meren slipped inside, glancing around the chamber hung with leopard skins and filled with gilded furniture. His gaze found the room's sole occupant, who was sitting on the floor sharpening the blade of a short sword. Meren took a step, sank to his knees, and touched his forehead to the deck.

The boy looked up from the blade and said, "You're angry."

"Aye, divine majesty." Meren sat up and glared at the king. "I am furious."

"I am pharaoh, you know. My will is as the will of my father, the king of the gods."

At once Meren smoothed the wrinkles of anger from his face and bent to touch his forehead to the floor again. "Thy will is accomplished in all things, golden one. May you have life, health, and strength forever. What is thy will?"

"Vulture dung! If you hide behind ceremony, I'll lose my temper."

Sitting up again, Meren put his fists on his hips. "Then I may speak to the divine one as a friend?"

"Yes, yes. You win." Tutankhamun cast aside the sword and jumped to his feet.

Meren stood as well and threw up his hands. "Then will you tell me, by all the enemies of Egypt, how have you come to be here and why, O divine one?"

The king laughed. Picking up the sword, he deposited it in a long box.

"I gave Ay a choice. He either allowed me to sneak away to see you or allowed me to pursue a horde of Libyan nomads who have been raiding villages south of Memphis. I'm supposed to be sick and confined to my apartments in the palace."

"Do you know that when I saw Karoya at my door, I nearly fell off the roof of my house?"

Tutankhamun gave him a quick glance, and in that brief exchange Meren glimpsed old hurts, dark and painful anxiety, and fear. He should have known that only the gravest of reasons would draw the king away from the possibility of engaging in his first real battle. This wasn't the time to play the stern adviser. Most of the king's life had been spent in duty, in preserving a remote divinity, and in learning diplomacy; how to manipulate powerful princes and kings, how to conciliate factions within his kingdom. But there was a limit to the maturity of even a divine king when that king was only fourteen.

Drawing closer to the youth, Meren said softly, "What has brought thy majesty to my house in secret?"

Tutankhamun lowered his gaze and hesitated. His face had yet to lose the gentle rounding of boyhood, yet his eyes were filled with the brooding sadness of a man thrice his age. The king looked up at Meren and began to speak in a whisper.

"I have to see him."

"Majesty?"

"My brother, you said the criminals had—had dese-crated his body. I know the priests have restored him, but still, I failed him, Meren. I was supposed to guard his house of eternity and preserve his body so that his ka could live forever, and I failed. I have to see for myself that he's restored." Tutankhamun turned away. "And I have to face him myself and ask him to forgive me."

"Majesty, thy divine brother is with . . ."

Meren stopped because he wasn't sure where Akhena-ten was. Akhenaten had tried to rid Egypt of the old gods who had formed the world and watched over the land from the beginning of time. He'd tried to establish his sun-disk god, the Aten, in their place. Had the Aten taken his disciple to some sun-disk netherworld? Or had the old gods punished the heretic and fed him to the Devourer when he reached the hall of judgment?

"Thy divine brother is . . . with the Aten, and he is a god. He knows who the true criminals were."

Turning quickly, the king burst out, "But don't you see? If I'd been stronger, or if I'd driven out the priests of Amun, Tanefer would never have dared plot such a crime."

"Evil finds weak hearts in which to lodge, majesty. Even you cannot prevent this."

He got a tortured look instead of a reply.

"Very well," Meren said. "Thy will is accomplished, divine one. You and Karoya and five of the royal body-guard will come with me."

"You understand."

"Aye, majesty. But you will return to Memphis at dawn?"

"I suppose it wouldn't be wise to visit your house?"

Meren shook his head. "Not if thy majesty wishes to preserve the secret that has brought us here."

"Then I'll go."

"Thy majesty is wise."

"Wise, ha! What wisdom is there in doing what I know you'll make me do anyway?"

"I would never force the divine one to do anything."

"And I'm a baboon in a fig tree. Don't answer, Meren. Pharaohs should be allowed a little humor. I'm going to need it before this night's work is through."

In little more than an hour Meren was on the journey he'd been anticipating for weeks, the one he'd expected to make unaccompanied and free of distractions from annoying relatives and from the presence of a living god.

The king's ship had carefully crossed to the west bank. Meren, the king, and their escort traversed the fields quietly, by foot, and set off into the desert. Their path skirted the mortuary temples of Meren's family and the modest tombs of the local villagers. The desert floor rose gradually to meet the limestone cliffs that formed a towering wall on the horizon. They climbed a ridge and walked down into a small valley formed by an ancient tributary. As Meren approached the valley he began to make out the walls of the old temple. Here, far from the sight of the river, surrounded by barren rock and dust, it had lain for countless centuries. The evil west winds had blown sand around its base and into its chambers. Time and weather had eroded its walls so that their tops were jagged.

Yet the place still stood, possibly because its unknown builders had used clay instead of mud in its bricks. One could still make out its facade—a series of buttresses and recesses like those of an ancient palace, like those he'd seen in Babylon. Like Babylon, the temple was alien, foreign, disturbing in its mystery. Around it lay a series of sand-covered mounds. And the wind was continually scraping the surface of the land to expose strange deposits of crudely painted pottery that bore images of sticklike figures in curved boats or engaged in warfare. Meren couldn't help feeling that whoever had made this place had done so long before the old ones recorded the deeds of the first pharaoh. The temple belonged to a time of darkness about which little was known.

Was it even a temple? The local villagers said that it was one of the resting places of Osiris, but that when his brother Set killed him, the god went to rule in the netherworld. After that Set sent the spirits of the dead to haunt the former domain of his rival. Even the steward Kasa claimed to have seen foul monsters abroad in this place at night.

As they emerged into the valley, the wind picked up, scouring the desert floor, flinging grit in their faces. Meren paused to bring a length of his headcloth over his face. Then everyone went still as a strange sound traveled to them with the breeze. It was like the distant, hollow call of trumpets heralding the approach of ghostly armies. And behind the trumpeting came high, thin wails, crashing upon them with infernal discord.

Several bodyguards drew closer to the king, facing outward and gripping their spears. Karoya set himself at the king's back, and Tutankhamun cast a wild, questioning look at Meren.

Meren smiled at him. "I've been here many times as a child and youth, majesty. Never have I met a demon or a netherworld monster."

"Never?"

"Never, but the villagers are afraid of this place. They say those who stumble upon the haunted temple return cursed with madness, or never return. Remember, that's why I chose it."

"Oh," the king said faintly. "Yes, how clever."

"Majesty, my cousins and I even spent an entire night in the temple. Djet dared us, and we dared him. We stayed the whole time and saw not one fiend."

"Of course. I'm not afraid, you know."

"Of course, majesty."

Meren led the way, approaching the temple's only entrance, a gap in the walls that must have been a door at one time. As they neared the structure, men rose from behind the mounds the surrounded it and saluted him.

"Reia, all is well?"

"Yes, lord, we—pharaoh!"

Figures appeared from behind various hiding places and dropped to the ground.

"Rise, Reia," Tutankhamun said, "and tell the men to keep silent. We're going inside."

Meren followed the king as he stepped through the gap in the temple walls. Before them lay a vast empty space, dark except for one lamp held by the waiting Kysen. Nento was beside him. When the king appeared, the men inside dropped to the ground. The lamp faltered as Kysen set it down, making shadows dance on the walls.

The king nodded at Meren, who gave permission for the charioteers to withdraw. Kysen and Nento stood, their eyes downcast. Oblong crates filled much of the interior.

"His majesty wishes to see for himself the results of the restoration."

His thighs brushing together, oiled hair covered in a film of dust, Nento bustled over to Meren and the king and bowed. "This humble cup-bearer greets the Lord Meren. I am Nentowaref, Scribe of the Royal Treasury, Overseer of the Seal, Overseer of the Magazines of the Temple of Amunhotep III. No effort has been spared by the priests, O divine one, but—"

"We know who you are, Nento," Meren said. "This is not the time for ceremony. It is the time for silence and hidden actions. Please show the golden one what he wishes to see."

Nento clamped his mouth shut and nodded. Bowing and shuffling, he conducted them to a tarp-covered mass set in the middle of the temple. Kysen lit the way with his lamp. Nento drew off the covering and the fine linen shroud that lay beneath.

There was a splash of reflected light as it hit a golden body. Meren heard the king suck in his breath. Nento began to chant spells from *The Book of the Dead* in a trembling whisper.

Like the body that lay within, the coffin had been cleaned and restored, and Meren thanked the gods that he'd ordered most of the work done before it was taken from Horizon of Aten. The old, solidified unguent, torn shrouds, and dead floral wreaths had been removed. Yet the coffin remained a strange sight.

Akhenaten had designed it, departing from the traditional form of the body of the god Osiris. Instead he'd used his own image, lying with his arms crossed over his hollow chest and holding the scepters of Upper and Lower Egypt. His figure, never the classic one of traditional art, emphasized wide hips, plump thighs, and spindly legs. Instead of being wrapped in the protecting wings of the goddesses of Upper and Lower Egypt, the heretic had wrapped himself in the symbolic rays of the Aten. The rays ended in stylized hands holding the ankh, the symbol of the breath of life.

"Meren, I want to see him."

Help was summoned so that the coffin could be opened. Pins of solid gold were removed, but it still took nine men to lift the lid. Meren dismissed the charioteers again, and he and the king went to stand by his brother's head. The body had been covered by another shroud, but one so sheer that the gold mask covering Akhenaten's face could be seen. True to his own doctrine, the king had ordered the mask in a style that exaggerated his already gaunt face, fleshy lips, and narrow, slanting eyes.

"See, majesty. The embalmer priests have made him whole again."

Meren asked forgiveness of the gods for this lie. The inlaid gold bands that surrounded the body were replicas, the originals having been stolen by the desecrators. Most of the outer protective amulets were also new. The gold covering on the hands concealed wads of linen bandages molded in the correct shape. The thieves had torn the arms off in their quest for the heavy gold bracelets and rings that covered them.

The king uttered a long sigh. "Indeed, they have made him whole. I was afraid there would only be pieces of him left."

"No, majesty. We discovered the atrocity before they could complete their evil work." Another lie, but if it would lift the burden of guilt from the king's spirit, a lie well told.

"And the queen?"

"If thy majesty commands, we will open her coffin as well, but there was no damage to her. I suppose they hadn't the time."

Tutankhamun gazed at the heavy-lidded, inlaid eyes of the king's mask. "I was so young when he died, and I'd almost forgotten what he looked like." The king lowered his voice. "Do you know how many times I've wished he and Smenkhare hadn't died? The priests of Amun and Osiris say the gods sent the plague to him because he tried to wipe them out. Perhaps they're right. But I wish they'd spared Nefertiti."

"She didn't suffer long, majesty."

"They wouldn't let me near her, you know. And because I wasn't there, I had to imagine what happened to her. Tell me what happened to her, Meren."

Tutankhamun's mother had been Tiye, the powerful Great Royal Wife of Amunhotep the Magnificent. Tiye bore her youngest son late and died when Tutankhamun was still a naked babe. Nefertiti had taken charge of him, and he remembered her more than his real mother. Meren had always feared pharaoh would ask such questions one day. The time had come to give part of the truth.

He glanced across the coffin to where Nento was still chanting spells. Then he began to whisper to the king. "I know little, majesty, except what my cousin's wife has told me. Anhai was in attendance on the queen when she fell ill. Ay has never spoken of it. I think his daughter's death still pains him."

"Did she suffer much?"

"Please, majesty. I know you're troubled by this terrible crime, and—"

"I want to know, and I can't ask Ay."

Sighing, Meren drew nearer the king and lowered his voice. "As with others, the plague allowed demons to enter the queen's body. She saw visions of them and yet couldn't see her surroundings. She was fevered, and the voice of her heart grew so loud it could be heard by those standing a few paces away." He hesitated at the pain in the king's eyes, but the boy had asked for the truth. "Her ka tried to fight the demons, and the struggle made her body convulse. She fought hard, but lost and lapsed into the deep sleep." The queen had died a few days after she came down with the sickness.

When Meren finished, the king said nothing. Meren stared at the mass of solid gold that housed the body of Nefertiti. Her features had been lovingly replicated by the artisans of the royal workshops—the hollow, fragile jaw, the long neck and full lower lip. She had been the embodiment of Hathor, goddess of love and beauty, and her ka had housed a spirit as sage and clever as Toth, god of learning and wisdom. A tragic end, and one upon which Meren never cared to dwell.

"Leave me for a moment," the king said.

Meren beckoned to Kysen and Nento, and they went to stand by the temple entrance. The king stood in the pool of gold cast by the lamp and the coffins, closed his eyes, and began to chant silently. It was Meren's misfortune that Nento couldn't be silent as well. The man uttered a litany on his responsibilities and excellent performance in an urgent whisper.

Like Wah, Nento had been a courtier at Horizon of Aten. But unlike his fellow servant, Nento had been clever enough to secretly desert the heretical faction once opposition to the king gained overwhelming strength. He constantly watched the shifting currents of power in royal circles, hopping from one nest of influence to another depending upon the ascendancy of one great man or another. Nento wasn't evil, just possessed of an all-consuming interest in his own advancement. Were pharaoh to suddenly declare that there were no gods at all, Nento would be the first to trumpet his agreement. Meren didn't like him much.

"Nento, I'm well aware of your work, now be silent. Kysen and I must return to Baht. Reia will be in charge of the charioteers here. In a few days you will sail south with the barge and complete the trading run as planned. I'll send for you if I need you."

Kysen coughed behind his hand. Giving him a suspicious glance, Meren decided that his son was trying to stifle a laugh. He frowned at the young man.

"You will meet me back at the house, and quickly. I don't want our guests to know we've been gone."

The king finished his prayers, cast a last, regretful glance at Nefertiti's beautiful features, and joined them. They all stepped outside into a world lit by stars. The moon had vanished, and with it the evil west wind. The men on guard had disappeared as well, hidden by rocks and slopes.

Karoya was waiting just outside the entrance. He scoured Nento with a contemptuous stare until the king dismissed the poor man and Kysen as well.

"Thy majesty has promised to return to court upon the morrow," Meren said.

"I know. But I'm not going to hurry."

"As thy majesty wills."

The king's escort awaited them behind one of the mounds that surrounded the temple. As they began the walk out of the valley, a high, laughing whine filled the night's emptiness. Another joined it, and another. Everyone stopped, and the guards formed a circle around Meren and the king. Hyenas usually preyed on carrion, but when food was scarce, they dared to attack children, the weak, or the unwary.

Meren surveyed the rocky slopes of the valley. It was too dark to make out much, but he thought he detected movement. Something on an incline to his right dislodged gravel and sent it tumbling toward them. Meren drew his dagger. Spears pointed in the direction of the rockfall.

Hardly breathing, Meren surveyed the starlit boulders. Another chorus of wails echoed off the rocks. Then he saw a black shape detach itself from the slope and scramble away on all fours. More shapes loped off in the same direction, and Meren sheathed his dagger.

"They're gone, majesty, but we should make haste for the river."

He escorted the king back to his yacht and exacted another promise that pharaoh would take himself back to Memphis the next day. By the time he got back home, Meren was exhausted. Having to sneak back into his own house didn't improve his mood either. Nevertheless, he was asleep by the time Zar had closed the door to his chamber after helping him undress and wash.

He seemed to have just closed his eyes when Zar roused him again. He sat up to find Kysen standing beside the body servant. It was still dark, and Zar's chest was swollen with disapproval as he stepped aside, holding an alabaster lamp.

"I'm sorry to wake you, Father, but there is a small difficulty."

"Small difficulty!" Sennefer pushed Kysen aside. "Is that how you describe it? My wife is missing, and he says it's a small difficulty."

Meren's head felt as if it were stuffed with natron and linen bandages. "Wait, Sennefer. Give me a moment."

He swung his legs over the side of the bed and stood. Zar returned with a kilt, which he wrapped around his waist.

Sennefer fidgeted, then burst out, "Are you awake now? Because I've no time to waste. I can't find Anhai."

"You mean she's vanished from your chamber?" Meren asked.

"No . . . uh, no."

Kysen gave Sennefer a look of disgust. "He hasn't seen her since before the guests began leaving."

"I thought she was among the crowd," Sennefer said.

Meren fixed him with a searing gaze, and he dropped his eyes.

"The truth, Sennefer. I've no patience with quibbling at this time of night."

"You want the truth?" Sennefer ran a hand through his hair as he paced back and forth by the bed. "I'll give you the truth, then, cousin. I didn't look for her, and I didn't ask for her. I waited, thinking she'd return, because I knew she'd gone off with your precious brother."

"How do you know this? Ra went off to the village of Green Palm."

Sennefer gave a bark of laughter. "A lie, no doubt, to disguise their meeting."

A noise at the door prevented Meren from arguing. Zar came forward, followed by a servant. Meren was surprised to see his steward Kasa. The man bowed, his face impassive.

"This humble servant requests an urgent word of the lord," he said. He gave the others in the room a sideways glance that stopped when it encountered Sennefer.

Uneasiness crept over Meren. In all the years he'd been lord at Baht, the steward had never disturbed him at night.

"Give me a moment, Sennefer."

"Gods! You're more worried about accounts than my wife."

Meren took Kasa aside and nodded for him to begin.

"The lord is discerning."

"Out with it, Kasa. What's wrong?"

"The workers were just beginning the day's grain grinding, lord."

Meren glanced at the high, grilled windows of his chamber and found that the first gray light was filtering through them. "Kasa, quit delaying. I've something else to deal with."

"The—the two are the same, lord. One of the workers has found a body in one of the large granaries."

"*In* the granary. In it?"

Kasa nodded, and Meren glanced at his cousin, who was still pacing and talking to Kysen.

"Not the Lady Anhai." Meren thought of the tall, beehive-shaped domes in the granary court.

"Aye, lord. Someone dragged her up the stairs and, well, dumped her in on top of the grain and replaced the cover."

"Meren, are you finished?" Sennefer asked. "We're losing time while you babble about your taxes."

8

Meren strode out of the house with Sennefer at his side and turned left to reach the gate in the wall that hid the granary forecourt from view. His eyelids felt as heavy as fishing weights. A mooring stake was being pounded into his head, and his mouth was dry as the fields outside Baht.

He went through another gate, with Kasa trotting ahead. Kysen walked behind them. A crowd of servants and laborers had gathered in the large granary courtyard that lay north of the house, between it and the outer wall. Within the courtyard sat four granaries in two pairs. Between each pair of domed structures stretched a high, solid mud-brick platform with attached steps. Loads of grain were brought up the steps to the platforms and emptied into the top of the dome through a circular opening.

Meren followed Kasa to the second pair of granaries. The servants were muttering among themselves and making the sign against the evil eye. The steward stopped at the bottom of the steps, beside which stood an older man with yellow teeth. He was Meren's overseer of the granary, Hray, who had discovered the body. The two bowed as Meren mounted the steps. Sennefer was on his heels.

At the top of the stairs, Meren barred Sennefer's way and said, "No. Let me look first."

"She is my wife!"

"That is the point I was about to make."

Meren walked along the platform to the first of the two granaries. Its round wooden cover lay on the ground, no doubt dropped there by Hray. Grain had been scattered on the platform and had fallen to the packed earth at the base of the granary. Bending over the opening, Meren peered inside. Rapidly growing daylight revealed the body. Anhai lay on her right side, her knees drawn up toward her chest, her arms bent toward her face in front of that short, sharp little nose. Her mouth was closed, concealing the razor tongue that would slice at its victims no longer. He could see nothing wrong with her—no wound, no blood, not even a bruise.

"Well?" Sennefer said as he came forward.

He stood beside Meren and looked down at his wife. Sucking in his breath, he held it, then expelled and whispered, "Anhai?" Gripping the edge of the opening, he stretched out a hand as if to shake her shoulder.

Meren grabbed his forearm. "Don't. Her ka is gone, cousin."

Sennefer stared at his wife's body and repeated her name on a questioning note. Then he began shaking his head.

"I don't understand. I don't understand. I don't understand."

Meren noted the dazed look in his eyes and the way he slumped against the side of the granary. As Sennefer's knees buckled, Meren quickly slipped an arm under his shoulder and helped him back down the stairs. He handed his cousin over to Kysen.

"Take him to his chamber—no—take him to my chamber and have Zar attend him."

Kysen gave him a quick look of comprehension that assured Meren that Sennefer would be guarded as well as attended and that his and Anhai's chambers would be quietly searched.

Meren went back up the steps and resumed his examination of Anhai. She almost looked as if she was asleep, except that her body was cool to the touch. The pallor of death was upon her, and he noted that her blood had seeped down to the portions of her body that rested on the grain pile.

Her clothing was arranged perfectly. Even the knot in the lengths of her robe that reached under her breasts was neat. The portion of her wig that was visible seemed free of grain, but there was grit on the back of it. The back of her gown was slightly dusty, but its pleats were smoothed and followed the bend of her torso and legs.

Meren lifted his face to the growing heat of the sun as he thought about what he was seeing—the odd resting place, the lack of marks on the body. The eastern sky was alight. Returning to his task, he reached inside the granary and tugged on Anhai's cool left arm. It moved, but was growing stiff with that strange paralysis that Nebamun, his physician, attributed to the shock of death and the flight of the ka from the body. He would have to get Anhai out of the granary soon, or she wouldn't unbend enough to fit through the opening.

Straightening, Meren rubbed his sore eyes, then took another look at the body. The overall impression was of neatness and peace. He glanced over the rooftops, into the distance over the trees. The scene around him seemed so mundane—the granaries, the workers and their tools, his daughters' pet cats. Not a place in which one expected to find the dead body of a noblewoman. The contrast between the prosaic scene he'd witnessed regularly as a child and the presence of death almost made him shiver. A sibilant whispering distracted him, and he glanced down at the servants hovering below.

"Kasa, take note of who was here at the discovery. Have them wait. The rest of you go about your chores."

Lapsing into thought once more, he evaluated the possibility of danger to his family. There didn't seem to be a threat at the moment, but he would have to be on guard. He glanced at the forecourt and saw Kysen standing in the gateway. Confronting him with excited irritation were Idut and Nebetta. Behind them stood Bentanta, silent, her lips pressed together. Kysen was shaking his head. Idut whirled around and stalked back to the house. Nebetta shook a finger at Kysen and followed her, but Bentanta delayed. Raising her eyes, she met Meren's gaze. Her face was impassive, yet severe, like a mortuary statue. Without acknowledging him, she turned and headed toward the main house.

Brushing away flies drawn to Anhai's body, Meren resumed his examination. He searched her for wounds and found none. He even removed the rigid bronze bracelet on her left arm. Drawing back the retractable pin, he bent the hinged half-cylinders and pulled it off. It bore an Eye of Horus inlay of white frit and lapis lazuli. Her arm was undamaged.

Meren was about to replace the bracelet when he noticed something stuck in the hinge, a small fragment of linen from Anhai's dress. He tugged on the tiny scrap, and it came free. Once he held it, he realized it wasn't linen but papyrus, a corner of a rectangular piece. Slipping the fragment into the folds of his kilt at his waist, he replaced the bracelet.

He noted the congealed unguent from the scent cone Anhai had worn last night. It had melted into her wig and streaked the broad collar of ivory and turquoise beads on her shoulders. The back of the collar, like the back of her gown, was covered with a fine layer of dust, yet it remained in place on her shoulders with the counterpoise positioned perfectly at her back.

While Meren studied the body, Reia and Iry entered the courtyard along with Kysen, who closed the gate to the forecourt. Backing away, Meren lapsed into thought while he glanced behind him to the rear of the courtyard. An awning was attached to the courtyard wall and two support posts. Beneath this shelter lay a row of seven concave querns of varying colors. Oblong grindstones lay on top of each quern. Nothing remarkable. Shaking his head, he motioned to Reia and Iry.

"Remove the Lady Anhai."

The two men extracted the body, whose left side was dark from pooled blood, and laid it on the platform. Meren knelt and lifted Anhai's robe, but could find no sign of the cause of her death. Kysen stepped past him and began to examine the interior of the granary where Anhai had lain.

Meren descended the steps to the ground. A knot of pain was growing in the space between his brows. Rubbing the furrows there, he ordered Anhai's body removed to one of the storage rooms in the service building before the back gate. Then he turned to the unfortunate Hray.

"Very well, tell me what happened."

Grimacing to reveal his yellow teeth, Hray bowed and said, "I came into the court with those men, the grinders, as I do every day, lord. I had my measuring container and went to the last granary, which is the one with the oldest grain, and I opened it and—and found her."

"So the cover was in its place?"

"Aye, lord."

"And did you notice anything unusual or see anyone who shouldn't have been here?"

"No, lord. There was only us, and all appeared as it should."

Hray indicated a group of men standing beneath the awning in a furtive clump. To Meren they looked apprehensive, but humble laborers tended to appear so when faced with situations that brought them unhappy notice from their lord. One of them shuffled backward and nearly stumbled against a yellow quern with a black grindstone resting on top of it. He looked down at it, scowled, and shoved another laborer, and a shouting contest ensued.

"You took my grindstone!"

"Liar! I never touched your foul grindstone."

"You did. I see it on your quern right there, you jackal."

Kasa rushed over to them and bellowed for order. Meren turned back to Hray.

"If you remember anything else, tell the steward." He motioned to Kasa, who hurried over to him. "You did well to come to me at once."

Kasa bowed. "Yes, lord."

Waving Kasa away, he began a circuit of the granary court. The ground was hard, packed earth covered with a layer of dust. Hundreds of footprints, both bare and sandaled, broke the surface of the dust. Useless to try to decipher them. Too many curious servants had trampled the area.

Much of the courtyard was empty space, left bare to allow donkeys to pass through, carrying grain from the threshing floors between the fields and the house. Baskets, sacks, and bowls were stacked near the grinding area. The day's requirement in grain was measured out and recorded by Kasa and Hray, then given to the laborers. These men first crushed the tough wheat in mortars, then sifted it to remove the bran. After this, the grain was ground on the quern. Then the rough flour was taken to the kitchens, where maids ground it further.

Meren walked around the perimeter of the courtyard, seeing nothing but ordinary equipment—stacks of extra winnowing fans, yokes for oxen, grain baskets. Under another shelter near the awning hung water jars. One of them rested askew within the ropes used to suspend it.

At last he came to the awning, beneath which still hovered the grain grinders. As he approached, he glanced at the querns. The yellow one now bore a grindstone that matched its color, and the black grindstone had been put on top of a black quern. Each set rested on a woven rush mat.

At Meren's command, the stones were removed and the mats lifted. His thoroughness yielded nothing, however, except a view of more packed earth and dust. The grinding area was next to the granary in which Anhai had been found, but appeared to bear no mark of her presence. Again Meren felt oddly disturbed by how normal everything appeared despite the presence of death.

"Why would she come here?" Meren muttered to himself.

"You spoke, Father?"

"Ah, Ky. Zar is watching Sennefer?"

"And I put one of the men outside your door. I've finished looking at the granary. There's nothing in it but grain, and I dug deep to see if there was anything below her body."

Meren nodded. Sweeping his arm around to indicate the courtyard, Meren said, "All this is a great puzzle. Why would Anhai come to this place? And what caused her death? There's no sign of a wound upon her, no mark of poison, no trace of evil magic, nothing. It's as if she decided to go to sleep in that granary, and her ka fled her body."

"Perhaps the gods simply ordained that she die now," Kysen said.

"Now, now of all times, when she seemed so full of humor, health, and venom? And if she just died, why would someone put her in a granary?" Meren asked. "I like not this coincidence—her dying just when we come to Baht for this special task. Gods, this business has distracted me. Have you received word that our visitor has departed?"

Kysen gave him a rueful glance. "Reia said the ship is still moored to the bank."

"Fiends of the netherworld!" Meren lowered his voice again. "Go to him and ask him to make haste in his departure."

Widening his eyes, Kysen thrust out his hands and shook his head. "You forget, Father. You're one of the few in the world who could even imagine saying such a thing to him. If you want him to leave, you're going to have to persuade him yourself."

"Damnation." Meren rubbed his eyes, then looked at his smiling son. "You're amused by my predicament, but it won't be so amusing if this turns out to be murder and *he* is here within reach of a killer."

"No, and that's why you must be the one to persuade him to sail out of harm's reach. He'll listen to you."

"All right. I'm going, but you'll have to stay here and make sure none of our unwanted guests leaves. Curse it. I was hoping to get rid of them today. Who stayed here last night? There was Sennefer, and there was Anhai and Bentanta. At least my other uncles couldn't come."

"Don't forget Nebetta and the loquacious Hepu, her upright spouse," Kysen said. "And Wah. Antefoker's family and the rest of the neighbors went home."

"And Ra? Has he come home?"

"I don't know, Father."

"Very well, I'm going now. And Ky, be certain to tell the men searching the house to look for any document or letter that looks suspicious." Meren withdrew the scrap he'd found on Anhai. "We're looking for something this could have come from."

"That's awfully small, Father."

"It may be nothing, but we have to be certain. Also,

none of the family or guests leaves Baht. You know what that means, don't you?"

"They won't like being treated like criminals."

"Then use diplomacy."

"There's nothing diplomatic about posting charioteers at the gates, Father. Nothing at all."

Meren had no sympathy to spare for Kysen. In his view, he had the worse task. He had to persuade his mischievous sovereign to return to the stifling and rigid ceremony of court. Without bothering to change his clothing, Meren left by the side gate in the granary forecourt used by those making grain deliveries. He skirted around the deserted threshing floors.

He drew little notice from the groups of winnowers working on a late batch of grain. Using pairs of wooden winnowing fans, they bent over piles of grain, scooped it up, and tossed it high in the air. The light chaff caught in the breeze and was blown away in golden clouds. As Meren left them behind, he heard them begin a winnowing song.

Retracing his journey of last night, he found the king's ship, as Kysen had said, still moored to the bank. Plainly garbed royal sailors and bodyguards lounged about in the shade of palm trees. Only to Meren was their tension and alertness apparent. His own anxiety reached greater heights when he realized that the king wasn't on his yacht. He was out in the middle of the river, spearfishing, alone except for Karoya.

Spitting forth every curse learned in barracks and on battlefields, Meren commandeered a skiff and poled out to the king's craft. As he neared the boat, Tutankhamun heaved his spear into the water with a cry. Pulling it back, he lifted a long silver fish into the craft, where Karoya removed it. The king then looked up as Meren drew alongside.

"Meren, a surprise. Did you see me get that one? What a size he is."

Bending low from his sitting position, Meren said coolly, "Thy majesty's prowess is bruited about the kingdom. Thou art Horus, Strong-Bull-arisen-in-Thebes, Golden Horus, Mighty-in-strength, Majestic-in-appearance, given life forever."

Arched brows drew together. The king threw his spear down and glared at Meren. At Meren's signal, Karoya picked up the weapon and exchanged places with him. Pharaoh sat down in the boat and pointed to a spot. Meren seated himself. As the Nubian rowed himself out of hearing, pharaoh scowled at his visitor.

"You're mocking me! Because I haven't done as I promised—but I was going to leave. I only wanted a few more hours of freedom."

Tutankhamun's shoulders slumped, and he seemed to lose the fire that prompted his outburst. "I have these dreams, Meren. I'm lying in the throne room in Thebes on a couch of ebony, on my back with my arms crossed, holding my scepters, dressed in all my finest jewels, and wearing the cobra and vulture of Egypt. My eyes are closed, as if I'm sleeping, but I'm awake, and I can see. It's like I'm a falcon hovering in the air above myself. All is in darkness except my couch, and I can hear the vastness of the throne room.

"Then the doors open, and pairs of priests march in, bearing vats of molten gold suspended on poles between them. Ay is their leader, and he comes to the couch. He raises his arms and shouts that I must be preserved for the well-being of the kingdom."

Tutankhamun swallowed hard before going on. "Then the priests bring forth the first vat, tip it, and pour the molten gold over me. I feel it splash over my body, hot, searing, scalding me. But it doesn't splash away. It clings to me. I scream, but they don't hear me, and I can't move. They keep pouring it over me until I'm encased in gold. It runs into my eyes, my mouth, my nose. I'm suffocating, but I don't die. The gold cools and hardens, and I'm left there screaming and suffocating. Forever."

This had ever been the problem. Pharaoh was so young, and saddled with the responsibility of divinity and an earthly empire as well. That haunted look of sadness had returned to the king's face.

Casting caution aside, Meren put his hand on the boy's shoulder. "I'm sorry, majesty. And I will try to ease your burdens when I return to court, but there is danger here. There has been a death at my house."

All sadness vanished from the king's features, to be replaced with eagerness and excitement. "A death! Whose?"

"My cousin's wife, the Lady Anhai, divine one."

"Oh, are you grieved?"

"I regret her death, but she was a woman with a scimitar for a tongue, which she concealed beneath a humorous and charming manner."

"What happened?"

"This morning my servants found her stuffed into the top of one of my granaries, majesty."

Tutankhamun's full lips formed an *O*.

"So thy majesty can see that he must return to court at once."

"Why? I'd rather stay and see what happens. Was she murdered?"

"I know not, golden one. I can find no cause for her death. But why else would someone stuff her in a granary?"

"Excellent. You're the Eyes and Ears of Pharaoh. You'll discover the cause and the one who is responsible, and I'll be here to see it all."

"Majesty, you don't understand. I like not this sudden and mysterious death coming hard upon our concealing the . . . the king and queen at the haunted temple. There is danger, and you must be away from here."

Tutankhamun folded his arms over his chest and drew his brows together. "No. I can come to your house to visit. I'll disguise myself as a foreign nobleman."

"Divine one, my family would recognize you, and even if they didn't, well—"

"Out with it, Meren."

"The golden one, if I may speak with frankness, does not behave like an ordinary nobleman, foreign or not."

"I don't?"

"No, majesty. Unlike the rest of us, you behave like a king of Egypt. How can I explain? Majesty, you don't even know the cost of a loaf of bread. You would be shocked if a nobleman addressed you without permission. And majesty, even without the crowns of Upper and Lower Egypt, you walk across the earth as if you owned it and the sky, which you do."

"Then I'll stay here."

Desperation crawled on scorpion's legs up Meren's spine, and he leaned toward the king. "If the golden one cares nothing for his safety, I beg him to consider mine. If you come to harm, Ay and General Horemheb will blame me."

He met the king's searching gaze without flinching. Tutankhamun was headstrong, but he wasn't callous. If Meren was found responsible for allowing the king to be harmed, his life would be forfeit.

"I don't want you hurt, Meren."

"Thy majesty is kind."

Pharaoh gave him a sidelong glance. "After all, you've promised to take me on a raid as soon as you're back in Memphis."

"A neat trap, majesty."

"I learned from you."

"A raid, then. Bandits or nomads, whichever occurs when I return."

"I'll be leaving as soon as the men can ready the ship."

Meren bowed to the king. "The divine one is as wise as he is strong. I will wait to see pharaoh embark."

9

▽

Kysen hurried toward the front gate, feeling as if he was
wading through steaming honey. He'd gotten less sleep
last night than his father.

"I'll have you disciplined, you son of a tavern
woman!"

Hepu shook his walking stick at an impassive charioteer. The guard stood, feet apart, a spear planted in the
ground, its tip tilted in Hepu's direction.

"Uncle, what's wrong?"

Hepu rounded on him, puffed out his chest, and
squawked. "You! You're the one who dared to keep us
here. What right have you to treat me like an unruly
child? My wife and I wish to go home. Tell your minions
to get out of my way at once."

"I'm sorry, Uncle, but I must ask you to stay awhile.
Anhai's death is most mysterious, and we must discover
the truth about it before anyone leaves."

Hepu turned carnelian, moved closer to Kysen, and
growled out his words. "You—you, with your polluted
commoner's blood—dare hinder me in any path I wish to
take? Get out of my way, and don't address me in that
familiar way."

"Guard your tongue," Kysen snapped.

"Meren was always wayward. Never would do his
duty the right way. What man refuses to remarry and

105

won't even keep concubines? And shames the family by adopting such as you!"

Kysen had spent too many years under his father's tutelage to reveal the humiliation and rage he felt. Using his hard-learned courtier's manners and warrior's composure, he merely sighed and took a step backward while glancing at the charioteer. The man banged his spear into the packed earth with a loud crack. At once, two more of his kind appeared from outside the wall to stand on either side of Hepu. Hepu was a large man, a fact he'd always used to intimidate his wife and his sons when they were small. But Hepu had never been a warrior. The sight of three spears hefted expertly finished him.

Hepu brandished his walking stick at Kysen. "Miserable cur! You'll regret this." He stalked back to the main house.

Kysen considered that it was almost worth enduring Hepu's insults to see him all puffed up like a pigeon and as red as a virgin at a feast of Hathor, goddess of love. Hepu and his wife had always resented Kysen. Which was why he'd enjoyed sending guards to the small house next door where they and Sennefer and Anhai had been staying along with Bentanta.

"An unfortunate exchange, my son." Meren walked through the gateway, and Kysen fell in step beside him.

"You heard?" Kysen said. "Hepu is a pompous old hyena."

"And you're a lion cub amusing himself by playing with him. Is he the first to try to leave? That's interesting."

"But it may mean nothing, as you're so fond of pointing out. I examined Anhai's room and found naught out of the ordinary. Neither she nor Sennefer have any papyrus with a missing corner."

"It was only a possibility. I'm probably being overly particular. Has Nebamun examined Anhai?"

"Yes, and he agreed with what you said. No marks of violence, no signs of poison or of magic."

Shaking his head, Meren said, "I was hoping he would find something I had overlooked. Come, it's time we spoke to Sennefer."

Sennefer was sitting in one of Sit-Hathor's chairs, a small table laden with food before him. A flagon of wine sat near his hand, which held a full cup. He glared at them as they entered, ripped a piece of bread off a loaf with his teeth, and chomped on it.

"You look as if you wish the bread were my leg," Meren said. "I see you've recovered from your grief at Anhai's death already."

Washing down the bread with a swig of wine, Sennefer wiped his mouth. "A man doesn't weep and wail like a woman. You know that."

"Yes, I know that," Meren said as he drew a chair near Sennefer's and sat down. He glanced at Kysen, who nodded imperceptibly.

"A terrible misfortune, nonetheless," Kysen said. He noticed that the wine flagon was half empty.

"We were having a disagreement, but that doesn't mean I'm not sorrowful, Kysen. We were married a long time."

Kysen placed a hand on the back of Sennefer's chair and filched a piece of date loaf from the tray. "But that was soon to end, was it not?"

"Gossip. You should know better than to listen to it. Anhai said she wanted a divorce, and she wanted to take my best land with her, it's true." Sennefer shrugged. "I wouldn't give her the land, and she wasn't leaving without it."

Sennefer moved the table aside and stretched his legs out in front of him. "You don't know women like I do, either of you. Anhai was jealous, and she was trying to punish me and get my attention at the same time. They're all alike. They cling to you and demand your undivided and total affection. Anhai had this strange notion that I should limit myself to her alone."

"And we all know you'd find that prospect unappetizing," Kysen said, "when there are so many other men's wives and concubines to raid."

Smiling, Sennefer said, "Why are we talking about the past? I want to know why you stuck me in your chambers and put that fool Zar to watch me like some criminal."

"You weren't yourself," Meren said. "I could see Anhai's death was a terrible shock to you, and I was worried about you."

"She was my wife, Meren. Of course I'm upset. If Bentanta hadn't brought me some of her magical pomegranate wine, I'd be most distraught right now. Have you found out what happened to her?"

"Not yet. I've ordered my physician to examine her. Can you think of any reason why someone would want Anhai dead?"

"No." Sennefer dipped his hands in a bowl of water and wiped them on a cloth. "Oh, Anhai was headstrong for a woman, I know. She was grasping and annoyed people, but not so much that they'd want to kill her. I don't understand what happened. Last night she seemed well. Too well. You saw how she behaved with Ra. And when everyone started to leave, I went searching for her and couldn't find her. Then I realized I hadn't seen her since before Hepu stopped torturing everyone with his Instruction."

Kysen said smoothly, "She was missing from the feast? And you said nothing of her disappearance so late at night?"

"Would you bruit your wife's absence when the last person she was seen with was Ra?" Sennefer asked.

Kysen glanced at his father, but Meren didn't react to this news and continued to study his cousin with deceptive concern and sympathy. If he were the object of that kind of attention from Lord Meren, Kysen would be as uneasy as a gazelle at a watering hole.

"She was with Ra?" Kysen asked as he leaned down to strain beer into an empty cup. "But you just said Anhai was jealous of you. Why would she risk scandal and disgrace with Ra if she coveted you?"

Sennefer hesitated, hardly blinking. "To make me jealous. Anhai liked to return blow for blow. Everyone knows that. Women like Anhai want you totally for themselves. I can't count the number who've shown their claws over me. That's when I tire of them. So many times I've seen a pretty woman, one with perfection of body and a delicate ka, turn into an underworld demon once she inhabits your bed."

"Who are these women?" Kysen asked. "I never seem to find them."

"Nor I," Meren said.

"Neither of you knows how to attract them as I do." Sennefer smirked at them.

"Do you know," Kysen said, "considering your habits, one would think you the more likely person to be killed and stuffed in a granary."

Sennefer only smiled at him.

Kysen smiled back and asked gently, "So why would someone want to harm your wife?"

"I don't know, unless . . ."

Kysen waited. Meren had taught him not to jump into silences. Patience and silence often forced people to talk when questions wouldn't. Sennefer was rubbing his forehead. He seemed to succumb to a spasm of grief before going on.

"I don't know of anyone who hated Anhai enough to kill her unless . . ." He glanced at Meren, then stared at the leg of the table, which had been carved in the shape of an elongated duck's neck and head. "Unless she decided she had no further use for Ra and dismissed him. You know Ra, Meren. He holds grudges, and he's hot-bellied when aroused. I didn't want to say anything."

Meren raised his gaze to Sennefer's. "But you have, haven't you?"

"Only because you both pressed me."

"It's important that we find out when Anhai was last seen alive," Kysen said, thinking it best to interrupt; his father was eyeing Sennefer as if he were a pile of dung. "You say she had vanished before Hepu finished reading his Instruction. We'll see if we can't find someone who saw her later than that."

"And you went to bed after the feast and remained there?" Meren asked. "Without knowing where your own wife was?"

"Don't play the royal inquiry agent with me, Meren."

"I'm only curious."

"You do want to know what happened to her, don't you?" Kysen asked. "Unless you're the one who caused her death."

"I didn't, and you know it," Sennefer said as he stood up. "And now, cousins, I'm going to my own room, if I've satisfied your suspicious curiosity. As I understand things, all we know is that my wife died, and then someone put her in the granary. A strange thing to do, but not necessarily a sign of murder. Am I not right?"

"Perhaps," Kysen said.

"I'm going to arrange for Anhai to be taken to Abydos to the Place of Anubis there," Sennefer said. "I've much to arrange before she's taken to her house of eternity." He turned to go, but paused beside Kysen. "And if I were you, adopted cousin, I'd refrain from casting suspicions on the innocent. You don't even know what killed Anhai, much less if it was murder."

Kysen watched him leave. "Do you believe him?"

"I'm not sure."

"Do you know what I think?" he asked, taking Sennefer's chair. "I think he doesn't seem to have cared enough about Anhai to murder her. But he's likely to get himself killed if he isn't careful about women. Has he always been such an ass?"

"No," Meren said, thinking of the past. "When they were small, he and his brother lived in terror of Hepu. You know how big Hepu is. Well, to a child, he seemed a horrifying giant. And Sennefer was little for his age. Hepu would come at him roaring with such violence, and poor Sennefer would cringe and whimper. I remember how Hepu would beat him, and beat Djet too. There was no need to hit them so hard. We were less than eight when he beat Sennefer and Djet with a staff so hard that they bled. He would call them stupid, worthless, other things, and Nebetta never tried to protect them."

"Stop," Kysen said faintly.

Meren put a hand on his arm. "I'm sorry. It reminds you of your father."

"I didn't know."

"If I'd been older, I would have taken that staff from Hepu and beat him worse than he beat my cousins. I wanted to."

Kysen was hardly listening. He was fighting off memories of his own blood father, blurred visions of fists coming at him, of being thrown across rooms. "Can we speak of something else? The past is dead."

"Very well," Meren said gently. "Reia and the men can question the servants and slaves about Anhai, but you and I will have to speak to the family."

"I haven't much hope. They're not afraid of you or me. To them we're only Meren and Kysen, not the Eyes and Ears of Pharaoh. This won't be the usual inquiry."

"Gods, I'd rather question a dozen princes and spies than try to get Aunt Cherit to answer me."

A knock interrupted them, and Zar opened the door to

allow Bener into the room. She hurried over to them and stood between their chairs.

"I've been looking for you, Father. I've heard about Anhai. Did she really drink poison standing on top of a granary and fall into it?"

Meren groaned. "The rumors have already started. No, Bener, she didn't drink poison and dive into the granary. At least, I don't think that's what happened. Now run along."

"I want to help, Father. Are you going to conduct one of your inquiries? I want to see how it's done."

Kysen almost gasped. "Bener, you're mad." Women didn't hold government office, much less insert themselves into murder inquiries.

"But I'm curious."

"No," Meren said. "Now run along. I'm going to bathe, and then I've much work to do. We'll play a game of senet tonight."

"Senet is boring. I always beat you, Father." When Meren only gave her a stern glare, she sighed and adopted a look of mock regret that alerted Kysen. "As you wish, Father. I suppose I'll just have to resume my studies under the steward, with Nu."

"You will not," Meren and Kysen said together.

"Then I'll just have to help Aunt Idut with the household. She's in such a state because of Anhai's death. It is a shame though," Bener said with a sly glance at her father. "I was looking forward to telling you all about the argument Bentanta had with Anhai at the feast. Ah, well, counting stores and learning the uses of herbs is more urgent, I suppose."

Kysen grabbed Bener by her shift as she tried to walk out of the room. She turned around and grinned at him.

"A girl with an intelligent heart is a curse," Kysen snapped.

Meren reached out, pulled up a stool next to him, and pointed at it. "Sit down and curb your impudence."

"She doesn't know anything" Kysen said. "She's only pretending."

Bener punched his thigh as she sat down. "Don't be a fool. No one would be stupid enough to do that to Father."

"Tell me what you know, my child."

Calmly arranging herself on the stool, Bener said, "You remember how Anhai and Bentanta quarreled at the feast? They didn't notice that I was nearby." At Meren's skeptical look, she tossed her head. "It may have been that I was looking at the flowers in that arrangement Aunt Idut had me design."

"You mean the one that was taller than I am?" Kysen asked. "The one behind which a squad of soldiers could hide? The one near the couch Bentanta was sitting on?"

"Yes, that's the one. I happened to decide to admire it when Anhai came over and sat beside Bentanta." Bener paused expectantly, only to resume when neither Kysen nor Meren urged her to continue. "Bentanta was angry. I could see the ire in her face, Father. Do you know what she said to Anhai? She said, 'It didn't work. He laughed at me, and when I tried to convince him, he got the idea that I was enamored of him, the fool.' Then Anhai said, 'You'll have to try harder.'"

"How interesting," Meren said without surprise. "Do *you* know who 'he' was?"

"No," Bener said. "But then Bentanta said, 'It's useless, as I told you it would be, so you'll just have to find another way. Now I've done what you said to do. Give it back.'" Bener gave Kysen a look of satisfaction and relish. "Anhai refused, and that was when Bentanta flew into a rage and left the room."

"Thank you, daughter. Now go help your aunt Idut."

"Father! Is this my reward? I want to know what has happened, and I want to help you."

"Your duties lie elsewhere."

Kysen's gaze went from Meren's stern visage to Bener's determined one. As he watched he could see Bener's disappointment vanish and knew that she'd come to some decision on her own, one that would get her into trouble.

"Father, perhaps Bener could help."

"You make a jest," Meren said. He shot Kysen a glance filled with warning. "I don't want Bener involved in an inquiry. There could be danger."

"But she could be our eyes and ears among the women."

They used women informants in their inquiries for pharaoh. At this moment there were several among the queen's household in Memphis.

"And if there is a murderer among the women?" Meren asked. None of them spoke Bentanta's name.

Bener scooted closer to her father. "Then I'm going to be in her company whether I'm trying to help you or not, and so is Isis; so is Idut. What if this is murder, and the guilty one is a woman? You'd better let me help you so we can catch her quickly. Poor Aunt Idut and Isis might be in danger."

"The gods have cursed me with an interfering daughter," Meren said. "You're only to listen, and use that clever wit of yours. Don't go off alone with anyone, especially Bentanta."

Bener jumped up and kissed him on the cheek. "I'll be careful, Father."

Kysen remained silent until Bener left.

"Don't rail at me, Father. Bener was going to pry and meddle with or without your consent. I saw it in her face. At least now we might be able to control her."

"I don't understand it," Meren said. "In but a few

months she's become headstrong and much too clever. And too curious. My only comfort is that she'll be too busy spying to seek the company of that young colt Nu."

"True. Then shall we pay a visit to Lady Bentanta?"

"Yes." Meren drummed his fingers on his thigh. "Last night she was quite adroit in telling me only part of the truth. I'll have to find out what it was she wanted back from Anhai."

"A document, perhaps?"

"It could be," Meren said. "But Bentanta isn't a fool or easily intimidated. I can't imagine her falling for any entrapment of Anhai's making."

A knock announced the entrance of Zar. "My lord, the Lord Nakht has been seen in a skiff nearing the dock."

Meren rose. "You see how Reia is progressing among the servants. I'll be back."

Kysen hid a smile when Zar looked as if he'd suddenly acquired an aching belly.

"The lord will wish to go to the docks in his red-and-gold sandals. I have a robe and the belt with the gold and red jasper beads in readiness."

"Not now," Meren said as he crossed the threshold.

"The lord has forgotten his walking stick. Again."

"I don't need it," came the answer.

Zar called after him in desperation. "The lord will need a sandal carrier and fan bearers!"

"No, I won't," came the distant reply. A door slammed, and Zar winced.

"Be of good cheer," Kysen said. "He'll let you attend him after he's seen his brother."

"I will be laughed at by chamber-pot carriers and field workers," Zar said with offended dignity. Bowing, the servant quietly closed the door in a manner that suggested that he would bear his suffering with fortitude and patience.

Kysen was left to consider his good fortune. He didn't want to be there when Meren confronted Ra and asked his brother if he'd killed Anhai.

10

▽

Ra's skiff, rowed by two of his friends, was gliding down a small canal toward Baht when Meren found him. Ra slumped in the middle of the boat, his forehead pressed against the side of the craft, his eyes closed, his complexion almost as green as a papyrus reed. Meren signaled the skiff, crossed a field, and met the vessel as it settled against the canal bank. He watched in silence while Ra's friends hopped ashore, reached down, and hauled him out by his arms.

Landing unsteadily to hang suspended between his fellows, Ra kept his eyes closed during this maneuver. They flew open at the jolt of his landing. Meren was gratified that the first thing his brother saw was himself, standing with arms crossed and legs planted apart. Ra's eyes were red around the rims and in the whites. He gave Meren a bleary stare. Then his mouth went slack, and his throat muscles rippled.

"Oh, gods!" Ra's head went down. His body heaved forward, dragging his supporters.

Meren jumped back, and Ra vomited on the spot where he'd been standing. The north breeze wafted putrid smells at him. Glancing around, Meren noticed two fishing boats and their sailors, several women with water jars on their heads, laborers shoring up a breach in a dike, more women and girls on their way to the river with loads of laundry. One of the girls giggled before her mother slapped her. The boats sailed on, but not before Meren caught a glimpse of disgust on the face of an old fisherman.

Each witness found something to look at elsewhere when Meren's gaze fell on him. Ra's groans attracted his attention again. His brother had fallen to his knees over a pool of thick mess. Meren's lip curled as he turned back toward the house.

"Take him to his chamber at once."

Without glancing back, he returned to the house, leaving orders at the gate for Ra's friends to be questioned and sent back to their neighboring homes. Porters, charioteers, and doorkeepers gave him wary looks as he strode down the path between the twin reflection pools. Servants scurried out of his way when he charged through the reception room. In the central hall Kysen was talking with Reia.

As Meren stalked past, Reia saluted him, but Kysen stopped him from intercepting his father.

"I wouldn't, Reia," Kysen said. "Not now."

Vaguely aware of his son, Meren was through the hall and approaching his own apartments in moments. Thrusting open the door, he slammed it shut and bellowed for Zar.

"Where are you, you pompous nuisance?"

"Here, lord."

Meren whirled around to find Zar standing on the threshold of the bathing chamber, a stack of clean bathing cloths in his arms. Untying his kilt, Meren yanked it from his hips and hurled it to the floor.

"Call my bathing attendants," he said as he headed for the inner chamber. "And send for my barber. I want a massage with that Babylonian oil you praise so highly. And then I want my finest kilt and overrobe, my collar and wristbands of gold, and my best sandals."

Zar followed him into the bathing chamber, clapping

his hands and calling for assistance. Meren sat on the anointing table.

"Send someone to Lady Bentanta for some of her pomegranate wine," Meren snapped. "And find my belt of gold beads with the red-gold clasp."

Zar bowed as slaves scurried into the chamber bearing soap pots, dousing vessels, and wide copper bowls in which rose lotuses floated. Meren was glaring at a frieze of papyrus painted on the wall when Zar's whisper reached him.

"No, Zar, I haven't taken ill." He rose and entered the bathing stall. Cool water splashed over his head and shoulders, and he sputtered through it. "This is what you wanted, wasn't it? Dignity, noble magnificence, stately demeanor. You're going to get them all, Zar. They have to come from somewhere, don't they?"

The body servant gushed with thanks, but Meren wasn't listening. He'd wanted to drop all ceremony and formality and take refuge with his family. Instead of refuge, he got a mysterious death. He was going to solve this mystery quickly, so that it didn't interfere with the concealment of the royal mummies or with what little time he had left to rest.

He didn't want to think about Ra. When he did, he nearly erupted into a rage. But he had to think about the murder—for Anhai had to have been murdered. Otherwise there was no reason to hide her body. And the murder couldn't have been planned, or the culprit wouldn't have chosen to stick the body in so strange a repository.

Sennefer had cast suspicion on Ra. Meren hadn't mentioned to anyone, even Kysen, his conversation with Ra at the feast. Ra had hinted that he was thinking of marrying Anhai. If Anhai had merely been playing him against Sennefer, Ra would have been furious.

Meren couldn't imagine being in love with the woman,

but Ra lacked wisdom, and thus might have been, simply because she flattered him. She might have fed his over-generous estimate of his own value. Ra was so intemperate, wild, and ungovernable; and he cultivated resentment as a farmer cultivates barley.

Still, Sennefer could have been lying. He had every reason to cast suspicion on someone else. But if Ra had discovered that Anhai had only been using him . . . The fires of his resentment were already hot from imagined abuse at Meren's hands. Anhai could have pushed him over the edge of control.

While Meren wrestled with this unpleasant possibility, his servants got him bathed and his body smoothed with oil. He went over the questions he wanted to ask Ra while he dressed. Zar fastened a gold broad collar and centered the counterweight at his back. Meren clamped a wide bracelet of gold over the sun disk branded on his wrist, the legacy of his imprisonment at the hands of Akhenaten. A beaded gold band wrapped around his forehead. Long black locks of hair fell over his shoulders.

His hand traced the groove etched down the middle of the dagger blade thrust into his belt. A memory flitted by—of being a youth proud of attaining the rank of charioteer, of his first court appearance as a warrior. That night, at a royal banquet, was the first time he beheld his fellow noblemen from the perspective of an initiate.

He had been struck by the contradiction. These men wore gossamer robes, earrings of gold and electrum, bracelets and necklaces of lapis lazuli and turquoise. Their eyes glistened with kohl. These men could laugh while thrusting a spear into the heart of a lion. They would ride a chariot into the midst of a charging army. The hand that wore elegant rings of silver wielded a dagger with unsurpassed expertise. Beauty and violence linked. One disguised by the other, merging, enmeshed, deceptive—fatal.

He had never told anyone of this insight, because no one else seemed to find it odd that creatures capable of such violence draped themselves in a veil of such beauty. That feeling of disjunction came to him now as he stood dressed in creamy linen, encrusted with gold.

But he was dressed this way for a reason. Shaking off his discomfort, Meren waved away the servants who were arranging the folds of his robe. He dismissed Zar with a nod and left his chambers, walking past two doors to his brother's room. There he found a charioteer standing guard.

"He's spoken to no one?" Meren asked.

"No, lord. He's, that is . . ."

"Say it," Meren snapped.

"He wasn't in a state to carry on a conversation, lord."

"You're a man of careful words."

The guard hurried to open the door for him. The interior was black. Meren took an alabaster lamp from the guard and motioned for him to remain outside. The door closed, and Meren marched down the length of the room to the dais on which sat a carved bed surrounded by sheer curtains on a frame. Thrusting aside the curtains, Meren went over to the lump in the middle of the bed and thrust the lamp in his brother's face.

Although his eyes were closed, Ra gasped and covered his face. "No light, damn you! Get out."

Meren set the lamp on the floor and yanked his brother off the bed by his arm. Ra slid to the floor, cursing and kicking. Then he groaned, drew up his legs, and put his forehead on his knees.

"What do you want, Meren? I'm sick. Go away."

"Anhai has been murdered," Meren said over Ra's groans.

The groans stopped. A red eye opened to blink at him.

"What did you say?"

"You heard. Where were you last night?"

"How can she be dead? She was in excellent health. Last night she was fine."

"Answer me," Meren said. "Where were you while Hepu read his Instruction?"

"Did he read another Instruction at the feast? When Anhai was dead? That's just like him, the hypocrite."

"No, no, no!" Meren sank to his knees and captured Ra's gaze with his own. "Answer my question, Ra. Where were you while Hepu read his Instruction? When did you leave for Green Palm, and who went with you?"

Ra put his palms to his temples and squeezed. "Oh, gods, my head. Send for that physician of yours. I'm dying."

"If you don't answer me at once, that ache in your head will seem like bliss compared to the way you'll feel after I've done with you."

Ra stared at him for a moment, then winced at the lamplight. The family's angular jaw was softened on his face, making him appear more youthful than he was. His eyes were as deeply set as Meren's, but not as haunted. Covering his eyes, he said, "Something's wrong about Anhai's death, isn't there? Where was I, where was I? I don't remember any Instruction. Most likely, I was already gone by then. It disgusts me to watch Wah and Sennefer and Antefoker and everyone else fawning over you as if you were pharaoh. I went with some of my friends to Green Palm. There's a tavern there with excellent beer and women with the talents of Hathor."

"You stayed there all night? There are those who will swear to it?"

Lifting his head, Ra leered at him. "Three of the women will swear. Are you asking me if I killed Anhai? By the gods, you think I might have done it." Without warning Ra reached out and grabbed Meren's gold necklace and pulled him close. "She's been murdered, and I'm the first person you suspect, you bastard. You think I killed her. You're hoping I did it."

"Let go of me," Meren said as he stared into his brother's contorted features. There was a moment during which neither of them breathed. Then Ra released him with a sharp laugh.

"You always were good at command, brother."

"You were never good at obedience."

"Not when you were giving the orders."

Meren stood and looked down at Ra, who had closed his eyes again.

"There has been a murder in the family, Ra. The victim is a married woman you told me you wanted. I would ask these questions of anyone who behaved as you have. Did she refuse you? Did you quarrel?"

"Although it grieves me to disappoint you, we didn't quarrel. You saw us. We played with each other, nothing more. I hadn't approached her yet. I'm no fool, Meren. I know better than to move too quickly. When I left, Anhai was alive."

"Sennefer says the last time he saw her she was with you."

"He's probably lying."

"And he says Anhai was only using you to make him jealous, because she coveted him."

Meren jumped at the loud laugh that issued from his brother. Ra held his head and groaned between chuckles.

"You're a fool, Meren." His laughter subsided when Meren continued to stare at him, unsmiling. "By the truth of Maat, you do want me to be guilty. It doesn't matter to you that Anhai was a grasping tyrant to Sennefer. You don't care that she chained him with her evil tongue. You haven't even considered the others she's turned from friend to lethal enemy. She's been quarreling with Bentanta since they arrived. She near drove Antefoker mad with her cheating, and Wah owed her fifty head of cattle. Ha! You didn't know that. She was growing rich off the folly of her friends, Meren."

"So you spent the night drinking and playing with women."

Meren walked over to Ra and offered his hand. Ra took it, and Meren pulled his brother to his feet and shoved him back down on the bed.

"Last night was just another evening of pleasure, then." Meren leaned down and touched a bruise on Ra's jaw, a scrape on his elbow, a red mark over his ribs. "But if it was, dear brother, then why do you look like you've been in a fight to the death?"

Ra shrugged. "Sometimes making love can be like a fight to the death. But you don't want to know about that, do you? You'd rather believe I fought with Anhai and killed her. Why haven't you mentioned the others who might have done it? How about Bentanta?" Ra paused, then sat up straight in the bed.

"What's wrong? You're not worried about her, are you? Gods! No wonder you're hot to cast suspicion on me. I've heard how the family is planning to unite the two of you."

"The family isn't going to interfere in my life. So you're saying you spent the entire night at Green Palm."

"All of it that I remember."

"What part don't you remember?"

"How can I know, if I don't remember?"

"I grow weary of these evasions," Meren said. "Your companions had better support your tale, or next time I won't be so gentle in my questioning."

"Have you talked to Bentanta yet?"

"I will."

"Do. I'll be waiting to see how you manage it. I've seen the two of you circling each other like two wary leopards. And, brother, you're going to be disappointed about me. I left Anhai alive. I know you want me to be the murderer, because it would relieve you of the burden of being reminded of how you've cheated me."

"I never cheated you, and I don't want you to be guilty. Why would I want my own brother to be guilty of such a crime?"

"Then why are you treating me like a criminal?"

"I'm not, Ra. You've just forgotten who I am."

"You're my brother."

"I'm the Eyes and Ears of Pharaoh. Before I am a brother, or even a father, I am the Eyes of Pharaoh."

"Poor Meren," Ra said as he slid down in the bed and covered his eyes with a forearm. "Always so serious, so merciless in duty. No wonder we never got along. Don't you see how empty you are?"

"What are you talking about?"

Ra lifted his arm and smiled at Meren. "Your life, brother. There's so little pleasure. You dislike me for being at ease with women, for knowing how to enjoy living, for being able to laugh."

"Did you kill Anhai?"

"You're the Eyes and Ears of Pharaoh. You tell me."

Kysen found Meren in the roomy chamber that served as his office on the second floor of the house. Four painted columns with capitals shaped like lotus flowers supported the roof. Estate documents, accounts, and letters lay rolled up and tied in bundles on shelves and in leather cases. A tall ovoid water jar sitting in a corner bore a necklace of flowers. There was a niche in which sat a statue of the god Toth. An ebony-inlaid cedar chair sat on the dais reserved for Meren. Over its back had been thrown a heavy collar of gold. Kysen recognized the gold of honor given by pharaoh as reward for service.

The collar's owner wasn't seated on the dais. He was standing beside a carved alabaster chest. He opened it and withdrew three weighted spheres painted Nile-blue and green. He glanced at Kysen without expression and began tossing the balls in the air and catching them. Kysen made sure he'd closed the door. It wouldn't do for the noble Lord Meren to be caught juggling like a common entertainer.

Meren tossed a sphere while he caught another, and a third seemed to hang suspended in the air. "What of the haunted temple?"

So there was to be no discussion of what had happened between his father and Ra.

"Before dawn someone approached the valley, but Iry and the men frightened him off. They couldn't see who it was. Probably a villager. He ran away upon hearing the spirit noises."

"Nothing else? No other signs of interest?"

"None."

"I have been thinking," Meren said as he strolled around the chamber tossing the blue and green spheres. "Anhai can't have been dead more than half the night. Her body hadn't stiffened much, and we were able to get her out of the granary. Yet she had to have been dead several hours or she would have returned to her chamber. Anhai wasn't a fool, and she wouldn't have risked scandal by staying away."

Kysen tapped a sheet of papyrus he held rolled up in his hand. "True. She left some time between the beginning of Hepu's Instruction and the end of the feast. Unfortunately, there were dozens of guests and servants coming and going, in addition to the family. Reia says that the doorkeepers were busy at the front gate. No one saw her leave the house and go around to the granary court, but it was dark, and there are all those trees between the gate and the house. She could have kept to the shadows."

"Which makes me wonder why she would steal away to such a place."

"She could have gone down the back stairs and around," Kysen said.

"But the servants coming from the kitchen would have seen her." Meren caught all three balls in succession and put them back in the alabaster casket. "I've been trying to remember what I saw of Anhai last night. When she came in with Sennefer, we spoke briefly, and I remember Wah was there. Then Ra came, and she talked to him."

"And she had that quarrel with Bentanta."

"I don't remember seeing her after that. I was too busy enduring Hepu's reading." Meren went to his chair, picked up the gold necklace, and sat down. Swinging the collar from his fingers, he frowned. "Now that I think on it, Anhai seemed to stir up everyone's passion in some way."

Kysen grinned. "Of course, Sennefer must have been furious at her for allowing Ra to come near her. He was talking to Bentanta but watching Anhai. The unguent cone on his head was just starting to melt, and I remember thinking if he turned much redder, it would dissolve from the heat of his anger."

"He may have been angry at her, but Bentanta was furious. She even said she wished she had the courage to kill Anhai."

Kysen whistled and came to sit on the floor beside Meren. "Have you spoken to her yet?"

"I was going to after I saw Ra. But I . . . decided to gather my thoughts first. I'm worried, Ky. Ra thinks I want to blame him for this disaster, and then there's Bentanta."

"I suppose the gods wouldn't send us the good fortune to find that the murderer is a servant," Kysen said.

"No servant had a reason to kill her," Meren replied. "Nor can I imagine a servant would dare. Although I might suspect a servant were Anhai at court or allied with the queen."

The Great Royal Wife, Ankhesenamun, resented her husband's return to the old ways and restoration of Amun as chief god. She seemed to have lost her reason, at least in Kysen's view, when she conceived of a plan to depose pharaoh in favor of a Hittite prince. The plan had failed, and now pharaoh said she seemed to regret her traitorous behavior.

Kysen shook his head. "No, you're right. Anhai must have gone to the granary court with someone and been killed there. Ordinarily she wouldn't go there at all, so she must have gone with one of the guests or the family."

"Antefoker was trying to corner her all evening," Meren said. "And he vanished from the feast with Ra. We'll have to send someone to his house."

"But the only one at the feast who fought with her was Bentanta." Kysen looked up at his father, who was frowning. "Would you like me to talk to her?"

"No, my son. I'll do it. She would rout you in a heartbeat."

"I was hoping you'd realize that," Kysen said.

They both rose as a high, clear voice floated to them from the stairwell outside the office.

"Father!"

"Enter," Meren called.

Bener hurried into the room, dragging Isis behind her. Upon reaching Meren, she shoved her sister in front of her.

"Tell Father what you said."

Isis shoved her sister back. "Don't push me, and don't tell me what to do."

"It might be important."

The younger girl smoothed the skirt of her shift and patted a stray lock of hair into place. "You think you're so quick of wit, but you're just trying to be important.

Father, she's been annoying Aunt Idut and Great-Aunt Cherit all morning, and now she's pestering me."

"I haven't time to settle arguments, girls."

"Father," Kysen said. "I think Bener is serious."

Bener gave him a grateful smile. "She saw Bentanta and Anhai go out the front door while Uncle Hepu was speaking his Instruction."

Kysen knelt in front of Isis. "Is this true?"

"She should have let me tell it."

Throwing up his hands, Meren said, "Then do so."

Having gained everyone's attention, Isis bestowed upon them one of her sunrise smiles. "I was standing near the door to the reception hall pretending to listen to the Instruction."

"She was staring at one of Uncle Ra's friends," Bener said. "The one with the long face of an ibex."

"I was not!"

Kysen poked his sister's arm with a finger. "Pay her no heed, Isis. Go on."

"I was standing by the door," Isis said with a defiant look at Bener. "And Anhai came swooping by. You know her manner. She looked as if she owned our house and everything in it. She sailed by me with her nose lifted. She never noticed me, but I noticed her because she looked angry, and Bentanta was following her. Bentanta looked sick. I don't think Bentanta likes Anhai very much anymore."

Kysen glanced up at Meren, who seemed unable to speak. He looked back at Isis. Her small face was alight with curiosity, a childish version of Queen Nefertiti without the air of dignified concern.

"Did you see where they went?" Kysen asked.

"They went through the reception room and out the front door. That's all I saw."

Bener put her hands on her hips. "I would have followed them."

"That's because you spy on your elders," Isis retorted.
"Enough!"

Meren's sharp exclamation made Kysen hurry the girls toward the door.

"Our thanks, sisters. You've been of great help. Thank you, Bener, but Father is beset at the moment."

Bener went out the door and turned back to him. "I know. Aunt Idut has ruined our peaceful visit. That's all Father wanted, and now he's going to have to solve this mystery instead of spending his time with us."

"If Aunt Idut hadn't invited Anhai here, she would have gotten herself killed somewhere else," Isis added.

"We'll find a way to be together," Kysen said. "I promise."

Bener put her hand on the door to stop him from closing it. "Lady Bentanta is in the garden. I heard her say she'd promised to meet Sennefer there and give him more of her pomegranate wine."

"Thanks, sister."

Kysen shut the door and faced his father. Meren was toying with a scribe's palette from a table near his chair. When he lifted his gaze, Kysen nearly winced at the pain he saw exposed and then concealed.

"I don't want it to be her. We were children together, Ky, and I don't want it to be her."

11

$\triangledown$

As he walked into the garden where the family had gathered for an afternoon meal, Meren decided that he'd rather face desert bandits than question Bentanta. He paused inside the gate to survey the tree-shrouded enclosure. Idut was presiding over a small feast under the branches of an old willow. With her were Nebetta, Aunt Cherit, and his daughters, who kept giving him sly glances. Hepu seemed to be giving one of his lectures to the entire group as they ate.

Everyone had a desperate look, a sure sign that Hepu had been speaking for some time. Only Wah had escaped. He lay on a couch, fanned by a slave, and snored, his food discarded on a tray beside him. Across the garden in a grape arbor sat Sennefer and Bentanta.

"It must be done," Meren muttered to himself as he directed his steps toward the arbor.

"Here he is, come to accuse me of murdering my own wife again," Sennefer said with his face in his wine cup. His speech was slurred, his eyes wide. "Don't let him belabor me, Bentanta."

"I haven't come to accuse you of anything," Meren said. "I would like to speak to Bentanta privately."

Sennefer lifted his head, and it wobbled on his neck. "Be most happy to leave you, cousin. Pleasure. Beware, my lady. He's playing the inquisitor."

Standing, Sennefer blinked sleepily at Meren.

"Don't stand there staring at me, go eat something," Meren said. "Look at you. You're red from drinking, and you can hardly stand."

"I'm thirsty." The wine cup fell from Sennefer's lax fingers.

"Drink water," Meren said as he signaled to a servant. The girl hurried over to pick up the fallen cup and retreated.

"Water?" Sennefer said, as if he'd never heard the word before. "Yes, water would be good." He embarked on a wavering course toward the group under the willow.

Meren watched him stagger over to a chair and almost fall into it. Then he went back to Bentanta, who had remained silent since he entered the arbor. She was sitting on a couch and seemed to be undisturbed when he took Sennefer's chair and trained a silent gaze on her. She lifted a brow in inquiry, but when he didn't speak, she turned her attention to the harpist who was playing music for the diners.

"You were seen leaving the feast with Anhai last night while my uncle read his Instruction."

"I'm sure many people left."

Irritated at her composure, Meren raised his voice. "But only one died, and she was last seen with you."

"Don't bark at me, Meren. I remember you when you were a naked, uncircumcised little boy."

"You don't seem to understand what has happened. Someone has murdered Anhai, and you fought with her and threatened her life."

At last Bentanta's gaze swung to him from the harpist. "You think I killed her?"

"We may have played together as babes, but that was long ago. We're almost strangers now, and all I know for certain is that Anhai died shortly after you said you wished you had the courage to kill her."

"I spoke to her on the front porch. Then I went for a walk under the trees by the reflection pools."

"Alone?"

"Yes, Meren. I'm not a fool. If there was someone who could vouch for me, I would have said so and saved myself the ordeal of this inquisition." She stood and walked around the couch so that her back was to him. "I don't suppose you'll believe me if I say I didn't kill her."

"I would like to."

"Then do so."

"Help me by explaining why you quarreled with Anhai."

She looked over her shoulder at him. "I've already told you why."

"Bentanta, I know there's more to this quarrel than you've said. She had something of yours, something you wanted back desperately. And she was trying to make you do something you didn't want to do. You failed, and she was furious."

For the first time, Bentanta's composure broke. A flush crept up her neck to settle in her cheeks. Then it faded, leaving her pale and making the kohl that darkened her eyes stand out.

"Do you always spy on your friends?" she asked.

"No," he said, hoping the heat in his face wasn't noticeable. "I came by this knowledge by accident. Tell me what was between you and Anhai. It was a grave matter, or you wouldn't have threatened her."

"It was a private thing, and I'll not spew out my secrets to you, Meren. I've heard the talk. Idut says you don't know what killed Anhai. And since you don't know, you shouldn't go about making false accusations. You've become a suspicious and evil-minded wretch. And you used to be so sweet-natured."

Meren rose and walked over to the couch. They glared at each other across it.

"This ruse of yours won't avail you," he said quietly.

"What ruse?"

"Since we began talking you've done nothing but try to distract me with foolish accusations and insults. You were always stubborn. I remember Djet used to say you had the ka of a donkey."

"And I'm not the only one spouting insults."

"Forgive me," he said. "Now tell me what Anhai had that you wanted."

"It's not your concern."

Meren threw up his hands. "Listen to me! I'm not your childhood companion anymore. This isn't the nursery. If you don't speak, I have to find answers by my own methods, and they are those of the Eyes of Pharaoh."

She was looking at him in astonishment. Then her eyes narrowed, and her lips curled. His frustration grew as he realized he hadn't intimidated her at all.

"It's easier this way, is it not?" she asked.

"What are you talking about?"

"Easier to deal with me as the Eyes of Pharaoh. Ah yes, I see." She waved her arm in the direction of the family. "You keep them at a distance. You keep everyone at a distance, except your children, whom you command. What frightens you that you must conceal yourself behind rank and duty?"

He almost let his mouth fall open. Clamping his lips shut, Meren scowled at the woman facing him. She had always been irreverent, full of pride. It came of spending the years of her youth under the tutelage of Queen Tiye and Nefertiti.

"You know I speak the truth," Bentanta said. "That's why you're speechless. I'm sure no one else has ever dared to confront you with the truth."

He was losing this battle, and he didn't want to hear any more of Bentanta's false truths. She was trying to vex him, stampede him in the direction she wished him to go. Narrowing his eyes, he studied her. Her hands were curled into fists. He hadn't noticed before because they were half hidden in the folds of her overrobe.

"I desire no conversation of so personal a nature," he said. "Since you refuse to tell me the truth, you leave me no choice but to make more formal inquiries."

"Don't threaten me, Meren."

He would have replied, but a crash and shouts sent him whirling around to face the group beneath the willows. Sennefer lay facedown over a collapsed chair. Hepu and Wah were trying to pull him off it. Idut was shrieking, while Bener tried to calm her. Isis stood by gawking, and Nebetta hovered over the men, calling her son's name.

Meren broke into a run, rounding the reflection pool and reaching Sennefer as Hepu and Wah lifted him off the fallen chair and laid him on the ground. Shoving Wah aside, Meren knelt beside his cousin. He hardly noticed Bentanta standing behind him.

Sennefer's eyes were closed, but he was muttering, calling out. Meren touched his forehead. It was hot, and he was breathing unnaturally. Nebetta, who was kneeling opposite Meren, began to cry.

Meren ducked as a flailing arm nearly hit him in the face. Sennefer cried out and sat up, hitting blindly. Meren pinned his arms to his sides and shouted orders. In moments several of his men came rushing into the garden.

"He's ill with drink. Help me get him to his chamber. Idut, send for my physician. Out of the way, Aunt Nebetta. You do him no good by hindering us."

It was a struggle to get Sennefer to the guest house and into his chamber. He fought them the whole way. The physician arrived while Meren and Hepu were trying to keep Sennefer in his bed, but as Nebamun attempted to examine him he subsided. Hepu comforted Nebetta while the physician looked at Sennefer's eyes, felt his skin, looked in his mouth. Before Nebamun could finish, Sennefer stiffened. Then his body began to jerk, and Nebetta screamed. The physician produced a wooden spoon from the wicker box he'd brought containing his instruments and medicines. This he forced between Sennefer's teeth.

"No!" Nebetta cried. "What are you doing to him?"

Hepu held her back when she tried to swoop down on her son. Meren went over to them and spoke to Hepu.

"Take her out of here. She shouldn't see this." He didn't wait for Hepu's agreement. Shoving them, he propelled them outside and shut the door before they could protest.

He returned to Sennefer's bedside. Nebamun was removing the wooden spoon from Sennefer's mouth. The violent spasms had ceased, and he appeared to have lapsed into a stupor. Nebamun pulled a sheet over his patient.

"What's wrong with him?" Meren asked.

"A moment, my lord."

Nebamun pulled a papyrus roll, thick with many sheets, from his physician's box. He unrolled it and leafed through the sheets. His finger ran across lines of cursive hieroglyphs, then paused at a group of words written in red ink. Hesitating, his finger tapped the red script. The finger moved again, down the page. Nebamun flipped through more sheets, reading in silence with constant glances at Sennefer. Finally he closed the papyrus roll and placed it back in the box.

"Well?"

"Many illnesses follow similar courses, my lord."

"Can you help him?"

"I think not, lord." Nebamun knelt beside Sennefer, who hadn't moved. "I've found the sacred writings about this illness. A fever, the possession by visions. The voice of his heart grows weak."

"But in the garden it wasn't," Meren said.

Nebamun inclined his head. "He seemed drunk, lord?"

"Yes."

"And his speech was slurred."

"Yes, yes. Can't you do something?"

"I fear not, lord. These signs are grave, and . . ."

"Nebamun, you're trying not to say something. I've no time for vacillation."

"I think he's been poisoned, lord."

Meren looked down at Sennefer. "Poisoned?"

"This illness is too sudden to be an illness, and we've found no signs of magic, lord."

Meren waved a hand for silence. He walked back and forth by Sennefer's bed, thinking rapidly. If Sennefer had been poisoned, there was more danger than he'd thought. But why would someone poison Sennefer? And how could it have been done? Sennefer ate the same food everyone else ate. It was prepared in the kitchens and served from large containers, with several people sharing the same portions.

Meren went back to Sennefer, knelt, and touched his cousin's arm. They hadn't been close. Meren and Djet had been like brothers, but Sennefer had been older and had his own friends. They shared blood and childhood memories, nevertheless, and now Sennefer was dying.

"How long?"

"His ka will fly to the gods before sunset, lord."

Feeling as if he had stumbled into a nightmare, Meren smoothed the sheet that covered Sennefer and stood. "I'll have to tell his parents. You will remain here, Nebamun."

At the door he paused, wishing he didn't have to perform this ugly task. Beside the door sat a tall jar with a clay seal around its top. Another sat beside it, its seal broken. Meren's glance fell on the writing that had been incised into the clay before it dried. Abruptly he turned around and searched the room. His gaze fell on a small table bearing a flagon and cup.

Nebamun darted out of his way as Meren rushed across the room. He picked up the flagon and inhaled its fragrance. Setting it back down, his fingers touched the pool of liquid in the cup.

"Wine, Nebamun."

"Wine, lord?"

Meren picked up the flagon again. His fingers drummed a rhythm on its side.

"Yes, wine," he said. "Lady Bentanta's special pomegranate wine."

Lord Paser was once again satisfied with the cleverness of his heart. Indeed, he was practicing more guile even than his recent unwelcome visitor. He sat beneath the awning near the bow on the small freighter while one of his retainers plumbed the depth of the water as they sailed south. A sailor manned the rectangular sail, and at the stern another man steered with a long, narrow paddle.

This boat wasn't yellow and green. It had no paint at all to distinguish it from the dozens of other small craft that swarmed with it upstream. Having been chased away from his pursuit of Kysen, Paser had pretended to sail north toward Memphis. But on the way he'd spotted this little freighter. It belonged to a small temple of the ram-headed god Khnum in an insignificant town near Elephantine. The complaints of a small temple in such a paltry town wouldn't be listened to, so he commandeered the freighter.

The captain and his crew hadn't been happy, especially when Paser shoved the three oxen that comprised their most valuable cargo onto the riverbank and sailed off with their feed. Now he was headed south. Surveying the baked fields, Paser estimated that Meren's estate wasn't far off. He rose and went to the prow where the pilot was pulling his pole from the water.

"We will lower the sail," Paser said. "What is that village, the one in the midst of those palms?"

"It is called Green Palm, my lord."

"Ah, yes. Not far from Baht. There will be a shore market near the village. We'll beach there."

Paser walked back to the awning, rubbing his bare upper lip. He'd made a great sacrifice, all in order to concoct a clever disguise. No one was going to accuse him of not being quick-witted. Still, it was hard to accustom himself to having no mustache or sophisticated pointed beard. He ran his palm over his skull. He'd even shaved his head. But what he missed the most was his fly whisk, the mark of a man of rank.

What he went through for advancement! He prayed to Amun, Osiris, and Ra that all these discomforts would be rewarded. Once ashore, he would send a sailor to the village to make discreet inquiries, to listen to the news of the great feast of rejoicing held for Count Meren. It would be one of the signal events of the year for those lesser beings.

No one was going to tell him to go home. No insufferable know-all was going to tell him that Kysen would leave pharaoh's side for a mere feast. He knew deep in his bones that Meren would only leave court to spin plots in secret. Something was going on in that peaceful country estate. And he was going to find out what it was.

All he had to do was be patient. Sooner or later Meren would make a mistake, one Paser could use against him at court. After all, the path to power lay over the bodies of one's enemies. And Paser's path to the favor of

Tutankhamun, may he have life, health, and prosperity,
lay in the rise of Prince Hunefer and the fall of Lord
Meren.

12

▽

The door to Sennefer's room opened to reveal Nebetta and Hepu huddled over their son's body. Nebamun stood beside the table with the flagon of pomegranate wine. Meren stepped into the corridor and closed the door. With his back to it, he appraised the sea of startled and agonized faces. Everyone was crowded into the narrow corridor—servants, his sister, his daughters, even Wah.

Great-Aunt Cherit occupied the threshold to the hall in her carrying chair. And Kysen stood near Bentanta. Meren gave him a wordless signal and glanced at Bentanta. Kysen nodded in response.

"Well?" Idut asked, her eyes shining with tears. "His ka has flown to the netherworld?"

"Yes. We'll have to send him to Abydos with Anhai tomorrow morning."

As Nebamun had predicted, Sennefer had died before dusk. Long before this Meren had given confidential orders to his men that the entire estate be searched and all the pomegranate wine confiscated. Their task had been made easier since all the family except Ra, who was still asleep, were keeping vigil in the guest house.

The family began to talk together in that quiet way people employed at a death. As at Anhai's death, none of the women fell to wailing and moaning. The only noise of that kind came from Nebetta. The others were too frightened to think of the proprieties.

A hand slipped into his. He glanced down at Isis and saw fear in his daughter's eyes. He pulled her against him, and Bener slipped beneath his free arm.

She pressed against his side and whispered, "This is terrible. There's some evil loose among us."

"I'm scared," Isis said.

Meren frowned at Bener. "You mustn't frighten your sister. Both of you take heart. I won't let evil come near you. I'm here. Your brother is here, and we have a dozen charioteers to protect us."

"They haven't done Anhai and Sennefer any good," Bener said. She seemed to have lost her enthusiasm for mystery.

"I didn't tell them to protect Anhai or Sennefer, but I am going to order them to protect you. You will be safe."

Wah thrust his way past a couple of serving women to approach Meren. "Perhaps I should leave."

"No," Meren said.

"Oh, of course," Wah said smoothly. "You need my assistance in this time of difficulty. I am honored to be of aid to my future brother. You have only to tell me what I may do for you. Anything—"

"Wah, not now." As he spoke, Meren glanced at Reia, who squeezed past Cherit and saluted him.

"Idut," Meren said. "Will you take everyone back to the garden? There's nothing to be done here."

"There's much to be done," she said. "I have to look after Aunt Nebetta and Uncle Hepu. They'll want mourners and ashes, and Sennefer must be prepared for the journey to Abydos. I must summon priests."

"Not now, Idut."

"Meren, you've grown callous, and I won't—"

"No!"

Idut jumped and scowled at him. Before either of them could speak, Cherit held up a wrinkled hand for silence.

"Idut, you're a fool. There's evil rampant in this house, and you're worried about conventions."

Wah sidled over to Idut. "The venerable Lady Cherit speaks with wisdom, my dear. Two people have died suddenly. This is no longer an ordinary matter. Let us all retire to the garden as Lord Meren requested."

The family complied, but as Bentanta tried to follow them, Kysen delayed her. Meren joined them.

"Lady, where is the pomegranate wine you brought with you?"

"Most of it has been drunk. Why?"

"You gave some to Sennefer?"

"Yes, this morning. He was distraught over Anhai. What's wrong?"

"But there's some in his chamber."

Bentanta glanced at Sennefer's door. "At the feast he asked for some. I had two jars sent to his chamber."

"When was this?"

"Early, not long after the feast began. He tasted it and couldn't stop praising it."

"So you instructed a servant to bring jars to his chamber. And the jars were sealed."

"Of course they were sealed." Bentanta looked at him closely. "My pomegranate wine couldn't have killed him."

"Not the wine, no."

"I'm not lackwitted, Meren. You think his wine was poisoned, so you suspect me of killing him. Use your own wits, will you? Why would I want to kill Sennefer?"

Meren glanced at Reia. "Escort Lady Bentanta to her chamber."

"I do not allow anyone to send me to my room, Meren."

"Then allow me to explain something," he said. "My cousin is dead from drinking tainted wine that you provided. His wife is already dead after quarreling with you.

She held something of yours that you wanted back, which you refuse to explain. You deny any evil-doing, but can't prove your innocence. This is no longer a matter between friends, Bentanta. It's an official inquiry into two deaths by the Eyes of Pharaoh, not a plea for help by your playfellow. Go to your chamber."

He signaled to Reia, who bowed to Bentanta and indicated the way to her room, which lay on the opposite side of the house. Bentanta pressed her lips together, but said nothing. Turning her back on Meren, she marched out ahead of the charioteer.

When she was gone, Meren opened the door to Sennefer's room and summoned Nebamun. Nebetta was rocking back and forth on her knees beside Sennefer's body while Hepu stood over her. The physician came out holding the cup and flagon of wine. Kysen went in and retrieved the opened jar. Then Meren shut the door on the grieving parents.

He led the way to the hall, took a chair on the dais, and waited while Kysen set the round-bottomed jar in a stand. "Now, tell me again what's in the wine."

"I'm not certain, lord, but I think it's been tainted with a poisonous plant, the *tekau*. It has long, deep-green leaves and purple-black berries. My physician's book lists the signs that come upon one poisoned with it, and states that it is an illness one cannot treat if too much has been eaten or drunk."

"And so far the only wine that's been tainted is this we have here," Meren said.

"Iry has examined all the other jars," Kysen said. "When she arrived, Bentanta had twelve jars delivered to the kitchen storage. Most of it was consumed at the feast with no ill effects. There were three jars left in storage, and they have been found untainted. It seems the only poison is in this one open jar."

Meren rose and bent over the vessel to study the bits of

clay clinging to the twine fastened to its neck. "It could have been poisoned before it was sealed, I suppose."

"Or someone could have tainted it after Sennefer opened it," Kysen said. "If he opened it after the feast, in his chamber, someone still easily could have stolen into his room after he was asleep and put the poison in the jar. Anyone in the guest house, that is."

Meren went back to his chair. "True. You've been invaluable, Nebamun. Please go back to my aunt and attend to her."

"She is making herself ill with grief, lord. Shall I give her a draught to calm her?"

"Yes, if she'll take it."

When Nebamun was gone, Kysen lowered himself to the floor of the dais and shook his head. "I don't suppose you've thought of a way to blame a servant or a slave."

"Ky, all of them have been with the family for generations, and most were too busy at the feast to be involved with Anhai's death. Kasa has worked with my men to account for their whereabouts that night. As for Sennefer, only those who handled the wine or had the opportunity to taint it concern us."

"Who brought the wine to Sennefer's room?"

"Kasa," Meren said. "And I don't think Kasa had a reason to harm Sennefer or Anhai. He barely knew them and had no dealings with either."

Kysen turned around and clasped his arms around his knees. "But Bentanta had a reason to harm Anhai, and if Anhai shared her secret with Sennefer, she had a reason to harm him too. What was this great secret?"

"She won't tell me, and the search of her chamber and possessions has yielded nothing, especially not torn papyrus."

"Then you haven't seriously tried to make her tell you."

"Don't worry. I'm through being the gentle courtier

and hesitant childhood friend. I'm going to her chamber now." Meren rose and smoothed the pleats in his over-robe. "However, I almost feel like changing into armor."

"Fear not," Kysen said with a wry smile. "Reia will be there to protect you."

"You think yourself fortunate, but you, my dear son, are going to question my dear sister's proposed husband."

"Not Wah!"

"I can't talk to everyone, Ky, and he's the only stranger who was here for both deaths. Perhaps the gods will bless us, and you'll find out he's the murderer of both. Unfortunately . . ."

"Ra?"

"Yes," Meren said. "Ra was at Green Palm, and he could have stolen back to kill Anhai and poisoned Sennefer's wine too."

"An evil prospect, but how likely?"

"I'm not sure," Meren said. "Once I would have said Ra doesn't care deeply enough about anyone or anything to be provoked into action. But if Anhai used him, and Sennefer laughed at him for it—" Meren threw up his hands. "I don't know anymore. At times he's rabid with anger. He thinks he's been persecuted his entire life, mostly by Father and by me, but he's fed this grudge for so long that he's made a habit of seeing injustice toward himself from countless sources."

"And he drinks."

"Wine has ruined many a man's judgment," Meren said.

Kysen rubbed his chin and stared at the flagon and wine cup. "The doorkeepers for both houses were back at their posts after the feast. Anyone outside would have had to avoid them, and none of them saw anyone sneaking around the grounds. I suppose it's possible that someone from outside could have used a rope to climb the outer wall and steal up the back stairs to the roof to enter." He rose and stood beside Meren.

"You're going to question Aunt Idut?"

"Yes, and Great-Aunt Cherit," Meren said. "I wish you could do it, but they wouldn't listen to you. And I'll have to talk to Hepu, and perhaps Nebetta. Gods, this day seems endless."

"I'll visit the temple tonight. You get some rest."

"After this day, I don't think I'm going to be able to sleep. I'm not going to rest until I find out who's killing people in my house. And gods, what a choice of culprits!"

"You've thought of the possibility that Sennefer could have killed Anhai, and someone else killed him in revenge?"

"Which leads to Ra again," Meren said.

"I'll find Iry and see if his searches have revealed anything else."

"Ky," Meren said as his son walked away, "while you're doing that, assign Reia's brother Simut to guard Bener and Isis. I don't think they're in danger, but I'll rest easier knowing someone is watching them."

"I should have thought of it earlier."

When he was alone, Meren summoned a servant and had him take the wine jar, flagon, and wine cup to his office. They would be safe there with a sentry posted outside the door. He could think of nothing else to do that would delay his visit to Bentanta.

The women's quarters lay on the opposite side of the house. As he directed his steps in that direction, he realized that he'd been hampered from the beginning of this inquiry. It was almost impossible to intimidate people who remembered him as a muddy, sticky-faced boy. He dreaded demonstrating his power and authority, but his family—and Bentanta—were fast forcing him into a position in which he'd have no choice.

Reia was outside Bentanta's room with another charioteer. He almost went inside alone but instead gave an order to Reia. Reia left, and Meren paced outside the door while he waited briefly for him to return.

Leaving the second man outside as guard, Meren stepped back from the door to allow Reia to knock and throw open the portal. Bentanta was stalking around the chamber and paused in midstride when they appeared. Her brows drew together as her gaze fell on the charioteer. Reia had a scimitar stuck in his belt and was holding a scribe's palette and papyrus.

"I've told you I didn't poison Sennefer or kill Anhai. Your trained colts have searched every possession I brought with me. My patience is wearing, Meren."

Meren didn't answer. Reia walked past Bentanta, picked up a chair, and brought it to him. Meren sat down, gathering the complicated folds of his robe around his legs. Reia drew his weapon, sat on the floor, and placed it beside him. Then he took a rush pen from his palette and mixed some ink with water. Placing the papyrus on the length of his kilt that stretched between his crossed legs, he dipped the pen in the palette inkwell. All the while, Meren remained silent.

"What are you doing?" Bentanta demanded.

Meren studied her as he would any person whom he had cause to suspect of a great evil, assessing, probing, looking for any sign of guilt. Sometimes this treatment worked, but often, with the quick-witted or those with experience at the imperial court, he was met with a facade of impenetrable innocence. Unfortunately, Bentanta stared right back at him without guilt, but with a bargeload of anger. Ah well, he hadn't expected her to succumb to simple tactics.

"Lady Bentanta, I'll send for another witness to this examination if you wish it."

"Examination?" Bentanta walked over to face him and

put her hands on her hips. "You're going to examine me like a common thief who steals honey from your beekeepers?"

"Then you don't require another witness," Meren said. "Very well. We'll begin, Reia." He leaned over the side of his chair and glanced down at the charioteer. "Count Meren, son of Amosis, the Eyes and Ears of Pharaoh, Nebkheprure Tutankhamun—may he have life, health, and prosperity—year five, season of Drought. He speaks as follows: the examination of the Lady Bentanta, widow of Lord Hekareshu the justified, in the matter of the deaths of Lord Sennefer and Lady Anhai."

He waited, staring impassively at Bentanta as Reia's pen brushed across the polished paper. She looked from him to the paper and back. Her eyes grew wide, and her hands dropped to her sides. He watched the muscles in her throat work as she swallowed. Other than this movement, her face was still. She'd learned to conceal her thoughts at the side of two queens.

"I've told you I've done nothing," she said.

"And I will have Reia record all your answers to me. I remember all of them. But now I will ask you what it was that Anhai and Sennefer held against you. And you will give me the truth."

Bentanta walked away from him. She paused beside a table laden with cosmetics—kohl tubes, unguent containers, spoons, tweezers, an ivory comb, and a bronze mirror. She touched the polished surface of the mirror. He could almost see the rush of her thoughts. Best not to give her too much time.

"Answer me," he said.

Her hand jerked back from the mirror. She clenched it and thrust it behind her back. Turning his way, she lifted her chin and gave him a slight smile.

"The Lady Bentanta answers thus. I wish to consult with my family."

"In time," he said. Bentanta's family was a powerful one. In one way or another she was related to Meren's friend, the royal treasurer Maya, to General Nakhtmin's wife, to the high priest of Osiris, and to the divine adoratrice of Amun.

"No, Meren. I want to consult my family now. Send for my father and for Maya. Both Anhai and Sennefer provoked anger from many people, and I'll not submit to your hounding without my family near me to help." She walked back to him again, her carriage erect, her manner confident.

Drumming his fingers on his chair arm, Meren leaned back and studied her. Suddenly he quit tapping the wood and closed his eyes. He summoned the spirit of warfare, that attitude that allowed him to face his own death and the deaths of friends and remain calm and battle-ready. When he opened his eyes, Bentanta blinked at his expression. Her lips moved soundlessly, but he spoke first.

"I had hoped to spare you humiliation and pain. You refuse to answer, and I will not allow this." He stood abruptly.

Using the advantage of his greater height, he looked down on Bentanta, unsmiling. "I've questioned those far greater than you. If you think I'll spare the whip and the cane because of our past, you're wrong. Someone is killing people in my house, and I'm going to find out who it is. I want the truth from you, Bentanta. It's your choice as to whether I use force to get it."

She was staring at him, eyes round, body rigid, like a startled ibex. At last he'd force her to take him seriously. He took a step toward her, and she backed away. Nodding to Reia, he went to the door.

"What are you doing?"

"A forced inquiry takes preparation," he said as Reia opened the door to reveal the sentry. "Perhaps by the time I return, you'll have realized you have no choice but to answer my questions."

He left quickly with Reia, before she could protest. For the first time there had been alarm in her voice; perhaps a night spent alone in fear would loosen her tongue. She would start each time she heard a footfall. Her fear would grow at every whisper, every raised voice. He had much to do to keep him busy in the meantime.

Besides, he had no great faith in confessions obtained by force. Often one got only what the victim thought one wished to hear. With his men on guard, there would be no more deaths. He would revisit the granary before dark, talk to Idut and Aunt Cherit. Yes, there was much to do, and he could afford to wait for Bentanta to lose her courage. But if she didn't, would his be as great when he had to follow through with his threats?

Not wanting to know the answer to this question, Meren left the guest house and walked toward his own. As he made his way through the trees that clustered around the high walls, he heard shouting. People crowded around the front gate, pointing and muttering. Reia strode ahead of him, parting the observers.

As the onlookers stepped aside, the shouting grew louder, then ceased. Abruptly those closest to the center of the commotion scattered, leaving Meren to stare at Kysen and Ra. At the same time, a roar erupted from his brother's lips. Ra sprang backward. A dagger leaped into his hand, and Kysen drew his own.

"I'll teach you manners, you lowborn son of a goat!"

Ra's arm darted at Kysen's gut. Kysen parried the thrust, and the blades clashed together. Metal slid against metal until the two weapons locked at the hilt. As the two pushed against each other, Meren jumped at them, grabbed Ra's dagger arm, and jammed his foot into his brother's chest. Ra flew to the ground, still holding his dagger. Meren stood between his son and his brother and glared at Ra.

"What demon possesses you that you dare attack my son?"

Ra wiped sweat from his upper lip with the back of his hand. "He tried to keep me from leaving. The cur told me to go back to my chamber as if I were some pubescent girl! He says I'm suspected of killing Sennefer and Anhai, the dung-eater."

Meren held his ground as Ra sprang to his feet and walked toward Kysen. He grabbed his brother's forearm, immobilizing the hand that held the dagger.

"You don't want to fight Kysen," he said. "You want to fight me. Why don't you do it?"

Ra jerked his arm free and glared at Meren. Then his lips twisted into a smile. "By the wrath of Amun, I've wanted to do this for a long time. Come then, mighty Eyes of Pharaoh, great and powerful Friend of the King, fight me if you dare. I'll kill you before the sun sets."

13

▽

Kysen hurried over to his father as Meren removed his
gold collar, belt, and overrobe. "He came charging out of
the house saying he heard you'd forbidden him to leave. I
was nearby when he tried to bully the sentry into letting
him out of the gate."

"Did you say he was suspected?" Meren asked. Reia
took his jewels and robe.

"Of course not. I said no one was above suspicion, and
he took offense." Kysen glanced at Ra, who was glaring
at them from across the clear space formed by the crowd.
"This isn't good, Father. Your wounds aren't completely
healed. Let Reia and the men take him."

Meren took Kysen's dagger from him. "No. He has
attacked you in front of my people and challenged me.
Neither of us can go back, and taking him prisoner would
deal him a humiliation he'd never forgive."

Kysen knew that set look on his father's face. Meren
had made a decision from which he wouldn't waver. He
stepped back, caught the eye of one of the sentries, and
gave him a hand signal. The man nodded, pursed his lips,
and whistled. Another whistle sounded inside the house
grounds, then another.

At the same time, Meren and Ra began to circle one
another. The sun hung low in the sky, just visible through
the trees. Meren kept his back to it, working his way

closer and closer to his brother while making Ra face the light most of the time.

More people joined the crowd—farmers, fishermen, servants. Several charioteers shouldered their way to the front of the throng. Kysen signaled again, and they spread out in a loose ring around the two fighters. Feeling helpless, Kysen moved with them, watching Ra's dagger. Meren was a warrior, but Ra was seven years younger.

The two drew close enough to strike, but Meren remained on the defensive. Crouched, balancing on the balls of his feet, Ra waved his blade back and forth in front of his brother. Meren refused to look at it, watching Ra's face instead. Finally losing patience, Ra thrust his dagger straight at Meren's gut. Meren hopped out of reach, almost forcing Ra to overbalance. He jabbed again, this time from the side. The blade caught Meren at the waist, drawing a thin line in blood.

The crowd gasped, and a woman shrieked. Kysen saw one of the charioteers holding Idut by the arm as she shouted at her brothers. Neither paid her any attention. Ra was smiling after his hit, but Meren ignored it and moved to keep his back to the sun. Ra darted at him, his dagger leading. At the last moment, he tossed his weapon to his left hand and struck. Meren ducked underneath the path of the blade, spun, and shoved Ra, causing him to stumble and fall to his knees.

Kysen wasn't surprised when Meren simply straightened and waited for his brother to recover. From the beginning Meren's stance and lack of offensive movements had told Kysen he didn't intend to fight Ra as he would an enemy. Ra seemed to realize this too, for he jumped up and turned on Meren, his sweating face red, teeth bared.

"Fight me, you cursed son of the Devourer." Ra walked quickly toward Meren. "I'll not let you take this from me as you have everything else."

Before he finished speaking, Ra launched himself at
Meren. He crashed into his brother, who fell backward as
he grabbed Ra's dagger arm with his free hand. They
landed with Ra on top. Meren pulled Ra's arm while
shoving with his body. Ra toppled to the side, ending up
on his face, spitting dirt.

Meren jumped to his feet, turned, and stood over his
brother, his chest heaving. "You've drawn my blood, Ra.
Surely you're recompensed for any insult." He lowered
his dagger and turned away.

Ra rolled over, wiped dirt from his eyes, and saw his
brother walking toward the front gate. Springing to his
feet, he sailed at Meren, dagger held high and pointed at
his brother's back. Kysen put his fingers in his mouth and
let out a piercing whistle that was accompanied by those
of the charioteers.

At the sound, Meren whirled around and brought his
dagger up just as Ra's blade descended. Metal slid
against metal until the weapons locked hilts. Meren fell
beneath the impetus of Ra's charge, planted his feet on
his brother's stomach, and threw him over his head. Ra
hurtled through the air. His head cracked against hard
earth as he slammed into the ground on his back,
stunned. His dagger flew from his hand.

There was a sudden quiet as Meren got quickly to his
feet and went to his brother. Flailing with arms and legs,
gasping for air, Ra tried to rise, but ended up looking like
a writhing fish tossed on the riverbank. Kysen picked
up Ra's dagger and joined Meren to kneel beside the
fallen man.

Meren grabbed a fistful of Ra's hair and pulled the
dazed man upright. "Remember. I wasn't the one who
wanted to fight, Ra. And remember this too. If you ever
touch Ky again, I'll fight you as I would an enemy
instead of a spoiled little brother." Ra slapped Meren's
hand from his head and cursed. "You're staying here,"

Meren said. "You can remain as a guest or as a prisoner. I care not which. Come, Ky. We've work to do."

Kysen had listened to his father's last words with growing surprise that kept him silent while Meren ordered his men to remove Ra to the house. Always, deep within his ka, there had remained a nagging feeling of disbelief that Meren could hold for him the affection a father held for a son of his blood. To be presented with such overwhelming proof of Meren's love was like being gifted with perfection by the gods. He didn't know how to feel or how to respond. Luckily, Meren seemed unaware of the magnitude of his actions. He handed his dagger to Reia, waved a hand to banish the crowd of onlookers, and then glanced at Kysen.

"We can only pray to Amun that my fool of a brother will think before acting in the future. Damnation. Here comes Idut. Delay her, Ky. I'm going to wash. Meet me in the granary. I want to look at it again before all the light vanishes."

"Aunt," Kysen said as he stepped in her path. "You don't look well. Didn't you enjoy Father's little game with Ra?"

"Game? That was no game. Meren! You come back here, Meren."

Kysen danced in front of his aunt as she tried to go around him and thought of a half-lie. "A royal messenger has just arrived. Father must attend to it at once. May I send for beer? You seem overheated, Aunt."

A messenger had come from the king, but he'd arrived long ago and was filling his belly in the kitchen while he awaited Meren's letters of reply. Kysen managed to divert Idut long enough for Meren to disappear into the security of his apartments.

Not long afterward Kysen entered the granary court to find Hray in the process of issuing ration payments to the workers. While waiting for his father, he questioned

Hray again. No, the overseer had seen nothing out of the ordinary, touched nothing when he found Anhai.

Meren joined them. "But there was one thing out of the ordinary, Hray."

"There was, lord?"

"Your grinders fought over their querns and grindstones."

"Aye, lord. They're a quarrelsome lot sometimes."

Kysen glanced at the bowed querns and the oblong grindstones. "It appears that several of the laborers have favorite implements. Two of them prefer the same ones."

"Yes, lord."

"Indeed," Meren said. "And when you found Anhai's body, two of the grindstones had been switched, precipitating an argument. What I want to know is whether the querns and grindstones were left in their proper order after the day's work."

"Oh yes, lord," Hray said, jerking his head up and down. "I make them keep the querns and grindstones matched, and I make the two laborers take turns with the set they both prefer. I don't tolerate fighting over the tools. Wastes time."

"And yet the stones were mismatched," Kysen said. While Meren dismissed Hray, he went over to the awning and picked up a black grindstone, hefting it in his hand. Returning to Meren, he pointed the stone at him. "It's heavy. Wouldn't it have made a mark if someone hit Anhai with it?"

Meren took the stone, grabbing it by the end. Something in that gesture bothered Kysen, but he couldn't decide how. They stared at the black stone together. The surface was smooth from constant grinding and had a dull sheen. Kysen rubbed it with his fingers, but they came away clean. No trace of any substance at all. He returned the stone to its quern.

As he did so, he passed a water jar hanging suspended

in a net. The vessel was made of clay, allowing some of the water to seep and keep the rest cool. He picked up a pottery cup and poured water into it. He drank all the water before he rejoined Meren, who was standing at the base of the granary in which Anhai had been found.

While the laborers and Hray filed out of the granary court, they stood contemplating the tall structure.

"Reia and the others have collected reports on all the servants and guests," Meren said. "We have yet to question Wah, Idut, Sennefer's parents, and Aunt Cherit."

"You don't think Aunt Idut or dear old Cherit—"

"Of course not, but they may have seen something."

"You spoke to the Lady Bentanta?"

Meren kicked at the door in the base of the granary. "That woman has more boldness and insolence than a she-falcon. I swear when she looks at me she sees a boy with a sidelock."

Kysen's glance took in Meren's greater height and charioteer's build. "I don't think so."

"She must, or she wouldn't have refused to answer my questions. I subjected her to a formal inquiry, and she threw it back in my face. She's hiding something, Ky, and I'm going to find out what it is. If she doesn't give in tomorrow morning, I'll—curse it—I don't want to do what I'm going to have to do."

"Don't worry. If you tried to frighten her, you succeeded. You're good at it." Kysen glanced around the courtyard. "It's growing dark. Time to eat. And I'm going to get some sleep before I have to go to the haunted temple."

"At least we've been successful there," Meren said.

"And what of Ra?"

"I'm going to Green Palm tomorrow morning and talk to those tavern women myself. Then I'll confront Bentanta."

"Which of them do you think did it?" Kysen asked.

"I don't know."

"Would you rather find Bentanta guilty?"

Meren's head jerked in his direction. His eyes widened, and Kysen heard a sharp intake of breath.

"Of course," Meren said. "Of course, I'd rather it was her than my brother, no matter how irritating he is."

"It's just that you seem uncertain."

Meren fixed him with a forbidding stare. "I'm uncertain about who has committed this evil, and I'm worried about the danger to the rest of us."

"Of course," Kysen said. "Shall I have the cook send food to your chamber? I don't think you want to eat in the hall with Idut."

After the evening meal, Kysen left Meren to deal with a pile of correspondence and went upstairs to the office. He was going over the results of questioning the servants and slaves when Iry arrived, escorting Wah. The man had been an ubiquitous presence at Baht. He hovered over Idut dispensing sympathy, compliments, and gifts. He listened to Great-Aunt Cherit's numerous stories of people long dead, nodding and feigning interest. He had tried to gain interviews with Meren, even tried to waylay him during Sennefer's fatal illness. Meren had remarked with venom that if Wah tried to leave as Ra and Hepu had, he might be tempted to let him go.

Now Wah trotted into the office, eager as a hound, his ever-present basket of dates in one hand, the other wiping runny kohl from his eye. Kysen offered him a stool and took Meren's chair. He had to force himself to do this, for his impulse would be to take the stool. But Meren wouldn't have approved. His rank as a royal inquiry agent demanded that he present an air of authority. Iry settled himself nearby to take notes.

Wah gave the charioteer an apprehensive look before folding his long frame to fit on the stool. "Such terrible happenings, dear Kysen. I've tried to comfort your aunt and the Lady Cherit. They need me, since you and your father are so busy trying to find the evil one responsible for these deaths. Poor Anhai and Sennefer. Have you found out who it is? I hear the Lady Bentanta is confined to her chamber, as is Nakht—um, Ra, that is."

"The charioteer Reia tells me you agreed with reports that during Hepu's Instruction at the feast Bentanta left with Anhai."

"Yes," Wah said as he popped a date in his mouth. "I saw them quarrel. Quite a few people did. And later they left together, which I thought odd considering how little tolerance they seemed to have for each other. Forgive me, but I don't understand why the Lady Bentanta was here at all. I know Idut said she was visiting Sennefer and Anhai when the invitation arrived for the feast."

This was why Meren disliked Wah. The man probed and pried and busied himself in affairs that didn't concern him, and he wouldn't stop talking. Kysen found himself trying to strangle the arms of his chair and grinding his teeth.

"Did you see Anhai at all after Hepu finished his Instruction?"

"No, but I saw Sennefer." Wah laughed. "I remember being able to spot him no matter how thick the crowd because he had a fresh unguent cone on, and it was lop-sided. It was a wonder it didn't fall off before it melted."

"And this was after Hepu had finished?"

"Oh, yes. Sennefer was talking to one of Antefoker's daughters. The poor girl was blushing and hiding her face behind a fly whisk. I never did understand how Sennefer escaped being garroted by some irate father or abused husband."

"Do you know of anyone like that who might have wanted Sennefer dead?"

"I hear there were many," Wah said, giving Kysen a

curious glance. "But I thought Sennefer died of poison wine, Lady Bentanta's pomegranate wine."

"And your servants at the guest house say you retired from the feast along with Nebetta and Hepu, before Sennefer."

"Am I under suspicion?" Wah drew himself up, but failed in his attempt at dignity; in his position on the stool, his knees stuck up nearly to his ears.

"I'm merely making a thorough inquiry," Kysen said.

"Well then, I retired after thanking Idut and your father for an enjoyable feast, and I slept through the night. You may ask my servant."

"I have," Kysen said. "And I've made other inquiries. You were with my aunt for most of the feast, and you even remained in the hall listening to Hepu's entire Instruction."

"I found it most rewarding. Your uncle is a man of high character and honor."

"You think so?"

Wah bit into another date and contemplated the remaining half fruit in his fingers. "I've tried to speak with your father several times without success, my boy. I'm worried about your aunt and your sisters. It might be safer for them if I took them to Memphis until you've solved this crime."

"You?"

"After all, I'm Idut's proposed husband. It's my duty to look after her, and as a future member of the family, I'm concerned for the well-being of my little nieces."

Kysen had no intention of letting this date-munching place-seeker get his hands on his sisters. "I thank you, Wah. I'll put your suggestion to my father. In the meantime you'll continue to lend your support to Aunt Idut by remaining with us."

"Of course. My, you've been busy making so many

inquiries. I had no idea you'd checked my every movement at the feast."

"Not just you, but yes, we have. We know that you
rose late after the feast, after Anhai's body was found,
and that you spent the morning lending comfort to the
family. I also know that you didn't speak with Sennefer
until everyone went to the garden to eat. He fell sick
while you were nearby, on the couch."

"You're surpassing thorough." Wah set his date basket
down on the floor. "So you already know that I didn't
come near poor Sennefer."

"But did you see anyone go near Sennefer's wine cup
when he was in the garden?"

"Oh, I suppose most of the family went near it, but
only Bentanta remained close to him long. But what of
Ra? I hear he claims to have been asleep most of the
day."

Kysen rose, causing Wah to do the same. "My thanks
for your help, Wah."

"It was my duty, especially since I'm soon to be a
member of the family. Soon I'll be your father's brother
and your uncle. Be certain I'll do everything I can to protect the family. In the future I hope to be of great service.
Would you like a date?"

"No, thank you."

"You will speak to your father about my taking Idut
and your sisters away?"

Kysen ushered Wah out of the room. "As soon as possible. A pleasant evening to you." He closed the door
before the man finished speaking.

"Iry, I don't know when I've felt my time more wasted
than when talking with that fool."

"Yes, lord, but at least the task is done."

"Get some rest. We'll leave after everyone's asleep."

Kysen took the record of Wah's interview from the
charioteer. Iry left while he was placing it in a document

case along with the dozens of others made during the course of their inquiries. There was a basket of ostraca, pottery shards on which the men took notes. He picked up one that recorded the statements of a kitchen worker, then tossed it back into the basket.

Because of the two deaths, he hadn't mentioned the situation at the haunted temple to his father. Some of the guards reported that Nento was growing more and more agitated. The long hours in the dark spent listening to the wind and the calls of hyenas were wearing down his courage. He jumped at the slightest sound. He refused to remain in the temple alone with his royal charges, insisting upon at least two guards for company.

The men had assured Kysen that Nento was alarmed about nothing. The only sounds that broke the silence around the temple were those of jackals, hyenas, lizards, and Nento's cries of alarm. The only movement was that of the wind. Kysen was going to talk to Nento tonight and tell him he was welcome to return to Baht. It would be amusing to see the man try to decide which was more dangerous, the haunted temple or a country house in which two people had been murdered.

14

Indigo darkness surrounded Meren in the garden at Baht. Although it was several hours after sunset, the sun's heat remained to envelop him in a stifling cocoon. His bare skin stuck to his chair, and no amount of fanning brought relief. He alone sat beside the reflection pool and watched the moonlight play over the still surface of the water and illumine the lotus flowers floating nearby. Still dismayed at his fight with Ra, he had sought privacy here after dining in his chamber. The recently healed wounds Tanefer had given him ached and stung with renewed intensity. It had been difficult to conceal his pain from Ra and the others.

He and his brother hadn't fought as children. Ra had been too young, and once he was old enough, Meren had been sent to the royal court to be reared among princes and the children of high nobles. To Meren, Ra had been a babe, an endearing child in need of protection. But as the years passed Meren had grown more and more confused and angry at the difference in the way his father had treated them. For him there could be no mistakes, no gradual progress in learning. He was expected to learn the skills of a scribe or those of a soldier at once, with no help.

For Ra, life had been different. Ra was young, Meren was told. Ra hadn't been given the gift of as clever a heart as Meren's. Ra was unique, his parents had said; his talents had to be nurtured, encouraged, aided.

Once, long ago, before he'd been sent to the royal nursery, his father had given him his first bow. He had shown Meren how to string the tiny replica of a man's instrument—once. Meren tried to bend the bow as his father had. It snapped in his small hands. Meren was surprised and brokenhearted at the destruction of this prize of manhood, but his father had erupted in rage. He still remembered the bewildered shame he'd felt as Amosis bellowed at him in front of the household.

Years later Ra had broken his first bow, and his second, and had lost his third. Each loss had been met with tolerance. Ra was so strong. No wonder the bow broke. Ra was so busy and popular with his friends. It was understandable that a bow could be misplaced. There was always an excuse.

Now Ra lived on excuses, and Meren was afraid his brother would never understand that the world wouldn't conform itself to his desires. He was afraid that Ra had so misunderstood the world that he'd committed murder with the notion that there would be yet another convenient excuse to save him from the consequences.

"You sent for me, lord."

"What?" Meren dragged his gaze from the silver spray of light on the water. "Oh, Nebamun, yes. You've examined the querns and grindstones? What do you think?"

"Lord, anyone hit with a stone roller would be bloodied."

"I know that, but is there some other way to kill a person with it?"

"I know not, lord."

"And there's still no sign of any *tekau* poison about the estate?"

"No, lord. I think the evil one must have used it all in that jar of pomegranate wine." Nebamun cleared his throat. "You asked who might have knowledge of the use of the *tekau* plant, my lord. A physician would, for it can be used in small amounts to induce sleep or visions, or relieve pain, but it is a dangerous thing. Otherwise, perhaps someone who was interested in gardens and plants might know of it; a mistress of a household, for example."

"But there's none in this garden."

"No, lord."

"So someone brought it with him. You may go," Meren said as he rose and walked to the edge of the pool. Kneeling, he touched the petal of a rose lotus. A frog croaked and hopped into the water, splashing his hand.

"This is madness," he said to himself. "Stop worrying about Ra and think of what you've discovered."

Anhai. She had been killed some time on the night of the feast after Hepu began his Instruction, in some mysterious way, and then dumped into the granary. But putting her in the granary must have been an awkward business. Yet her clothing and wig had been neatly arranged. Why repair her appearance after she'd been killed?

"And there's that scrap of papyrus," he muttered.

Had the killer searched Anhai for a piece of papyrus and then rearranged her clothing? Since finding the scrap, he suspected it might have something to do with the woman's death, but a search of the house had yielded no papers that would have been worth a murder. Of course, the evil one might have destroyed it, or still be carrying it. Did he dare search his own family and Wah? He might have to. Still, he might be chasing a phantom. The scrap might mean nothing.

And who had reason to kill Anhai? Bentanta, and possibly Ra. Meren was skeptical that Antefoker or Wah would kill over debts, and he knew his sister wasn't a murderer. Besides, Ra and Bentanta had both been involved with Anhai, and both had been in a position to kill her the night of the feast.

What was worse, they also had a reason to kill Sennefer. Anhai might have shared her damaging knowledge of Bentanta with her husband, thus provoking Bentanta to kill him. Ra might have killed Sennefer out of jealousy over Anhai, or out of revenge if he suspected Sennefer of killing her.

Meren groaned and pressed his palms against his closed eyes. What a miserable choice of guilty ones. And Bentanta appeared the most likely, since it was her wine that killed Sennefer. But Ra could have stolen into the house from outside and poisoned it. So, too, could the other inhabitants of the house—Wah, Nebetta, and Hepu. His parents wouldn't have killed Sennefer, and Wah had no reason to do it.

"Damnation," Meren muttered. "I'm making no progress at all. I should have brought my juggling balls. Think, you fool. Go back to the beginning—no—to the feast."

He cast his thoughts back, trying to remember if anyone had acted strangely. Idut had dragged him to the reception room to greet the guests. Aunt Cherit had been annoyed with him for refusing to accede to the family's plans for his future. The Antefokers had arrived. Antefoker had been determined to corner Anhai about her cheating him in trade.

Then he remembered Sennefer coming in with Anhai and Bentanta. And at once husband and wife had begun slashing at each other with their tongues. Only Wah's appearance saved everyone from witnessing a fight. There had been talk of the days at Horizon of Aten when both Anhai and Wah had served Nefertiti. But Wah had made even discussion of the fabulous Nefertiti tedious.

Until Ra had arrived. Meren swerved away from

considering the ugly reunion with his brother and the annoying discovery that Ra had linked himself with his cousin's wife. His next memory was of being cornered by Wah, succeeded by that quarrel between Bentanta and Anhai. Why hadn't Sennefer stopped it? He'd been nearby, reclining on a chair and footstool, touching his slightly melted unguent cone and sniffing his fingers. Yet he'd done nothing to stop his wife and her supposed friend from quarreling at so important a celebration as Meren's feast of rejoicing.

After the fight and his unsuccessful attempt to make Bentanta confide in him, Meren had been waylaid by Antefoker, then rescued by Kysen, only to be forced to listen to Hepu's Instruction. During this ordeal he remembered seeing Sennefer, Nebetta, Idut, and Wah, but not Ra or Bentanta. However, he'd been distracted by Isis's conversation with Ra's dissolute friends.

He leaned over the pool and spoke to the black reflection of his body. "It's no use. I see nothing that points the way. No signs of guilt, no marks or traces to lead me to the evil one."

And he was beginning to suspect Anhai had been killed by magic. How else could she have been dispatched without any trace of violence or poison? Yet a search of the house and grounds had revealed no signs of the use of magic—no replicas of Anhai, no collection of the dead woman's hair or nails, no evidence of ritual burning of sacrifices. However, if someone had performed magic while in the midst of some household ritual, at the shrine, for example, such behavior might go unnoticed.

No, that didn't make sense. If someone was using magic, he wouldn't need to dump Anhai in a granary. The magic could have been worked while the murderer was at the feast among those he could call upon as witnesses to his innocence.

Several loud cracks and a yelp, then another, interrupted his musings. The door to the garden banged opened, and Idut marched in, holding an ivory fan. Behind her the two men guarding his privacy bent over, one rubbing his head, the other his shin. Idut descended upon him, shaking the fan in his face.

"No more of this skulking and hiding, Meren. I want to know what's happening. What demon possesses you? How could you take a dagger to Ra?"

"Me! I'm not the one who—"

"Never mind," Idut said. She slapped the fan against her palm. "Not only have you accused your own brother of murder, but Kysen has accused my poor Wah. Wah, of all men, isn't a murderer. He's gentle and sweet, and, and . . ."

"And a sycophant and a place-seeker."

"He doesn't need to seek a place. He was steward to Queen Nefertiti. And how can you make Ra and Bentanta prisoners in their rooms? They've done nothing."

Meren looked at the pool, wishing he could dive into its black waters. "Idut, I'm trying to solve two murders, and I need to be alone."

"Nebetta blames you."

Turning to stare at his sister, Meren said, "Me? What have I done?"

"I don't know. She says you're responsible for both her sons' deaths. She says if Sennefer and Anhai hadn't come to the feast, both of them would be alive."

"She doesn't know that. If the same person killed both, then that person was determined to get rid of them and would have tried elsewhere. And I was nowhere near Djet when he killed himself."

"I tried to tell her that," Idut said, "but she wouldn't listen to me. No one listens to me. You have to find out who killed Anhai and Sennefer. The whole household is fearful. What if there's some evil demon loose among us? I think I should take the girls and go to Memphis. Wah says he'll take us on his yacht. You can stay here with the murderer."

"My charioteers are on guard now. There will be no more deaths, and I'm not sending Bener and Isis anywhere with that fool Wah."

"There you are!" Hepu strode toward them like a colossus with a sagging belly and jowls. "I hear you've confined Ra and Bentanta to their chambers. Did they kill Sennefer?"

"I don't know," Meren said.

"Why not? It's been hours since my poor boy died."

"Catching a murderer isn't a simple task, Uncle."

Hepu seethed with barely contained rage. "But that woman poisoned him!"

"That isn't certain," Meren said.

"Oh, Uncle," Idut said. "I can't imagine Bentanta killing anyone."

"Ah-ha!" Hepu pointed at Meren. "You're protecting her. I see it now. You're all in some evil plot together."

Meren walked over to Hepu. Even now the older man was taller, but Meren wasn't a child anymore. He studied Hepu's indignant face for a moment, then asked quietly, "Are you accusing me of murdering Sennefer?" Hepu's indignation turned to uneasiness as he watched Meren's expression. "I thought not, Uncle. It's your grief. It's taken hold of your heart and interfered with your reason."

"I'm going to see how Nebetta fares," Idut said. "The physician's potion was wearing off before the evening meal."

As Hepu turned to accompany Idut, Meren held up a hand. "A moment, Uncle." Idut left the garden.

"What do you want now?"

"Have you any idea who might want to kill your son or Anhai?"

"My son was beloved by all who knew him," Hepu said.

"Perhaps by the women," Meren said, "but not necessarily by all the men."

"I don't understand you."

"Surely you knew about Sennefer's dealings with women, especially married ones."

Hepu gave him an openmouthed stare. "You're mad."

"Are you saying he never talked to you about his adventures? He talked about them to everyone else."

"My son knew the advice of the great man who said beware of approaching women in a man's home. He was a man of honor and upright judgment."

"Hepu, Sennefer made a habit of seducing married women. It's a wonder some wronged husband hadn't already taken a knife to him."

"My son didn't do such things," Hepu said as he drew himself up to his full height so he could look down his nose at Meren. "It wasn't possible for him."

"Why not?"

Hepu went as still as a temple relief before answering. He looked away from Meren and said, "Because I taught Sennefer well. Unlike Djet, he learned virtue, respect, the conduct of a decent man. No doubt Bentanta killed him in a jealous rage because he refused her. Perhaps she killed Anhai so she could have my son."

Meren could find no reply to this fanciful reasoning. Anyone should know a woman like Bentanta wouldn't want Sennefer. Hepu's conception of his son had more to do with imagination than with Sennefer's true nature.

"I must return to Nebetta. She isn't well at all."

Left alone, Meren tried to regain his calm so that he could resume contemplating what little evidence he had for the two deaths. Eventually he gave up and went to bed. He fell asleep wondering if he could face arresting his own brother for murder.

* * *

Early the next morning a vessel arrived with priests of Anubis. Along with the grieving parents and the family, Meren witnessed the ceremonial removal of the two bodies to the ship that would take them to Abydos for embalming. Then he went to Green Palm.

Now he walked down the main path of the village. It was lined with the trees from which its name was derived, and between the palms squatted stalls covered with goods—vegetables, fruit, basketry, pottery, amulets, cloth. He and Reia stopped beside a rickety awning that sheltered a vendor of melons and surveyed the two-story structure. In the door's stone lintel was carved "The Green Palm," the name of the tavern and village alike.

"Reia, you're staying outside. I don't need a guard to visit a tavern."

"Lord," Reia said. "Captain Abu would flay the skin from my body if I allowed you to go in there without me."

"Abu answers to me—oh, very well. You'd think I was an untried youth. But I can't speak to these women if you hover over me, so you stay away. Watch from a distance and try not to look intimidating."

"But you're you, lord. It's not I who will frighten them."

"I haven't been to Green Palm since before my father died. No one knows me."

Reia gave him a skeptical look. "As you say, lord."

Meren went inside, leaving behind the white light of the new day for the darkness and dim yellow glow of pottery lamps. The main room of the tavern was long, with a central fireplace filled with dead embers. Reed mats lined three walls, and on these were thrown cushions and pallets. Several women reclined in a group on the cushions, while some distance away a man snored on one of the pallets.

Against the fourth wall sat a table on which rested jars of varying sizes and stacks of cups. A man came through a door at the back, his arms loaded with beer strainers, clay straws, and more cups. A girl followed him with two baskets, one filled with bread, another with melons.

The man piled his burdens on the table and began arranging the cups. Meren went over to him, but he didn't look up from his work. "I understand Lord Nakht was here on the night of the feast at Baht."

"I don't flap my tongue about my customers," the tavern keeper said.

"He recommended your tavern to me as a place of comfort and pleasure."

The tavern keeper looked at Meren for the first time. He took in the fine linen, the bronze pectoral necklace, the leather sandals.

"Ah, good master, I'm honored. Yes, yes. Lord Nakht was here and had a merry time drinking my fine beer. My family has brewed the best beer in the entire nome for generations. And I have the most beautiful of women."

"These women, my friend said he liked them well, and I'm interested in seeing them."

"Of course, good master."

The tavern keeper hurried around the table and ushered Meren over to the women. None of them got up. There were three, each wearing a beaded girdle around her hips and nothing else. Although they were more painted than the young female servants of Meren's household, he found none of them more remarkable. The tavern keeper pulled one of the women to her feet.

"This is Tabes, one of the women Lord Nakht favored. Greet the good master, woman."

"Stop snarling at me, Kamosi." The woman bowed to

Meren and kept on lowering her body until she was lying on her cushions again.

Kamosi glowered at her, but Meren dismissed him. "I'll spend a while with these lovely women." When the tavern keeper went back to his beer table to serve Reia, Meren sat down among the women.

"We seldom receive visitors so early in the day," Tabes said with a yawn. She reached out with a languid hand and patted Meren's thigh. "But for so handsome a visitor, I would rise before dawn."

"My thanks," Meren said.

"Oh," said another, who had great painted eyes. "I would rise in the middle of the night." She sat up on her cushion and smiled at him while plucking a lotus from a bowl and handing it to him.

The third woman, small and with quick, darting eyes, touched his ankle with her toe. Meren moved out of reach.

"Good women, I'm here only for conversation." He watched surprise give way to disbelief among the three, so he hurried on. "I understand Lord Nakht was here with several friends the night of the feast at Baht. Tabes, he was with you?"

Silence. The small woman got up and left through the back door.

"Was he here?" Meren asked.

"A tavern woman with a loose tongue soon finds herself cast out of her village," Tabes replied.

Meren leaned closer to her and lowered his voice. "You may speak to me. I'm Lord Nakht's brother."

"But he only has one broth—Gods!"

"Shhh."

"Tabes, this is Lord M—"

Tabes jerked the girl's arm. "Be quiet, Aset. Let the great lord conduct his business in peace and with the secrecy he desires."

"You've an intelligent heart, Tabes."

"The lord is kind," Tabes said with a bow from her sitting position. "The lord wishes to know if his brother was with us on the night of the feast. He came late and in a merry mood. He bought several jars of beer for the entire tavern, and we danced for him."

"He was here the whole night?"

Aset began to chatter. "Oh, the whole night, great lord. He went upstairs with Tabes, Sheftu, and me. Ra is quite generous. He gave me a shift of fine Delta linen, and he gave Tabes a bottle of perfume from Byblos. He kept us busy far into the night. Ra is so funny. He even makes jests while we're—"

"Aset!" Tabes quelled her friend with a severe look. "Lord, we all have great affection for your brother."

"He was here until morning?"

The two women glanced at each other, then at him.

"I woke first," Tabes said. "Around dawn, I think, and he was already gone."

"With Sheftu," Aset chimed in.

"Who is Sheftu?"

"Our other friend," Tabes said. "She's the one who just left, lord."

"Where has she gone? I want to talk to her."

"There's no need for alarm, my lord. Ra and Sheftu probably went to her house. Her grandmother is a wise woman known for her preparations of herbs to enhance pleasure. Sheftu often provides them to those who can pay, and Ra always has plenty of grain or other goods."

Meren's heart battered in his chest like a war drum. He drew closer to Tabes and said, "Herbs, preparations. You mean potions?"

"Aye, lord."

"Flowers, seeds?" Meren asked. "Berries?"

Tabes looked at him curiously. "Yes, lord."

Closing his eyes against pain, Meren spoke again. "I want to talk to this Sheftu who deals in herbs and potions."

15

Meren kept his eyes closed as Tabes rose and disappeared into the back of the tavern. He opened them when she returned, leading Sheftu, who hung back and had to be pulled along. Recognizing her fear, Meren questioned the girl gently, assuring her that she wasn't in danger.

"Yes, lord. Ra woke me while it was still dark. He was drunk, but sober enough to want one of grandmother's preparations. We went to my house, which isn't far away."

"You gave him what he asked for?"

"Yes, lord, and then we went to sleep again."

"Both of you?"

Sheftu hesitated. "I fell asleep first, but I'm sure Ra did too."

"And he left the next morning?"

The girl nodded.

"When?"

"I know not, lord."

"Why?" Meren asked quickly.

"He was gone when I woke," Sheftu said.

"So he left you between the time you fell asleep and the next morning when you woke. Would anyone else have seen him go?"

"There's no one else except Grandmother, and she doesn't see or hear very well."

"When did you wake, Sheftu?"

"The sun was up, lord. We drank more than usual, and I had a terrible ache of the head."

"Then my brother left you before sunrise."

"I suppose so, lord."

"And my brother's friends?"

Tabes said, "Two live not far upriver. They stayed the night in the tavern and left that morning. The third? He's still here. He sampled Sheftu's preparations that night and has been using them ever since." She pointed to the man who still snored on his pallet across the room.

Meren got up and went over to the prone figure. Turning him over, Meren straightened, put his fists on his hips, and shook his head. He didn't want to deal with this fool now.

"Antefoker, Antefoker, wake up."

The man smiled in his sleep until Meren kicked him. Then he snorted himself awake and looked up at Meren with a slack-lipped leer.

" 'SMeren. How're you? Howas th' feast last night?"

"You seem to have lost a day, Antefoker. You'd better go home."

"Lost a day? What day?" Antefoker yawned, smacked his lips, and began to snore again.

Meren threw up his hands and went back to Tabes and her friends. Feigning a casualness he didn't feel, he said, "Sheftu, I'm curious about your grandmother's preparations, especially the ones my brother might have obtained. You will take me there at once." To Tabes and Aset he said, "You've been helpful. I'll have my steward send the three of you a length of cloth. However, I expect your mouths to remain closed about my visit. If I hear differently, I will be displeased."

He and Reia followed Sheftu out of the tavern after fending off the entreaties of its keeper. The woman lived down the street and off an alley formed by the walls of two-story houses. At the end of the narrow lane, Sheftu's house clung to a much larger structure. Its walls were cracked, and the roof sagged as if it was about to fall in. The grandmother was asleep in the front room on a pallet. As he passed her, Meren paused and clapped his hands several times, causing Sheftu to start. The old woman slept on.

The young woman led them through the sparsely furnished chamber to the kitchen in the back. From a rickety frame suspended from the ceiling hung bundles of roots, leaves, flowers, and berries. Dozens of pottery jars covered the only table and much of the floor. There was a stone mortar and pestle, along with wooden spoons, strainers, and stirring sticks. Meren gestured to Reia, who began opening jars and inspecting their contents.

Touching a bundle of feathery dried leaves, Meren asked, "What are these?"

"Dill, my lord," said Sheftu. "And those are acacia pods, and these are chervil seeds. This is celery. Grandmother crushes it and applies it to burns."

He picked up a bowl of hard kernels. "Balanos?"

"Aye, lord."

Reia left the kitchen to search the rest of the house while Meren opened a square basket. In it were more dried leaves, rough, with five lobes.

"Those are white byrony, lord. To purge the stomach or to relieve an ache of the head, but it mustn't be used more than once."

"Poisonous?"

"It can be, lord."

Reia reappeared. Meren raised his brows, but the charioteer shook his head.

Meren set down the basket of white byrony. "Now, can you show me the preparation my brother took?"

Sheftu plucked a small bag from a pile on the table and handed it to Meren. It contained a quantity of finely ground powder that smelled slightly of black pepper.

Meren touched his finger to the powder and was about to taste it when Reia lunged and caught his hand.

"No, lord!"

Meren pulled free but wiped his fingers on a cloth taken from a pile on a shelf.

Sheftu was eyeing them, her brow sweating. "You fear that our preparations are harmful?" She found a cup and poured water into it. Dumping the powder into the cup, she stirred it with a stick, then gulped it down.

"You see? I'm unharmed."

Sighing, Meren said, "We're looking for *tekau*."

"Oh, you should have asked, my lord."

Sheftu found a stool, mounted it, and reached up among the herbs. Her hand came out with a bundle of dried, ovate leaves and flowers that might once have been violet. This she handed to Meren. Then she found a round clay pot with a wavy red pattern painted on it. Shriveled brownish-black berries filled the vessel.

"Grandmother says the stems can be used to treat bad breathing, catarrh, and aching bones."

Meren took the pot from Sheftu. His hands had grown cold, and he felt as if he were in a waking dream.

"Demons and fiends," he muttered. Reia took the pot from him, and he collected the leaves as well. "Sheftu, I must take these."

The woman picked up a tall jar and hugged it to her breast as if it would lend her protection. "Have I done something wrong, lord?"

Meren looked around the dark, cramped little kitchen, at the sparse quantity of grain for bread and wood for fires. A few shriveled onions rested in a bowl.

"Did you give my brother some of these berries or leaves?" he asked.

"No, lord. Your brother was quite healthy except for sickness from drinking."

"You know this plant can be dangerous."

"Of course, but everyone knows better than to put more than a little in a potion. Who would be so foolish as to—" Sheftu wet her lips. "Oh, by all the gods, lord. I've done nothing!"

The woman crumpled to the floor at Meren's feet and babbled protestations of innocence.

Meren backed away. "Be calm. Sheftu, listen to me. Be calm. I have no reason to think ill of you. At the moment. But I must ask you if any *tekau* is missing."

Sheftu straightened. Using the table for leverage, she stood and looked at the herbs Reia was holding. Biting her lower lip, she shook her head.

"I don't know, lord. We haven't used it for a while, not during the whole Drought season."

"Very well," Meren said. "I will send my steward with payment for the herb. You will remain in the village, Sheftu."

"Of course, lord. Where would I go?"

Meren left Sheftu's house scowling and muttering to himself, with Reia striding behind him. The charioteer knew better than to ask questions, and Meren was left to deal with his agitation without interference.

At first he'd been pleased to know that Ra had been indulging in his usual excesses. But Sheftu had ruined his pleasure. Ra could have left the girl in her beer stupor, taken some of the herb, and stolen back to the estate to poison Sennefer's pomegranate wine. He then could have returned to meet his friends at Green Palm. There he could have feigned sickness so that they would offer to bring him home. When questioned, his friends had said they met Ra at the riverbank the morning after the feast. They had assumed he'd come from Sheftu's house. He might have, but if Meren couldn't find someone who saw him there . . .

In a nasty mood, Meren reached the skiff that had

brought them to Green Palm. He got into the boat and snapped at Reia.

"Hurry. I've done an excellent job of implicating my brother in murder, and now I'm going home to threaten a woman with the whip and the brand. Sometimes I disgust myself, Reia."

Back at the main house, Meren went directly to the servants' block to the rear of the compound. It was here that the charioteers had been housed, and it was here that he'd ordered Bentanta brought before dawn. She had been waiting for him there in a narrow, dark room with no windows and no lamp. The building consisted of a row of similar rooms meant for storage, and one long common chamber with half a dozen beds. In the common chamber Meren put on a leather and bronze corselet that wrapped around his chest, wrist guards of the same materials, and a belt into which he shoved a dagger. Still distracted by his discoveries in Green Palm, Meren failed to hear Reia when the charioteer addressed him.

"Lord? Lord, are you well?"

Meren lifted his gaze from the floor to find Reia holding out a charioteer's whip.

"You asked for this, lord."

"Oh, yes. Where are the others?"

"Outside waiting, lord."

"Yes, yes." He cleared his throat. "You've given them their orders? Good." He looked down at the whip to find that his hand was trying to strangle it. He loosened his grip. "Yes, well, it's time, is it not? Come."

Outside waited the four tallest and brawniest of his men. With legs like palm trunks and chests as wide as pyramid blocks, they made even Meren feel slight. He walked down the row of doors to the last one and signaled to Reia. The charioteer pulled back the latch silently, then took a step back and kicked the door open with a crash.

Sunlight pierced the dark void within. Reia took a lamp from one of the men and strode inside. Next Meren motioned for the remaining charioteers to enter. They marched in with spears, nearly filling the room. Only then did Meren follow, stalking in slowly, tapping the coiled whip against his leg. He had drained himself of compassion, separating his ka from all softness, forcing himself to meet this woman as a stranger and an enemy. It was the only way he could carry out this task.

Bentanta stood inside against the back wall, her arms at her sides. He usually preferred not to notice her appearance, as it further disturbed his comfortable, removed perspective of her. But she wasn't in the usual elaborate dress of her station, and he was left with nothing to regard except her unadorned appearance. Without heavy paint on them, her eyes still glinted with that annoying look of calm amusement. They were large and tilted up at the outer corners, adding to the impression of cool humor. Her long, heavy hair was loose except for a thick lock at her temple. Unlike many women he'd questioned, she didn't catch her full lower lip between her teeth to attract attention to her mouth. She simply faced him with the dignity of a Great Royal Wife.

Acknowledging a salute from his charioteers, Meren took a position opposite Bentanta, directed a frigid stare at her, and almost felt his jaw unhinge. Bentanta's expression had changed as his men crowded into the small room. Now she was glaring at him as if he were a slave who had disturbed her in a nap beside the reflection pool.

"I've had enough of this bullying, Meren."

Recovering from his surprise, he asked, "Are you ready to tell me the truth?"

"I've told you the truth."

All at once his shoulder sagged, and he let out a long

breath. Touching the bridge of his nose, Meren thought for a moment.

"Oh, Bentanta," he said gently. "Forgive me."

Bentanta shifted uneasily from one foot to the other. "For what?"

"I am so, so very sorry." He lowered his gaze to the whip, then wearily looked at Reia. "I must leave this to you."

"I will be careful, lord."

"I know you will, but it's difficult."

"What is difficult?" Bentanta demanded.

Reia took the whip from Meren. "It would be best if you went to your chamber, my lord."

"You're right."

"Wait a moment," Bentanta said.

Meren hung his head. "I must leave, Bentanta. I regret this. I truly do."

"I'll be careful, lord," said Reia.

"Very well. I've decided you may use the fire."

"What fire?" Bentanta asked.

Meren glanced back at her. "Fear not. I'll send my physician at once. He's excellent at treating burns. There might not be scars at all."

"You're leaving!"

"You were right," he said. "I can't bring myself to question you by force. You've beaten me."

Meren turned his back on Bentanta and shouldered past the wall of charioteers. He slowed his steps as he crossed the threshold. The door closed, and he was left in the sunlight, sweating and shivering. He forced himself to walk to the shade of an acacia, where he whirled around and glowered at the door to Bentanta's cell. Long, long moments passed. He jumped as a whiplash cracked through the air. He heard a cry, a woman's cry, but it was one of fury. Then there was a slap.

"Meren! Meren, you come back here, damn you. Serpent's spawn! Demon's whelp! Meren? May the gods curse you if you aren't out there."

He counted to twenty before entering the cell once more. Bentanta was still standing against the wall. Her long obsidian hair hung wildly about her shoulders, and she was breathing heavily. The skirt of her shift had a slice in it from hip to thigh. Reia was beside her, gawking at her, his hand pressed against a red cheek. The whip lay discarded on the floor. Retrieving the whip, Meren glanced at Reia. The charioteer gave him an embarrassed glance, saluted, and left, herding his men before him.

Standing in a pool of lamplight, Bentanta raked him with her gaze. She gripped her upper arms, and Meren realized that if she didn't, her hands would tremble. Walking away from him, she suddenly whirled around and spat her words at him.

"Spawn of a scorpion, you were going to let them torture me."

He wasn't about to admit the truth. "I must find out who killed Sennefer and Anhai. I'm sworn to uphold Maat, the harmony and balance of the Two Lands."

"And you're officious as well. Gods, why have I tried to spare you? You don't deserve it."

"Spare me? Spare me how, Bentanta? No more quibbling, no more maneuvers. Tell me what happened with Anhai. Tell me everything, at once."

Abruptly she gave a bitter laugh. Setting her back against the wall, she lowered herself to a sitting position and drew the lamp to her. "Sit down, Meren. This will take a while, and it will be—hard."

He sat down so that the lamp was between them. She glanced around the room at the blank walls.

"No windows, only one door, an isolated building. I suppose I should thank you for providing secrecy."

"Get on with it," he said.

Bentanta was wearing a thick lock of her hair strung with gold ring beads. She reached up to it with both hands, lifted the bright strand, and began to pull something that had been inserted within the encircling beads—a tightly rolled paper. This she uncurled and smoothed, holding it at both ends. The papyrus had been folded and refolded so that there were tears along the fold lines. Its edges were ragged, but the script that covered the rectangle was dark and readable. Meren had been expecting to see something like it. Bentanta gave him the papyrus.

"Djet can tell you the truth better than I."

"Djet?" Meren began to read.

Bentanta,
You were right, as you have always been. How can I explain to you? How can we justify what we've done? You and I took comfort from each other when both of us knew we really wanted Meren. When Ay called me home to care for him, I thought he might turn to me. He did, but only as he always has, as a brother. He writes to me, begging me to come home. How can I tell him I have no home because I made the mistake of telling my parents I loved my cousin? I can't endure being near him. Living with this pain will slay my ka. I don't know how much longer I can contain this lake of fire in my soul. You say there is a child within you from our uniting. I will send a messenger from Babylon with gold for you and the babe, but I see no remedy but silence. It has ever been thus for me, condemned to silence, living amidst many and feeling alone. I'm weary, so terribly weary.

The letter ended with Djet's name. Meren stared at the script until the lines blurred. A confusion of memories came to him—of Djet helping him spear his first fish, of their first real taste of warfare, in which he'd saved Djet from a beheading by scimitar. His ka refused to reconcile the meaning of the letter with his experiences. Raising his head, he looked at Bentanta as if he'd never seen her before.

"He never told me."

"Could you have responded to him as he wished?"

Meren lowered his face to his hands, shaking his head.

"He knew that," Bentanta said. "Why burden you with remorse? He told me he felt that way since he was a boy."

"But he was famed for his exploits among the women."

"And men. But you and I know that adventures have little to do with love." Bentanta looked away. "And after that terrible time when he brought you home after Akhenaten had you tortured, he turned to me. You remember I was here visiting your aunt Cherit with Anhai."

Meren stood up suddenly. "You . . . and Djet. You and he came together. I don't understand this—this taking of each other as replacement for someone else. You bedded my cousin to comfort him?"

Standing, Bentanta reached out to touch his arm, but Meren jerked away as if stung and stepped out of reach. His vision filled with images of Djet and Bentanta.

"Do you think I want to speak of it?" she asked. "Gods, Meren. I was married to my husband when I was thirteen. He was much, much older. I had babes by the time I was fifteen. Babes, a household, a husband, duties, so many to care for. Women are no different than men, you know. They lust, Meren. They give their affection. I was so young still, and you were a royal charioteer."

She reached out to him, but pulled her hand back. "You don't remember that time in Horizon of Aten when we attended the king and queen at their pleasure garden.

You and your wife had quarreled, and she went into the palace. I asked you to row one of the skiffs for me so I could pick a lotus flower. No, you don't remember, because you ignored me the whole time. After Ay persuaded the king not to kill you, and he brought you to your house in the city, bleeding and wandering in your wits, I was there. I stayed with you until Djet came."

"I don't remember." He ran his fingers through his hair and paced back and forth in front of her. "I don't understand why he would kill himself just because I couldn't be what he wanted me to be. There were so many others. There was you, and—" Meren stopped and stared at a wall, then slowly turned his gaze on Bentanta. "A child. He said there was a child."

"There were two, actually. The twins."

"Your son and daughter." Meren heard his voice crack. He looked down at the papyrus in his hands, confused, shaken more than he'd been since Akhenaten's death. He sought refuge in duty; in duty lay escape from that which he couldn't understand and didn't want to know. Touching a torn corner of the letter, he said, "Anhai had this and was using it against you somehow."

"Yes. It's odd how long and loving friendship can turn to bile. As children we were close, and as women we remained friends, but one day when she was visiting me, she asked me to persuade Sennefer to give her his fortune and a divorce. I knew she could be ruthless, but I never thought she'd do something so mad. I refused, and she seemed to accept my decision. Until a few days later. She invited me to stay with them at their home in Memphis, and when I got there, she told me she had the letter. She'd found it in my chamber while I left her alone to confer with my cook on her last visit. She said she'd return it if I helped her, but if I didn't she was going to give it to you."

Meren rolled the papyrus and slipped it into his belt. "You could have told me the truth."

"You know the penalty for adultery. I have no wish to be flogged or have my ears and nose cut off."

"That wouldn't happen."

"Perhaps not, but I didn't want you to find out. You can't see yourself, Meren. You look at me as if I were some plague-ridden hound."

Meren dropped his gaze to the whip he'd discarded. Picking it up, he threaded the lash through his fingers.

"So, this old folly is the reason you quarreled with Anhai."

"Yes, and when I couldn't make her return the letter, I left her alone on the front loggia."

"I see."

"Then you must see that I wouldn't kill Anhai over it."

"I'll tell you what I see," he replied. "I see that you have the letter now. Yet Anhai had it the night of the feast. She had it in her bracelet."

"How did you know?" Bentanta asked in a faint voice.

"You weren't careful enough when you took it out of the bracelet. A piece tore from the corner." Meren pulled the letter from his belt and used it to point at her. "Tell me. Did you take it before or after you killed her?"

16

▽

Meren waited for Bentanta's answer, all the while feeling as if he'd been raped across the distance of more than a dozen years. But he couldn't succumb to confusion and misery now. Now he needed to find the truth. Thus he performed a monumental effort of will—one that would cost him later—and set aside in a tiny, dark vault in his ka his bewilderment and renewed grief.

"You're surprised," he said. "You gave yourself away by tidying up after you dumped her in the granary. I knew someone had interfered with the body and searched it for a reason. The only sign I found was a scrap of papyrus. Since my men never found the rest of it when they searched Baht, I knew someone had it on them or had destroyed it."

"I grow weary of repeating that I didn't kill Anhai. How could I carry her up those stairs to the granary?"

"Fear makes one strong. If you'd ever been in battle, you'd know this."

Bentanta picked up the lamp and came over to him. Holding it up so that she could study his face, she curled her lip. "You still want me to be the murderer. That way you're rid of me, if not of the past. I hate to cause you grief, but I'm innocent. And you have to believe me, because I know who did kill Anhai."

"Oh? How beneficial for you."

"Just before he was murdered, Sennefer told me he killed Anhai."

Lifting a brow, Meren said, "Indeed. And why didn't you tell me sooner?"

"Because you were convinced I was a killer, Meren. You wouldn't have believed me, not without me revealing the whole story, and I didn't want to tell you about Djet."

"Tell me the whole of it now."

Lowering herself to the floor, Bentanta set the lamp down again. Meren crouched a few cubits from her, near enough to see her face, but not too close.

"The night of the feast, while Hepu was speaking, Anhai and I quarreled again, but I left her. As I came back inside, I saw Sennefer go out, and I decided to follow him to see if he was going to give in to Anhai. If he had, there would be no reason for her to keep my letter. When I reached the loggia, they were already sneaking away in the shadows along the wall that runs from the corner of the house to the outer wall to form the front of the granary forecourt. All the doorkeepers were busy at the front gate or elsewhere because of the feast, and no one saw them go inside. I waited, thinking to intercept them when they returned, but they never came out. After a while, I crept up to the forecourt gate and looked in. It was deserted, so I went to the opposite gate and saw Sennefer coming down the steps of the last granary."

"And you didn't see Anhai or anyone else?"

"No," Bentanta said. "He was coming in my direction, so I hid behind a stack of wicker boxes. When he was gone, I went into the court and up the granary stairs. I could see the whole court, and Anhai wasn't there. Then I noticed that the granary cover was ajar. I don't know what made me open it. Perhaps it was only seeing Sennefer up there, in a place he would have no reason to be."

"And you found her."

"Yes, she was on her side with her uppermost leg drawn up to her head."

"And you searched for the letter, found it, and straightened her body and clothing afterward."

"Yes, and the rest you know."

"I don't know what he told you before he collapsed."

"Isn't it enough that he's dead? Why stir up more ugliness?"

Meren leaned forward, holding her eyes with his. "Because you haven't convinced me you're telling the truth." He gave her a slight smile. "After all, you could have planned the murder with Sennefer." Bentanta only gave him a disgusted look.

He remembered opening the granary cover the morning they'd discovered Anhai. Sennefer had been stunned. If he'd simply dumped his wife in the granary, it would have been a nasty surprise to find her lying neatly on her side, her clothing and wig perfect. "Did Sennefer tell you exactly how he killed Anhai?"

"You're an ass, Meren. You work hard to be good at it."

"Just tell me what he said."

"He was quite drunk."

"He was suffering the effects of poison," Meren said.

"His speech was slurred, but I understood him well enough. Still, I don't think he would have told me without a lot of wine, or perhaps it was the poison that loosened his tongue. And he was frightened of you. He told me Anhai had asked him to meet her in secret again, and when they found a place where they wouldn't be heard, she threatened him again. Only this time, she used a weapon she must have been reluctant to use, considering the results. I think she may have suspected how dangerous using it could be."

Bentanta paused, her eyes growing sad. "You see,

she'd been hinting at it for weeks, and he'd been growing more and more desperate."

"What threat could she have made that would disturb him so? He didn't seem worried to me."

"He concealed his fear, just as he concealed his secret, Meren. Because Anhai was hinting that she was going to tell everyone the truth—that Sennefer was impotent."

"Impotent."

"Cursed by the gods, he said."

Meren thought back over the last few days. When Anhai had insulted Sennefer about her lack of children, he'd assumed it was just another of her sudden and malicious attacks, lacking any real foundation. Then he recalled Sennefer's many boasts and the rumors of his conquests. Had it all been a facade? Sennefer had been diligent in his pursuit of a reputation for sexual mastery—perhaps too diligent.

Unwilling to admit he believed her, he said, "Go on."

"This time, Anhai said that if Sennefer didn't do as she wanted, she would tell his whole family he was less than a man, and that she'd do it while everyone was gathered for your feast of rejoicing."

"By the Devourer," Meren said.

"You knew she was vicious. Sennefer fell into a rage then, and they fought. She picked up one of those grindstones and swung it at him, but he grabbed it. She rushed at him, and he fended her off with it, holding it lengthwise like a sword. He hit her in the chest. He said she grunted and dropped like a duck hit by a throw stick. He tried to rouse her, but she was dead."

Meren was shaking his head. "Not from one blow to the chest."

"That is what he told me. He said he didn't understand it, that he hadn't meant to kill her. He had been trying to make sense of it, but he couldn't."

Drawing his legs up to his chest, Meren propped his

arms on his knees while he thought. Bentanta's story made sense. It accounted for all the signs he'd discovered—the too-neat arrangement of the body, the scrap of papyrus, the disposal of the body in the odd location, the timing during Hepu's Instruction—everything except . . .

"Even if I believe you, there's still the question of Sennefer's death. He was poisoned with your pomegranate wine."

Bentanta uttered a gasp of aggravation. "I had no reason to kill Sennefer."

"None to which you've admitted. Perhaps Anhai had shown him that letter you've been hiding for sixteen years."

"Someone else killed Sennefer, Meren, and you know it. You're just afraid you know who it is. By the gods, you'd rather condemn me unjustly than face the possibility that Ra killed Sennefer out of jealousy and revenge."

He'd had enough. If he stayed, the misery he was hiding might escape and reveal itself. Getting to his feet, Meren opened the door, stepped outside, and kept his gaze away from Bentanta. She followed him. Reia was waiting for them.

"Take the Lady Bentanta to her chamber. Set a guard outside her door and see that she remains there." He kept his gaze trained on the palm tree.

"I'm going home in the morning, Meren."

"You'll leave when I give permission."

"If you try to stop me, I'll tell your family about the letter."

Meren looked at her then. "I might have believed that threat if it had come from Anhai. I don't believe you."

"Did you know you're one of the few people I'd like to kick?"

"Take her to her chamber, Reia."

He didn't watch her go. He was too busy praying

he wouldn't give way to misery and confusion before
she left.

Late the same afternoon Meren stood beneath the awning
of the deckhouse of *Wings of Horus*. Kysen was talking to
Nebamun not far away. After the interview with Bentanta
he'd sought refuge here, hiding like a wounded antelope.
Flooded with remorse, he had relived the grief of Djet's
death. Now he understood Nebetta's and Hepu's ani-
mosity on account of Djet, but he also blamed them for
Sennefer's impotence. Hepu had beaten and sneered at
his sons almost from infancy, and Meren was certain that
this mistreatment had robbed Sennefer of his manhood.
His aunt and uncle were like two demons sent to spawn
evil and spread it throughout the family.

It had taken him a long time to regain his composure,
but he'd climbed out of the refuse pit into which he'd
fallen. He had to, because it was urgent that he confirm
Bentanta's tale of Anhai's murder. He'd sent for Kysen
and told him what had happened at Green Palm and in
Bentanta's cell. Kysen was now giving a censored version of the tale to Nebamun.

"So there it is," Kysen was saying. "He jammed one of
these into her chest." He hefted the oblong grindstone.

Nebamun took it, his arm sagging under the weight.
He held it in one hand and thrust it against the palm of
the other. Meren watched him for a moment, then beckoned Kysen.

"You said Nento is growing more and more agitated at
the haunted temple. Should I send him away?"

"I'll go again tonight. If he's no better, you can dismiss him in the morning. Father, you don't look well."

"I feel as if I've brought a curse home with me."

"Anhai is the one who brought the curse," Kysen
replied. "If she hadn't been so vicious, Sennefer wouldn't
have fought with her."

Meren turned his face to the north breeze, but even that beneficent wind couldn't banish the deathly heat. Nebamun set the grindstone down on the deck and approached them.

"What say you?" Meren asked. "Could my cousin have caused his wife's death in such a strange manner?"

"My lord, I think it is possible."

"Why?"

Nebamun pointed to the casket he'd brought with him, in which were stored his medical texts. "The wisdom of the ancient ones has been passed down for countless generations. Wisdom learned from the study of our brothers, the cattle, the ox, the goat, and others, as well as experience from great healers such as the great Imhotep."

"I know that, Nebamun. You don't have to convince me."

"Yes, lord. And we also know that the heart is the house of the soul. Within it resides a person's reason, his character and feelings. The gods speak to us through the heart, and through it they let us know their will. But also, from the heart issue channels linking all parts of the body. These channels convey blood, air, tears, sperm, sustenance."

"Nebamun, all I want to know is whether a sharp blow could kill Anhai."

"That is what I'm trying to explain, lord. The heart is the center of the soul, the crux of all channels in the body. A sudden blow could disrupt the flow of blood, air, everything." Nebamun held up a finger. "And such a blow could murder the ka in its house."

"Then Sennefer could have killed his wife with one strike."

"Aye, lord. I think it possible."

Meren nodded and walked away to stand at the ship's railing. He heard Kysen thank Nebamun and dismiss him. When his son joined him, he was leaning on the railing watching a royal trading vessel sail by, its decks laden with incense trees, several baboons climbing on its mast.

"Bener was looking for you this morning," Kysen said. "She accused Isis of flirting with poor Simut."

"Was she justified?"

"I'm afraid Simut isn't wise in the ways of young women. He's caught between the two and wishes to be relieved of his duties as their bodyguard. He said he's suffering greatly."

"I'll ask Aunt Cherit to supervise them. They won't be able to fool her."

"I can already hear Bener's howls of dismay," Kysen said with a smile. Then the smile faded. "Now what do we do?"

"This tale of the grindstone, I've been thinking about it. Even if Nebamun agrees it's possible, I can't justify believing Bentanta without something more to confirm what she says."

"You could, but you won't."

"Please, Ky, not now. I've been thinking about that night at the feast, and what various people have said about how Sennefer behaved."

"Even Wah noticed him," Kysen said with a grimace of distaste. "After hinting that your brother and Bentanta were guilty, that is. He said he saw Sennefer after Hepu finished speaking."

"Which doesn't help verify Bentanta's tale."

Sighing, Kysen propped his forearms on the railing and gazed out at the deep blue water. "I know, especially since Wah offered a convincing detail. He said he was able to spot Sennefer because he had a fresh unguent cone on, and it was lopsided."

"Then I don't see how—" Meren turned to look at his son. "An unmelted scent cone?"

"Yes."

"But not much earlier, the one he had on was already melting."

They looked at each other.

"Between the time Bentanta and Anhai quarreled and when Hepu finished his interminable Instruction, he used two scent cones." Meren turned back to gaze across the river at the desert.

"Why would he do that?" Kysen asked on a note of suspicion.

"He may have lost the first one."

Kysen said, "In a struggle."

"Perhaps. I must think about this, Ky." Meren closed his eyes. "But it's as I said. If Sennefer killed Anhai, then who killed Sennefer, and why?" Meren opened his eyes reluctantly to face his son. "And since we've been so astute in confirming what Bentanta has told us, we've just increased the likelihood that my brother is a murderer. Ra is the only one I've been able to link to Sennefer's death except Bentanta."

"Even if she's told us the truth about Anhai's death, she still might have had a reason to kill Sennefer. One we don't know about. And anyway, from what you've told me, I wouldn't put it past Hepu to kill Sennefer rather than allow anyone to find out his son was a murderer."

Meren straightened and eyed his son. "By the gods, Ky, you've grown as suspicious as I am."

"I'm only using the reason Nebamun says is one of the properties of the heart. Hepu is bloated with pride in his virtue. His heart is unbalanced near to madness with it. I can imagine he would fear for his sacred reputation enough to get rid of a son who was both impotent and a murderer. You have said he is violent."

"But if he thought Sennefer killed Anhai," Meren said, "Ra could have murdered him out of revenge. You forget that I had Sennefer confined immediately after finding

Anhai's body. Ra would know that such an action meant I suspected him."

"I only meant that Ra isn't the only one who had a reason to kill Sennefer."

Meren smiled bitterly. "And there's still Bentanta. She feared the discovery of her adultery. Who knows what her husband's family would have done had they found out? She was right. An adulterous woman can lose everything, including her life."

"What are you going to do?" Kysen asked.

Turning to gaze downriver in the direction of Memphis, Meren breathed in deeply and exhaled. "I'm going to set a trap, Ky, a trap for my own brother. Come with me. We'll stop by my chambers and then go to the garden."

It wasn't long before they were ensconced on couches in the shade of a stand of palms. Two slaves waved tall fans over them while a servant appeared with a tray full of fruit dishes. This was set on a low table between Meren and Kysen. Meren picked up a copper bowl that had been set beside his couch and put it on the tray. As he did so, Ra came toward them accompanied by Reia.

"You sent for this lowly prisoner, O master of all?" Ra said with a sneer.

Meren waved Reia aside. "Curb your tongue. I sent for you in order to beg your forgiveness."

"You never begged for anything in your life," Ra snapped.

"I was wrong to begin that fight, Ra. I ask your forgiveness."

"Are you ill?" Ra asked. "Or is this some kind of trick?"

"No. I've just discovered that Sennefer killed Anhai."

"Ha! I knew he did it." Ra planted his fists on his hips and gloated. "For once the mighty Eyes of Pharaoh has made a fool of himself."

"I knew you'd be happy."

Ra laughed, went to the table, and poured himself a cup of wine. "I feel like celebrating."

Meren grinned at him. "I am truly sorry, brother." He picked up the bronze dish. It was filled with shiny black berries the size of grapes. "Here. Have some fresh berries."

Ra was gulping down his wine. He tilted the cup and finished the last of the brew, wiped his lips on the back of his hand, and glanced at the berries.

"I have no appetite."

"You will if you taste these."

"They're good? Give them here."

Ra snatched the dish from Meren's hand, grabbed a handful, and stuffed them in his mouth. Meren and Kysen jumped up at the same time.

"No!" Meren cried. He pounded him on the back as Kysen slapped the dish from Ra's hand. Ra gasped and spewed out berries and curses. Meren thrust a water flagon to his lips. "Did you swallow any of them? Good. Rinse your mouth and spit."

Ra complied and then turned on Meren. "What in the name of Amun are you doing?" He looked at the scattered berries and swore. "Those are poison. You tried to poison me!"

"You know what they are, then," Meren said.

"From the way you're acting, they must be poison. That's twice you've tried to kill me."

Meren rolled his eyes. "Do you know what kind of berries they are?"

"Poison berries."

"Ra, you're going to drive me mad," Meren said through clenched teeth.

"They're the same kind we found in Sheftu's house," Kysen said as he picked up berries and put them back in the bronze dish.

Understanding dawned on Ra's face. "You've been spying on me, Meren."

"I found the same poison used on Sennefer there," Meren said. "And I wanted to know if you knew what it was."

"I do now."

"I thought that if you ate them, I would prove your innocence."

"By killing me?"

"I didn't let you eat them. Unfortunately, you seem to have managed to cast suspicion on yourself anyway."

"What! You nearly poison me and still accuse me of murder?"

"You said the berries were poison."

"Because of your reaction, O clever one."

"I'm trying to be fair. I'm trying to prove you innocent."

Ra threw out his arms. "Don't. Don't try to help me. The next time you do, I might end up dead."

"I have to do something, brother, because all you do is dig a deeper hole for yourself. You didn't tell me about Tabes and Aset, and you especially didn't tell me about Sheftu, her grandmother, or their preparations and potions."

"Everyone knows about Green Palm and its tavern, and anyone who has an ailment goes to Sheftu's grandmother."

Meren sat down on the couch and said quietly, "You could have stolen back here from Green Palm with poison from Sheftu's house and put it in Sennefer's wine jar."

"I was so drunk my friends had to bring me home!"

Kysen set the bronze dish on the table. "You could have been feigning illness."

Ra walked over to Meren and looked down at him. "And I suppose that vomit you saw was a pretense."

"I've witnessed stranger things," Meren said wearily.

"You've spent too much time at court," Ra replied. "It has corrupted your reason."

Lifting his gaze to Ra, Meren said, "Perhaps my reason has only been sharpened. I learned long ago how to dissemble and conceal my true ka behind a guise as blank as a death mask. We share the same blood, Ra. If I'm capable of such deceit, I would expect my brother to be as good at it as I am."

"Then you have a problem," Ra said. He bent over Meren and whispered in his ear. "By that kind of reasoning you could ask yourself another question. Are you capable of murder?"

Meren felt an inner jolt as Akhenaten's death flashed through his thoughts.

Ra gave him a taunting smile, stood erect, and walked away. "The answer to that question should tell you if I'm guilty. Don't you agree?"

17

Standing in the haunted temple in the midst of shrouded coffins and canopic chests, Kysen listened once again to Nento's complaints. He'd arrived several hours after sunset but wished he hadn't been forced to leave Meren, who was still reeling from the day's discoveries. But someone had to attend to the sacred guardianship; Nento hadn't proved to be much good at it. He could barely make the required sacrifices and recite a proper spell.

"And then last night I was certain I heard footsteps," the man was saying. "Your aide said I was imagining it, but I insisted he send the men out to search the rocks and the valley slopes. I'm sure the demons who inhabit this place are angry at us for invading their refuge."

"But the guards didn't find anyone."

Nento bobbed his ostrich-egg head. "If it was a demon, they wouldn't." He tugged on his oiled mustache. "I tell you, we should light fires to frighten evil spirits away."

"We've discussed this dozens of times. Campfires would be seen. Everyone has amulets for protection, and you're qualified to do the appropriate rituals of warding."

Waddling closer, Nento crowded Kysen with his melon-shaped bulk. "Torches, then. Small ones, like when pharaoh—may he have life, health, and prosperity—came to us."

"No, Nento. That was a matter of extremity. We're not

going to do it again. If you don't like it inside the temple, join the men."

"Listen! You can't tell me that's just the breeze."

The evil west wind whipped through the valley. Kysen listened over Nento's labored breathing to the hollow wail of a trumpet signaling the approach of some unseen, ghostly army. Nento darted glances around the temple. The back wall was cracked, allowing the wind to whip around the interior and toss the draperies over Akhenaten's coffin. Nento's head jerked in that direction, and he gasped as the coffin appeared to disturb the cloth that covered it. His agitation was beginning to make Kysen uneasy.

"I'm going outside," he said.

Nento was on his heels. "I'm coming with you."

The wind blew grit in their faces as they emerged from the temple. Kysen paused as a particularly fierce gust brought with it a long, hollow groan that soared through the valley. Everyone knew that lost souls roamed the deserts—those whose descendants had ceased to provide nourishment in their eternal houses. They fed on hapless ones foolish enough to venture near their abandoned tombs. What if there were such eternal houses buried beneath the temple?

Excellent, Kysen thought. You're going to end up like Nento if you don't take care. Have patience. The new tombs will be ready soon, so you won't have to endure the temple or Nento much longer.

He surveyed the valley in the silver glow cast by the moon, then went over to a spray of boulders at the base of the north slope of the valley. Nento trotted after him. Iry was sitting between two of the largest rocks scanning the top of the incline.

"All seems quiet as usual, lord," said Iry.

"Good. If things continue this way, I'll return to the house. I'm not sure what Lord Meren will do now that—"

He paused as the screech of a falcon echoed down from the slope before them.

The figure of a charioteer shot up from behind the ridge and pointed toward a rock at the top of the slope shaped vaguely like a reclining bull. Then the man sprinted for the rock. As he ran, another figure catapulted from hiding behind the bull rock, ran a few steps, and plummeted down the opposite side of the slope. Kysen let out another falcon call and sprang up the slope with Iry. At the same time Nento yelped, spun around, and ran away, legs churning beneath his melon belly.

Kysen had no time to worry about Nento. He scrambled up the side of the valley, feet slipping on loose gravel and stone. Half the guards in the valley, along with Iry, climbed with him, while the other half remained on alert at the temple. Kysen reached the summit, stopped to find his bearings, and saw the charioteer who had signaled sliding to the base of the incline. Then he set off after a man who was but a darker spot in a nearly black landscape.

They were headed east, toward the river. If the invader reached a boat, he might escape. Kysen plunged down the slope along with his men. Once at the base, he set out at a run, heedless of sharp rocks and sudden dips in the ground. Whoever the spy was, he was fast. Kysen's chest heaved, and pain accompanied every breath as he sprinted across the desert toward the fields that bordered the Nile.

Kysen and Iry ran side by side. Behind him a guard stumbled and fell with a cry. Neither Kysen nor Iry looked back. They reached the dormant, baked fields. The ground suddenly flattened and became softer. Kysen realized he'd run onto a bank of one of the small canals that brought water to outlying fields. He had to watch his footing now, or he'd fall into a channel.

His progress slowed; he watched the lead charioteer

cross the fields at an angle that told him their quarry had
turned south. He put on a burst of speed, springing across
a narrow canal, and headed for the riverbank. Soon he
was at the water's edge, scrambling around palms, stumbling into water where the bank had collapsed, shoving
his way through reeds with Iry still a step behind him.
Abruptly he heard a cry, then burst through a stand of
reeds to come upon the charioteer they'd been following.
He was lying against the stump of an old palm, holding
his leg.

Running up to him, Kysen asked breathlessly, "Which
way?"

The man pointed back to the west. "He suddenly
turned back, lord."

Swearing, Kysen ran out into the fields again and
stopped. Iry came running up to him, followed by the rest
of the men.

Kysen was scanning the fields to the west. "He
doubled back. Three of you go north. The rest of you
follow me." He set off at an angle to the river that
brought him to the bank just ahead of the injured charioteer. As he reached the bank he heard a cry, then a terrified scream and a watery thrashing. There was a great
splash, and more screams as Kysen bolted toward the
noise.

The screams stopped as suddenly as they had risen.
Beside him Iry cried out and pointed. Not far ahead, in a
fan of moonlit water, a long, dully gleaming body rolled
in the water. A crocodile. And it had something in
its jaws.

As Kysen reached the bank, the creature twisted and
rolled again, over and over and over. A portion of its
prize tore away, and the crocodile tossed a dark shape,
caught it in the back of its jaws, and gulped. Kysen
looked out into the river and vaguely discerned arrow-

shaped patterns in the water that signaled the approach of more predators.

He, Iry, and their men waded into the water, slashing with their scimitars. One man plied a whip. The lash wrapped around a dark bulk. The crocodile slithered toward them. Kysen gave a cry and helped the man pull on the whip while they sprang for shore. Iry sliced at the water in front of the animal's jaws. It uttered a grunting bark, snapped at the blade, and then back-pedaled. Twisting its body, the creature sank beneath the surface and disappeared.

Chest heaving, sweating and bruised, Kysen helped the charioteer pull the dark mass onto the bank. Men crowded around them, then separated, making the sign against evil. Kysen stood up and looked down at the mangled body of a man. An arm had been torn off at the shoulder. Large puncture wounds dotted the chest, neck, and head.

Kysen was glad it was dark and wished the moon wasn't so bright; it highlighted bloody, wet chunks of flesh. They'd reached the crocodile before it had had time to drag the remains of its booty underwater. Any longer, and more predators would have arrived to tear the body to pieces. Still, Kysen didn't count himself lucky, for he'd wanted the spy alive and able to answer questions.

One of the charioteers was trying to light a handful of field stubble. Kysen studied the dead man, swore softly, and exchanged rueful glances with Iry. Then he heard snuffling. To a man they all spun around to behold Nento creeping toward them through the tall water plants, bawling at the same time.

"Help, help, help, help! Help?"

Kysen sighed, stooped down, and hauled Nento up by one arm. "Shut up."

"He just appeared, out of nothing." Nento held his

head in both hands and moaned. "We knocked heads, and he fell off the bank into the shallows."

"This is your fault?" Kysen asked. He jerked on Nento's arm. "Did he say anything?"

"I've cracked my skull. Can't you see I'm bleeding? I need help. Get me a healer. Get me a physician. I'm dying."

Knocking Nento's hands from his face, Kysen growled, "Stop babbling or I'll throw you to that crocodile. Now tell me, did that spy say anything to you?"

"I can't remember. Ohhh, I'm bleeding." Kysen drew back his arm as if to backhand him, and Nento rushed on. "Say anything? Let me think, let me think. No. We cracked heads, he stumbled backward and fell into the water. There was no time."

"Curse it."

Kysen turned back to the charioteers around the body. Suddenly the dry stubble flared, and a guard held it close to the dead man's face.

"Lord," Iry said. "This is one of the men from Lord Paser's yacht."

"Paser? You're certain?"

"Aye, lord. I remember him because he was always on lookout at the bow, and one of his eyebrows was higher than the other." Iry glanced at the disfigured face. "Of course, you can't see it now."

Kysen climbed back up the bank to stand on the edge of a field. Iry followed and joined him in looking up- and downriver.

"You haven't seen Paser, have you?" Kysen asked.

"No, lord, not since we reached Baht."

Peering in the direction of the house, Kysen said, "If he's returned and found out about the haunted temple, we're in a bit of trouble."

"No one has seen his yacht, lord."

"He might have suddenly acquired a clever heart and

left the yacht behind," Kysen said. "But at his cleverest, Paser is barely intelligent. He'll be lurking somewhere close, but not close enough for us to see him."

His gaze met Iry's, and they said together, "Green Palm."

"You take the men there at once," Kysen said. "I'm going to the ship. We may need it if Paser has already missed his spy and decided to run."

Having been awakened by the messenger from Kysen, Meren hurried out of the front gate of his villa. He'd just sent most of the men on duty at the house to the temple on the chance that there had been more than the one spy lurking around the valley. His features grim, he headed for the dock.

"Meren, Meren you wait right there!"

Grimacing, he turned around as his sister flew toward him. "Not now, Idut." He headed for the dock again, but Idut was at his side, matching her steps with his and chastising as they went.

"Do you know what a scandal you're creating?"

"It's not my fault Sennefer accidentally killed his wife. Now go away. I've business to attend."

Idut quickened her pace when he did. "Oh no, Meren. You're not running away this time. Why can't you see that Sennefer killed himself because of remorse at Anhai's death? Why must you keep the family and Wah like prisoners? All the intrigue at court has twisted your wits. Everyone wants to go home. Nebetta and Hepu wish to be free to mourn their son, and Wah grows more anxious with each hour that passes."

As they neared the dock, Meren lengthened his stride, but Idut only walked faster. "Sennefer didn't kill himself, Idut. Only you would think of such a tale, because only you, and possibly his parents, are capable of ignoring how little Sennefer cared for Anhai. He wasn't greatly disturbed because she was dead, he was disturbed because he'd been the unwitting cause."

"Then it must have been Bentanta who poisoned him," Idut said as they stepped onto the dock, "but you're too delighted at having an excuse to blame Ra to admit it."

Meren stopped suddenly and stared at his sister. "You believe that I—" Idut wasn't looking at him. She gazed over his shoulder, her mouth falling open, and pointed.

"By the mercy of Amun, what is happening?" she asked.

Coming toward them with the current, a small freighter zig-zagged back and forth on an erratic course that threatened the early traffic on the river. Fishing boats and skiffs scattered before the careening vessel. On its deck, a bald-headed man screeched at the two men manning the oars. As he did so, he gripped the steering oar and dragged it with him as he danced across the deck in his agitation.

Meren cursed as he heard a low, steady thud accompanied by the watery slap of many oars cutting through the water. *Wings of Horus* rounded a bend in the river and aimed at the freighter. The steersman on the smaller craft looked over his shoulder at the sleek black vessel and screamed. He jumped and scurried back and forth in his fright, then lost his grip on the steering oar. The boat spun around, then settled sideways in the current as *Wings of Horus* gained on it. A sailor at the bow of Meren's craft yelled a warning. Long lines of oars lifted up out of the water.

Standing on the dock beside Meren, Idut cried out as well. "Look, it's Paser! Paser, make way, make way!"

Paser was too busy scrambling about the deck of his freighter in terror. Kysen appeared at the bow of *Wings of Horus* to shout at Paser, to no avail. Meren watched in irritation as the prow of his ship smacked into the freighter amidship. There was a loud crack of wood against wood, and the sound of bodies hitting the water as men dove for their lives.

"If he's damaged my ship, I'll take payment out of his hide," Meren said.

"What is Paser doing on a freighter?" Idut asked as they watched Kysen's men throw ropes to those in the water. "And why was he trying to sail it himself?"

Rolling his eyes, Meren said, "Go home, Idut."

"And where has Kysen been this early in the morning?"

"He said he was going to Green Palm. Now will you go home while I see what's happened to that fool Paser?"

"You're not making sense, Meren. Kysen wouldn't take *Wings of Horus* for so short a sail."

"Damnation, Idut! Perhaps he wanted to impress a woman. I know not, and it isn't important. Are you going to go home, or do I have to take you there myself?"

"I'm going, I'm going. But don't think I'll let you get away with this high-handedness much longer. The whole family is going to revolt against you if you don't release them from this half-imprisonment." Idut glanced at the men pulling Paser on board *Wings of Horus*. "Bring Paser to the house. I'll find some clothes for him."

Meren's head was beginning to ache, and he rubbed his neck. "Just go home, Idut."

Once his sister was out of sight and his ship docked, Meren walked across a plank and hopped onto the deck of *Wings of Horus* beside Kysen, his face set, his jaw tense. "Where is he?"

"In the deckhouse. I shoved him in there to contemplate what we might do to him."

"Good." Meren walked toward the deckhouse and paused under its awning. He glanced over his shoulder. The pomegranate colors of sunrise lit the horizon. "I don't want to bring him to the house. You saw Idut, and she's already curious. The whole family is furious with me, except for your sisters."

Kysen nodded in the direction of a group of men squatting around a brazier full of coals. "I thought you wouldn't want any delay in getting the truth out of our simple-witted spy." One of the men held a long bronze rod, the end of which was embedded in the white embers.

Meren touched the wristguard over the sun-disk scar. Three deaths. Three deaths on what was to have been a respite from murder and treachery. "You're certain you've captured everyone on that freighter?"

"I still have men out searching, but the villagers said there were only three in the crew, and we have them all if you count the dead one."

"I don't like this, Ky. I know Sennefer's killing Anhai had nothing to do with our sacred charge across the river, but still, I don't like it that these deaths have happened so close together. Oh, I know what you're going to say. My ka is riddled with distrust from being raised at court. I'm trying to control my suspicions. Let's get on with it."

Kysen picked up an alabaster lamp that had been resting near another brazier and preceded Meren. Inside, Paser sat hunched on a stool between two charioteers. He blinked at them as lamplight filled the antechamber. The charioteers saluted Meren, and Paser, who had been staring at Kysen, widened his eyes. Meren walked over to him and surveyed his shaven skull and face.

"What were you doing spying on my men?"

"Spying? Spying?" Paser croaked. "I know naught of spying. I was but taking a pleasure sail in my new boat when your son pounced on me as if I were some nomad bandit."

Kysen set the alabaster lamp on a stand. Meren picked up the stand and placed it nearer Paser.

"I'm not going to spar with you," Meren said. "That was a freighter you were on, Paser, not a yacht. And you've shaved your face and head. Tell me what you were doing."

Paser tried to stand up, but the charioteers shoved him back down on the stool. "My friends at court will hear of this abomination. I'm a free man. I may sail the Nile as any nobleman might."

Listening to Paser's ranting for a few moments, Meren abruptly picked up the lamp and tipped it. A thin stream of oil poured down on Paser's head. Paser yelped and jumped from the stool. The charioteers moved with him, but stayed at a distance while he howled and rubbed his head.

"Curse you, Meren, that was hot!"

Meren set the lamp down and folded his arms. "I shall explain your situation only once. One of your men was found skulking around a deserted temple that happens to be near my ancestors' tombs. There have been two murders at my house, and I find you sneaking around. I want to know why. You're in trouble, Paser."

"Murders!" Paser was still rubbing his red scalp. "I know nothing of murder."

"You've been following me for days," Meren said. "Why?"

Paser gave him a sly, sidelong glance. "I was traveling in the same direction as you, not following."

"I've no patience for your clumsy lies," Meren said. "Kysen, tell them to bring in the brand."

As he finished speaking, Paser's eyes grew round. He gave a squeak, sprang past Meren, and was outside before his guards could move. Kysen ran after him, and Meren was close behind. As he left the deckhouse, Paser sprinted across the deck. He saw the men around the brazier, swerved, and ran for the railing. He might have jumped overboard if his foot hadn't tangled in a coiled rope. Paser tripped, fell forward, and banged his head on the railing.

At the sight, Meren slowed to a trot and joined his son in kneeling over Paser. They turned him over. He was bleeding from a gash on his forehead. One of the charioteers pressed a wad of cloth to the wound.

"Knocked senseless," Meren said with a frustrated smile as they stood. "I wonder which god I've offended to be so cursed with ill luck." His smile faded. "This isn't good, Ky."

"Depend upon it, Father. Paser knows nothing. We discovered his man before he could tell what he knew."

"But he might have been spying at the temple before last night."

"Do you think even Paser would be foolish enough to remain if he'd discovered what was in the temple?"

"Perhaps not." Meren began to walk back across the deck. "I sent more men to the temple before dawn, but that meant there were but two to stand guard over the family. I had to use doorkeepers to watch Bentanta and Ra. Send for me when that fool wakes. I'm going back to the house."

By the time he reached Baht, the household was stirring. He could hear the bray of donkeys in the granary court and the steady grinding sound of the querns. Hurrying to his office, he dismissed Reia and sat down with a pile of reports from the interviews his men had conducted with the household. He tried to fix his attention on them, but visions of Djet and Bentanta kept distracting him.

Wincing at a particularly vivid scene his imagination had called up, he dropped the reports on the floor and brought out his juggling balls. Tossing one in the air, he threw another from one hand to the other and caught the falling sphere. The rhythm established, he began to walk around the office while he concentrated on the balls.

He was desperately worried. The family was furious with him for the way he'd treated Ra and Bentanta, Idut especially. Nebetta still wouldn't speak to him and continued to blame him for Sennefer's death. And he hadn't found Sennefer's murderer. That is, he didn't think he'd found him. Or did he simply not want to admit he'd found him? If he didn't solve this murder soon, he was going to send the women to Memphis. Bener wouldn't like it, but she would have to go. He couldn't take any more chances with the murderer, not when this new danger threatened.

He needed more time, and now that the secret at the haunted temple was threatened by that worm Paser, he wasn't going to get it. Paser was part of Prince Hunefer's faction. Could Hunefer have found out about the desecration of Akhenaten's tomb? Secrecy was vital if another atrocity was to be prevented. There were still many at court who would love to deprive the king's brother of eternal life by destroying his body. He must make Paser speak. And he would, of that he was certain. Paser wasn't just dull-witted, he was a coward. It wouldn't take long to break him, once he woke.

Until then, he would do what he shouldn't—try to think of anything that would cast suspicion of Sennefer's murder elsewhere than on Ra. His plan to prove his brother's innocence hadn't worked as he'd thought. True to his contrary nature, Ra had cast even more doubt upon his own innocence.

He returned to the casket that held his juggling balls. Catching the three he'd been using, he took out a fourth. He held two balls in each hand, then began to toss the two in his right hand. Then he started with his left. When he had the rhythm going, he tried the exchange and missed. He grabbed for balls in two directions. They all fell.

Sighing, he picked them up and set the fourth ball aside. Soon he was juggling three again. Trying to add a fourth made him feel as frustrated as he'd been at the feast of rejoicing. He recalled that burning irritation, that trapped feeling he'd suffered while surrounded by bickering relatives. His temper was already short, and now Paser had added a new dose of disaster to his already overflowing cup.

Meren's hand froze in mid-toss. Balls dropped to the floor and skittered across the room. Virulent suspicions returned. Paser's invasion might be related to Sennefer's death. No, Kysen was right. Too many years at court had driven him to suspect that every event had a hidden meaning, every person a secret design. Sennefer had never been important at court. No one at the feast had been influential.

It was true that Anhai had once served the Great Royal Wife Nefertiti, as had Bentanta, but neither was high in the favor of Tutankhamun's queen, Ankhesenamun. Wah had been Nefertiti's steward for a brief time before her death, but Wah had no place at court. He had no power, and Meren didn't think Wah even knew Paser.

But still, he didn't like it that Paser and his spies appeared at the same time he was hunting a murderer. And there was something bothering him, something about the night of the feast, about his relatives, all gathered around him talking, talking, talking. Ra talking to Anhai. Bentanta whispering with Sennefer. Wah whining at him. Hepu moralizing. Meren was certain he'd missed something, something important.

Bending over his ebony chair, Meren fished beneath it to grab a juggling ball. He was feeling sorry for himself when Sennefer was the one to be pitied. Sennefer had lived in fear of having his impotence exposed. At the feast, he must have been terrified when Anhai threatened him. No wonder he drank so much pomegranate wine, both before and after her death. And when he'd been poisoned, Meren had assumed he was only drunk or ill . . .

only drunk or ill. Holding the one juggling ball, Meren suddenly sat down in the ebony chair.

"By all the gods of Egypt," he murmured. After a long silence, he began to toss the ball in one hand, slowly, as he cast his thoughts back to the feast of rejoicing one final time.

18

Murder at the Feast of Rejoicing

Kysen hurtled up to his father's office and burst
through the door. He started talking at the same time
Meren thrust himself out of his chair and spoke.

Kysen hurtled upstairs to his father's office and burst
through the door. He started talking at the same time
Meren thrust himself out of his chair and spoke.

"Paser's awake, and he says he'll only talk to you."

"Ky, I was wrong about the poison."

"What?" Kysen stared at Meren, breathless.

Meren hurled a juggling ball into its casket and
brushed past Kysen. "There's no time. Curse of the gods,
I hope I haven't endangered anyone else."

Kysen ran down the stairs after Meren. "Wrong about
the poison! How wrong? Father, wait."

Meren vanished around a turn in the stairs, and Kysen
didn't catch up with him until they ran down the hall to
stop before Ra's chamber door. At the threshold squatted
a doorkeeper who cradled his head in his hands.

"Where is my brother?" Meren snapped.

The man groaned. Suddenly cries issued from the central hall. This time Kysen was right behind his father as
they ran into the chamber. The family was supposed to
be partaking of a morning meal. Now they and several
servants had gathered in a huddle around Aunt Cherit's
carrying chair like geese around bread crumbs. At the
rear door of the long chamber an ovoid wine jar had been
tipped from its stand. Its shards littered the floor, and
wine stained the mats.

"What's happened?" Meren asked as they reached the group. "Ra is missing."

Cherit was patting Nebetta's hand as she wept. "He came charging through here like a netherworld fiend, and he would have escaped except that your men blocked his way when he tried to go through to the front."

"He went out the back?" Kysen asked.

Cherit nodded. "Simut and the other guard ran after him."

Kysen moved toward the rear entrance, but Meren put a hand on his arm. He glanced around the group. Cherit was muttering imprecations against foolish young men who ruined good wine. Isis was calmly munching on a slice of melon while Nebetta snuffled.

"Where are the rest?" Meren said.

"Why aren't you chasing that murderous brother of yours?" sobbed Nebetta.

Kysen grew alarmed at the killing look Meren gave her.

"Isis, where are the others?" Meren asked.

"Uncle Hepu is working on a tribute to Sennefer in his chamber. Aunt Idut and Wah left before Uncle Ra came, and Bener followed them." She finished the last bite of her melon and continued. "She was going to spy on them. I told her not to, but she never listens to me."

"The guards let them go?" Kysen asked.

"They were only going to the garden for a moment, and they promised to come back quickly," Isis said. "You know how Aunt can be. She wouldn't leave poor Simut alone until he consented. Then, when Simut and the other guard chased Uncle Ra, Bener stole away."

Kysen heard a lurid curse from Meren, who was already through the door. Kysen ran after him, calling over his shoulder, "All of you, stay here."

Racing out of the house, he caught up with Meren as he shoved open the garden gate. They charged inside only to come up short at the sight of Idut screaming at an acacia tree that grew next to the side wall.

"Bener, you contentious, wretched girl, come back here at once!"

They sprinted over to Idut.

"Where are they?" Meren asked.

Idut threw up her hands. "This is what comes of your soft discipline, Meren. That girl has been sneaking around the house for days, spying on everyone, asking impertinent questions, implying things."

"Idut!"

Even Kysen jumped at Meren's roar. Idut cried out, then glared at her brother, but she stopped babbling.

"Where did they go?" Meren demanded.

"He said the walls of the house were crowding in on him. He's sensitive, you know, what with all this death. They'll be back in a moment."

"Idut," Meren said as he jumped up to catch a limb of the acacia, "you have the wits of an oryx."

Kysen swung himself up into the tree after Meren and joined him on top of the wall. This section of the wall was also the outer privacy wall for the compound. From it they looked past a couple of sycamores and a vegetable garden. Beyond them ran the canal that fed water from the Nile to fields that marched past the house. Meren pointed to a leaping figure in a shift. Bener flew across a field at a diagonal to the canal. Her course would allow her to intercept a skiff being paddled rapidly toward the river.

"We have to catch her before she reaches him."

"Who?" Kysen asked, but Meren had already leaped from the wall.

Kysen measured the distance to the ground, then lowered himself over the side of the wall before dropping. His caution put him behind Meren and forced him to put on a burst of speed to catch up. For the second time in less than a day, Kysen found himself hurtling across a field littered with stubble and hard clods of earth baking in the sun.

As he ran, he saw the skiff reach the junction with the river and turn toward the dock and *Wings of Horus*. Bener reached the bank while the occupant of the skiff paused, then stood up, balancing with the long pole used to shove the little boat along in the water. Kysen got his first good look at the man and nearly tripped over his own feet.

Without warning, there was a shriek from the deck of the ship. Paser stood at the railing, one hand on his injured head, the other pointing at the intruder in the water below. At the sound, the intruder hefted the pole, swung it, and bashed Paser in the head. Paser dropped like a fishing weight over the side. At the same time Bener stooped, picked up a clod of earth, and hurled it at the attacker. It hit the man square in the back.

Both Meren and Kysen cried out a warning as the man was thrown off balance and almost fell into the water. Meren hurled himself at Bener at the same time the attacker turned on her. Kysen shouted a warning as the pole swung at Bener's head. Meren pushed his daughter out of the way, ducked under the stone-crushing blow, and grabbed the pole. He jerked it toward himself, then jammed the end into the attacker's chest.

"Huh!" The man doubled over, still gripping the pole. Meren jerked on it again and pulled the assailant off his feet. He landed half in the water and half on the bank, where he scrambled for footing. He thrust his upper body up out of the mud. Kysen palmed his dagger and stuck the tip of it under the man's dirty chin.

"Quitting our hospitality so soon, Wah?"

Wah went still as he felt the point of the dagger. His kilt and chest were caked with mud.

"Get up," Kysen said.

Meren pulled Bener behind him. "Slowly, if you value your life."

"What madness is this?" Wah asked as he complied.

On the dock, charioteers had jumped from *Wings of Horus* and were running toward them. Sailors were fishing Paser from the river. Women who had come to the river to do laundry, fishermen, and travelers began to gather at a discreet distance and stare.

Bener poked her head around Meren's bulk and beamed at him. "You see, Kysen. I knew it. I knew I'd discover who the murderer was if I was vigilant."

"Be quiet!" Meren turned on her. "What madness possessed you to take such a risk? You should have come to me, not chased after him yourself. He tried to kill you, you lackwitted goose."

Bener pointed at the skiff. "He might have escaped if I hadn't followed him."

"Father," Kysen said with a nod toward the curious onlookers. "Shall we retire to the ship?"

Meren glanced at the fishermen and the women with their laundry, then glared at Bener. "Go home, daughter. I'll speak to you later." Without waiting to see if he was obeyed, Meren turned and marched toward the dock.

Kysen shoved Wah in front of him, and soon they were on board and surrounded by charioteers and sailors. Kysen held his dagger on the prisoner while Meren went over to the soaked heap of flesh and linen being guarded by several men. He bent over Paser for a moment, then returned to confront Wah.

"He's dead."

Meren turned and walked to the deckhouse awning. He took a seat in a folding chair of carved cedar. Kysen pushed Wah over to kneel in front of his father. Then he signaled the charioteers. They lined themselves around the perimeter of the awning so that neither Meren,

Kysen, nor Wah could be seen. Wah glanced at the wall of soldiers as he wiped mud from his face and chest.

"What folly is this, my lord?" he asked. "I but wished to take a bit of respite on the cool water after being cooped up inside those walls for so long."

"And murder Paser along the way?" Kysen asked as he sheathed his dagger.

"Oh, that was an accident. Idut told me you'd captured him for some reason. I thought he was trying to escape when he cried out, so I tried to stop him." Wah gave Meren an uneasy glance, but when his captor remained silent, he went on. "And then—and then your daughter startled me by hitting me with a dirt clod. I—I reacted without thinking."

Kysen gave me an impatient laugh. "Wah, you're a fool if you think we're going to believe that tale."

Wah gushed with a deluge of protests, but as he babbled, Kysen was distracted by Meren. His father had remained silent far longer than expected, and he was sitting there absently rubbing his sun-disk scar. Kysen could tell from his distant expression that Meren wasn't listening to Wah at all. Then he caught a glimpse of something in Meren's eyes, a haunted look of dread that appeared and vanished in less than the space of a breath. Finally Meren stirred and beckoned Kysen. Kysen went to his father and bent down to hear his whisper.

"We must question him alone. No guards, no one else except us."

In moments Kysen had snatched Wah and thrust him into the deckhouse. Charioteers and sailors alike responded to Meren's command and left the ship. Only Reia remained on board, standing guard at a distance from the awning so that he wouldn't hear anything said inside the cabin.

Once the ship was almost deserted, Kysen followed his father inside the deckhouse. They hadn't brought a lamp, and the only light filtered in from the high, rectangular windows. Wah was facing the door, shifting his weight from one foot to the other and looking from Meren to Kysen and back.

"I don't understand this rough treatment, my lord. I swear by the feather of truth that I—"

"Wah."

Meren had spoken barely above a whisper, but Wah broke off with a cry and backed away from him. Kysen almost felt sympathy, for Meren's manner was disturbing.

"You've been under a great strain for a long time, haven't you? Keeping unspeakable secrets, fearing retribution, in terror of discovery. And finally, when you were beginning to think yourself safe again, my garrulous sister told you about seeing Paser," Meren said calmly. "That's why you lost your sense and ran. You knew I had him, and that I'd force him to talk. You were afraid of what he'd say."

"Paser had the wits of a goat!" Wah cried. "He was trying to ingratiate himself with Prince Hunefer by spying on you. The ass was stumbling around and keeping you alert and wary when I was trying to gain your favor. That's all there is to this matter."

"Keep quiet for a moment," Meren said in that same calm, pitying tone. "There will be no more dissembling, Wah. I know there's more to this than Paser's blundering. Do you understand what I'm saying? Ah, I see that you do. Then you know I cannot allow you to continue. I hope you understand that well enough to abandon this absurd pretense."

Kysen was growing more and more uneasy. He knew Meren had discovered that Wah killed Sennefer, but that didn't account for his father's gravity, or his carefully concealed fear. Meren was frightened, and that made apprehension crawl down Kysen's spine on scorpion's legs. Wah was mumbling more protests, but they faltered when Meren continued to look at the man as if he were already dead and lying in a sarcophagus.

At last Wah stumbled against the back cabin wall and asked in a weak voice, "You know?" He swallowed hard as if he might vomit at any moment. "How did you find out?"

"I remembered the conversation between Anhai, Sennefer, and you at the feast of rejoicing." Meren glanced at Kysen. "But I haven't had a chance to tell my son, who doubtless already has concluded that you murdered my cousin."

"But why?" Kysen asked.

Meren walked back and forth in front of Wah. "You weren't there when Wah arrived at the feast, but Anhai and Sennefer were, and Anhai remembered Wah from the days when they both served in the household of the Great Royal Wife Nefertiti."

"But what has that to do with Sennefer or Anhai?"

Meren's path took him back to Kysen, where he paused and asked, "Do you remember how Sennefer died? The fever, the mad visions, the loud voice of his heart, and then the stupor that ended in death? He died so unexpectedly that I failed to relate the features of his illness with any other event. Anhai's death was different from his. And Paser's spy was killed by a crocodile in a seemingly unrelated matter. But I am suspicious, as you have pointed out, and when Paser and his men appeared, I couldn't help suspecting some common influence might be responsible for the other deaths. I began to go over what had happened at the feast, but I found nothing odd until I remembered Wah speaking to Sennefer and Anhai."

Meren glanced at Wah, who was looking at his captor in horror. "You see, Ky, they had been making conversation about Nefertiti and mentioned her death. But it wasn't until just before you came to my office that I realized that the queen's plague closely resembled Sennefer's poisoning."

Wah whimpered, and Kysen turned a wide-eyed stare on him. The kohl around the man's eyes had smeared yet again and streaked his face. In spite of his lankiness, he seemed to be shrinking.

"It was Anhai who made the mistake, wasn't it?" Meren asked. Wah nodded, his bony knees seeming to turn to paste. "You see, Ky, Anhai said that she hated to think of the queen as she'd been while suffering from her last illness—her skin red and dry, the voice of her heart so loud, and the visions. All of these Sennefer suffered, and his body convulsed as well. But Sennefer had been poisoned and died quickly. Not like the queen, who died over the course of days. I would have seen the similarities sooner, but the two deaths were separated by many years, and the queen died when others were succumbing to the plague."

Meren approached Wah and said, "One died slowly, the other much more quickly, yet they suffered the same complaints. If Sennefer was poisoned, then the queen must have been poisoned too." Meren paused, but Wah said nothing and avoided his gaze. "You thought Sennefer was threatening you when he said his wife had mentioned you many times, didn't you, Wah? You had carried your secret for so long without anyone suspecting, and then without warning, Sennefer and Anhai appeared and began to speak of Nefertiti's death and of how they'd talked about you together. You were terrified, weren't you? You expected to be exposed or forced to pay for their silence."

Wah paled, even to the folds of skin beside his mouth and over his eyes. He licked his lips, tried to speak, then simply nodded.

"You must have been delighted when Anhai turned up

dead in the granary," Kysen said in wonder. "Was that it? Did you decide to take advantage of the confusion and get rid of Sennefer before he could threaten you?"

Wah's voice croaked. "I thought you would blame the Lady Bentanta or Lord Nakht, or both."

"I was close to it," Meren said. "Until Paser blundered and made me suspicious. What has he to do with any of this?"

"The dullard! He thought you were about some secret business for the vizier or General Horemheb. I told him you were simply going home for a rest, but he wouldn't believe me. I should have killed him sooner."

Kysen shook his head, trying to accustom himself to this strange twist to what should have been a murder for private reasons. Sennefer hadn't been killed out of revenge by Ra or to conceal Bentanta's transgressions. He'd been murdered for what Wah thought he knew.

Looking at Meren, Kysen said, "But Sennefer didn't—"

Meren banged his fist against the cabin wall. "No! Sennefer knew nothing. That's the worst evil of all. This bastard killed my cousin for nothing. If Sennefer had known such a secret, he would have told me. He may have been an ass about women, he may have lied to conceal his weakness, but he wasn't a traitor." Meren whirled around and stalked over to Wah. "And now I want the truth, you murdering piece of refuse. Who told you to murder Nefertiti?"

Wah backed away from Meren. His mouth clamped shut, and he whipped his head back and forth.

"You're going to tell me," Meren said. "My patience is gone. I warn you. You're going to die, Wah. Your only choices are how slowly, and in how much pain. I want to know who ordered the queen killed. I'll ask you but once more. Tell me the whole of it."

Clutching his head, Wah finally gave way to his terror. He doubled over and began to moan. Meren raised his eyes to the ceiling, and Kysen winced at the noise. He raised his hands to his ears as the moans turned to a high screech, and thus was unprepared when Wah suddenly sprang at him, grabbed his dagger, and knocked him to the floor. Caught off guard as well, Meren leaped after Wah, who scuttled out of the cabin with a cry.

"Worse will happen to me if I speak!"

19

▽

Meren hurtled out of the deckhouse after his prisoner. Wah scrambled out of the cover of the awning, hesitated when he saw Reia with his back turned, then charged at the charioteer, dagger pointed, bellowing as he ran. Startled, Reia whirled around to face a shrieking madman. As he moved, he brought his spear around to fend off the attack. Meren shouted a warning, but Wah rushed forward, raising his own weapon.

Reia tried to back away, but Wah jumped at the last moment and lashed out with his blade. Reia's spear thrust forward, knocking the dagger aside, then swept back in a defensive move that brought the tip into Wah's path. Meren heard a grunt and the muted sound of flesh being punctured. He reached the two as Reia pulled the spear out of Wah's gut and tossed it aside. Wah was still standing, clutching his belly while blood streamed through his fingers. Kysen appeared at Meren's side as he and Reia lowered Wah to the deck.

"He rushed at me deliberately," Reia said. "What madman charges a spear with a dagger?"

"A man who wants a quick death rather than a slow one," Meren said as he surveyed Wah's distorted, sweating features. Blood wet his arm when he touched the man. "Wah, can you hear me? Tell me who commanded you."

Wah stared up at him. "A pity I used all the poison on Sennefer." Blood seeped from his mouth. "You were going to tell the vizier." A long spasm of coughing stopped him. "Ay w-would have staked me out and flayed the skin from my flesh while I begged for death."

"Don't face the weighing of your heart in the hall of judgment without telling me the truth," Meren said. "Wah?"

Wah's eyes were closed now, and he began to gasp. Meren leaned close, turning his ear to the man's lips, but all he heard was a bubbling gurgle. At the familiar sound, he straightened and moved away from the man. Kysen, who had been holding Wah propped on his knee, allowed the body to slip to the deck.

"Lord, forgive me," Reia said as Meren stood. "He attacked so suddenly that I had no time to think."

"I know," Meren said. "He caught us off guard as well. Who would have expected that a fawning place-seeker would do himself such violence? Wrap the body and take it to the house with Paser's. Kysen, I want to talk to you."

He walked back to the deckhouse with a calm pace that belied his apprehension. When they were alone, he took a chair and beckoned his son to him.

"All this time it was Wah," Kysen said as he sat on the floor beside Meren. "He thought Sennefer knew he murdered Nefertiti and was threatening him?"

"He wasn't thinking clearly. If Anhai and Sennefer had suspected him of such a crime, surely they would have confronted him years ago." Meren rubbed his neck. The muscles felt tight enough to snap. "I think bearing such an evil secret for so long warped his reason. He lived with the fear of discovery for many years. I think he'd begun to count himself safe, or he wouldn't have sought my favor."

Kysen slapped his thigh. "And just when he thought he glimpsed a path back to power and riches, Sennefer and Anhai blurted out his presence in the household of the dying queen."

"And Sennefer's death had nothing to do with Ra or Bentanta after all."

Kysen glanced up at him. "You don't look relieved."

"Ky, Nefertiti was murdered, and we don't know who was responsible. Wah wouldn't have done it on his own, and once word of his death gets about—well—you saw his terror. Even the Devourer doesn't evoke such fear."

"Then we have to find out who his master was."

"How do we do that? Do we start telling royal ministers, high priests, and our friends we think the queen was murdered?"

"Dangerous?" Kysen asked.

"Extremely. I wouldn't wager on our chances of living out the year."

"Then what do we do?"

Meren rested his chin on his fist and thought for a while. Then he said, "Paser's death was an accident, as was Wah's. He tripped while we were showing him how to spar with a dagger."

"Two accidents on the same day?"

"Everyone knows it's a miracle Paser's stupidity hasn't killed him before now. As for Wah, people may suspect there's more to his death, but no one will challenge us. After all, he was going to marry Idut, so we had no reason to want him dead. I know there will be talk, but nothing can be proved. If we say nothing, the rumors will die for lack of nourishment."

"There's little choice, I suppose."

"Keep silent about the queen's death, Ky. One word could get us both killed."

"You're just going to leave it?"

"No, but we have to be careful. This matter is intricate. We don't know why Nefertiti was killed, much less who commanded it and who benefited." Meren touched Kysen's arm. "We don't even know if Ay knows the truth."

"If he did, wouldn't he have searched out Wah and killed him?"

Meren hesitated, wondering whether to voice his own suppositions. "He may already have discovered and dealt with the one who commanded Wah . . ." The less Kysen knew, the safer he'd be. "Yes, most likely you're right. He doesn't know."

"So we're left with a tale of lies," Kysen said. "Sennefer killed Anhai, then killed himself?"

"Yes."

Lifting a brow, Kysen said, "The story will please Idut."

"But not Nebetta and Hepu. However, I suspect they will be anxious to keep secret Sennefer's impotence. Remorse over accidental death makes a better explanation than admitting your son was cursed by the gods and less than a man."

They lapsed into an easy silence broken only by the sounds of Reia and the men working outside.

"Father, how much danger is there?"

Meren sighed. "A great deal. In the last years of Akhenaten's reign, many factions vied for power. There were those who tried to use the king by professing devotion to the Aten, and those who suffered because he wouldn't support our foreign allies and vassals. And there were some who decried Nefertiti's influence, either because she failed to stop him from casting out the old gods or because she refused to use her power to enrich them. She also protected and favored Tutankhamun, may he live forever."

"And if we make inquiries about Wah?"

"If we're clumsy, we could be inviting death. I'll have to think about this carefully to decide upon a course." Meren rose. "Meanwhile, there seems to be no threat to the haunted temple, but we've still the family to deal with."

"Shall I find out what happened to Ra?"

"Yes, and I'm going back to the house. I'll have to write letters accounting for these deaths and send the bodies to the families. Gods, Ky, I think I would have gotten more rest at pharaoh's side than I have in my own home."

"I tried to warn you."

Meren left *Wings of Horus* and walked slowly back to the villa. Although it was still morning, waves of heat rippled up at him from the baking earth. Zar would sulk when he beheld Meren's disheveled state. His kilt was splotched with blood, and his legs were splattered with mud. Meren trudged through the gate past an aged doorkeeper, intent on bathing before he faced Idut and the others.

Unfortunately, a phalanx of relatives waited for him on the loggia, barring the front door. Everyone except Ra seemed to be there. Meren paused to survey the group, then mounted the steps. A walking stick was thrust in his path, knocking against his shin.

"So, boy, you've returned at last," Cherit said as she withdrew her stick and settled back in her carrying chair. "Come here and explain all this absurd running about. Have you decided to accuse your own brother of murder?"

"No, Aunt."

"Injustice!" Hepu loomed over Meren, his bulk expanding with righteous indignation. "I know you've been to Green Palm and found those who implicate Ra in my son's death."

Cherit whacked Hepu's arm with her stick. "Shut your teeth and let Meren explain."

Meren looked around the group. Idut was gazing at him, startled. Behind her Isis and Bener fidgeted. Isis looked eager, as if she expected to enjoy the impending confrontation, while Bener's avid expression was tempered by apprehension. Nebetta wore her now-habitual air of sorrow mixed with condemnation. Refusing to meet her accusatory stare, Meren faced Hepu instead.

"Uncle, I would have a word with you and Nebetta."

He walked to the end of the loggia and stood beside a column. Looking injured and hostile, the two joined him.

"Not long ago," Meren said to Hepu, "you made a curious remark when I spoke of Sennefer's dealings with women. You said he didn't seduce them, and then you said that it wasn't possible for him. I remembered being confused by your choice of words."

"My son was a man of honor—"

"Let me finish. Certain knowledge has come to me that makes plain your meaning. Sennefer was impotent, wasn't he?"

Nebetta gasped. "What lie is this?"

Hepu's chest swelled, and he directed a furnacelike stare at Meren. "Who speaks such calumny? Is it Ra? He has good reason to lie."

The two began to yammer, causing Meren's head to pound. He'd had his fill of hypocrisy and blame. Filling his lungs, he let out a roar that rivaled any Hepu had ever emitted.

"Be silent!"

Nebetta squawked and clutched her husband's arm. Hepu worked his jaw, but no sound came out.

Meren continued in a lowered tone. "I know the truth about Sennefer. Out of respect I refuse to speak of the— the misfortune from which he suffered, and I'll remain silent. This is what I've discovered."

He told them of Anhai's accidental death, then called upon his skills in dissembling to create the tale of Sennefer's remorse and suicide. He hated lying, but could think of no other way to conceal the dangerous truth. As he spoke, he saw understanding wake in the faces of his aunt and uncle.

"This is terrible," Nebetta said.

"Unendurable," Hepu moaned.

"I know it's a tragedy," Meren began.

Hepu reddened. "What will people think?"

"The disgrace. Everyone we know will find out. What are we going to do, husband?"

Meren waited for a few moments, then left the two to plan their strategy. If he had to listen much longer, he would be tempted to shove a wad of Instructions down Hepu's throat. He returned to Aunt Cherit and gave the family the tale of Anhai's death and her husband's, without mentioning Sennefer's impotence. Then he announced Wah's mishap and dealt with Idut's confusion and sorrow. By the time he'd finished, he longed to bathe and obtain some draught for the ache in his head.

"But, Father," Bener said. "Wah was running away. I saw him."

"You were mistaken."

"But he . . ." Bener's words faded as she met the glare he turned on her.

"Bener, Isis, come with me to the hall. I want to speak to you."

When they entered the central hall, serving women appeared bearing a jar of beer, cups, and strainers. He took a cup and dismissed the servants. Alone with his daughters, Meren drained his cup. Then he handed the empty vessel to Bener.

"He was running away, wasn't he?" she asked.

Isis sniffed. "How do you know?"

"Because he climbed a tree and galloped over the fields as if a Hittite army was after him, Mistress Doubt-all."

"Cease this chattering," Meren snapped. "Bener, never again will you chase after someone you think might be a killer, or anyone else for that matter. Am I understood?"

"But I was trying to help."

"And could have gotten yourself killed!"

"I was right," Bener said, beaming at him. "He was the guilty one."

"You're not to speak of matters that are none of your concern."

"She thinks everything is her concern," Isis said.

Meren fixed Bener with a stare that wilted her defiance.

"You're not going to explain?" she asked.

"I've already done that, just now."

"Oh, that." Bener and Isis exchanged glances. "We know when you're performing like a player in a festival drama."

For their own protection he had to silence them. Summoning the air of derisive authority he'd used on some impudent recruits, he said, "If I wanted to deceive you, I assure you I would have done it without detection. However, I'm not accustomed to having my words doubted, and I'll hear no more, or I'll be forced to deal with your disobedience. Now go. I'm sure your aunt is in need of aid in conducting the affairs of the household."

They left him, dissatisfied but compliant, although Meren was certain they wouldn't be for long. He took refuge in his chambers and tried to allow Zar's ministrations to ease the pain in his head and the disquiet within his ka. The mystery of a long-dead queen threatened his peace, but the prospect of facing Ra and Bentanta disturbed him almost as much. His misery reached new heights when Karoya suddenly appeared in his bedchamber as he was slipping on a pair of dyed leather sandals. He looked up at the royal bodyguard and cursed.

"By all the gods of Egypt, you had better have come alone."

Karoya never changed his impassive expression. "I have. I come as royal messenger."

"Good. Then you bear a letter?"

"No." Karoya glanced at Zar and the two other servants who had attended Meren's dressing.

"Leave me," Meren said.

When the servants had gone, Meren lifted a brow at Karoya. The Nubian planted his feet apart and lifted his gaze to the ceiling while he recited.

"Horus, Strong-Bull-Arisen-in-Thebes, Enduring-in-Kingship-like-Ra-in-Heaven, Mighty-in-Strength, Majestic-in-Appearance, King of Upper and Lower Egypt, Lord of the Two Lands, Nebkheprure Tutankhamun, given life forever, saith thus: At the command of my majesty, the new houses of eternity have been prepared. All is in readiness. Lo, my majesty commands the attendance of the Lord Meren in Memphis that we may take counsel for the disposition of thy charge."

"This is awfully soon," Meren said.

"The son of Ra commanded speed, and it was done," came the serene reply.

"Very well. I hear the command of pharaoh, may he live forever. His will is accomplished. Will you rest and take refreshment?"

"I am commanded to return at once."

"Then may Amun protect you on your journey."

Karoya left, and Zar reappeared, carrying a transparent overrobe, then proceeded to load Meren down with a broad collar of turquoise, ivory, and bronze beads, a heavy beaded belt, and a decorative dagger. Too weary to protest, Meren waited until the dagger had been shoved into his belt. Waving aside the inlaid bronze bracelets Zar proffered, he left his chambers, intent on making an official record of events. This he would present to Ay personally so that it could be lodged in the office of the vizier. He would have to be vigilant at court when Wah's death was announced, send out orders to his various agents and close friends to watch for any sign of interest. He was crossing the central hall on his way to the stairs that led to his office when he heard a familiar voice.

"There you are!" Ra called as he entered the hall, flanked by the charioteer Simut and another guard.

Behind him came Kysen, supporting an aged woman who took three steps for every one of her escort's. Ra marched over to Meren ahead of his guards. He planted himself with feet apart, arms folded across his chest, and gave Meren a contemptuous look that started at his carefully groomed head and ended at his gilded sandals.

"Where have you been?" Meren demanded.

"To Green Palm," Ra said bitterly, "to prove my innocence before you tried me for murder. But you won't be able to carry out your evil plan." Ra stepped aside to make way for Kysen and the old woman. His arms swept out, indicating the two, and he glared at Meren as he burst out loudly, "I'm innocent, and—"

"I know."

"This is Sheftu's grandmother, who is a wise woman— What?"

"I said, I know you're innocent."

"But you've kept me prisoner!"

"Forgive me," Meren said, feeling heat creep up his neck to his face. "I was mistaken. Sennefer killed himself in remorse." He explained the accident that caused Anhai's death while Ra listened with a dazed expression.

"But how do you know?" Ra asked.

Not wanting to mention Bentanta without privacy, Meren fell to studying the design on one of his bracelets.

"Hepu has agreed that this is what happened. Now why have you brought this woman to me?"

"Nedjmet is a wise woman, Meren. Many villages consult her on matters of truth and controversy. She has given testimony of the manifestation of gods that has solved cases of theft, disappearance, and rape. I asked her to help. Tell the Lord Meren what you know, Nedjmet."

Nedjmet had been listening with a hand cupped to her ear and her neck craning toward the speakers. She squinted at Ra, then tried to lower herself to the floor, but Kysen stopped her.

"Respected elder," Meren said. "What have you to tell me?"

Nedjmet held up a finger. Its joints were swollen, the skin cracked, but it was steady. "Great lord, I am Nedjmet, a *rekhet*, a knowing one. Thy brother has come to me seeking testimony that he was in my house late on the night of the feast of rejoicing, and into the early morning. This I cannot do, for I slept without hearing anything that night. But a manifestation of the goddess Maat came to me when Lord Nakht entered my dwelling and asked for my help. Maat, goddess of truth, is with thy brother. His ka is untouched by the sin of murder."

"There," Ra said in triumph. "You see?"

Meren clasped his hands behind his back, lowered his head, and walked back and forth. It was well known that the gods manifested themselves to people in situations of great import. Once he'd seen a man swear his innocence in the matter of a theft, only to recant when visited with a manifestation that struck him blind. Knowing ones in villages throughout Egypt served as intermediaries between humble Egyptians and the gods, dispensing wisdom and aiding in judgments. It was a comfort that he had this additional testament to Ra's honor.

"I am grateful for your help, knowing one. The wisdom of Amun already has revealed the truth of my cousin's death. However, this manifestation is a further sign of my brother's innocence. Kysen, have someone take the respected elder home, and tell Kasa that Nedjmet and her granddaughter are to be provided with a regular portion of grain and beer."

The old woman bowed repeatedly as Kysen backed away from Meren and guided her out of the hall. The charioteers followed, leaving Meren alone with Ra. He met his brother's accusing gaze, feeling like a criminal watching his miserable heart weigh down the feather of truth on the celestial balance scales before the gods. Forcing himself to speak, he told Ra the official version of the murders.

"Damn you, Meren. You wanted me to be guilty."

"I didn't. I know you, Ra. If you'd discovered that Anhai was using you . . . Don't you see? You could have wanted revenge against them both, and you made things worse for yourself by refusing to be clear and honest with me."

"I should have known you would blame me for your mistakes."

"No, no, I don't. I was wrong. I suspected the worst of you." Meren drew closer to Ra, who maintained his rigid stance and scowled at him. "But I never stopped trying to find another explanation for these deaths. Do you think I'd have done that if I hadn't wanted to absolve you?"

Ra's scowl faded a bit. "I suppose not."

"I have asked for forgiveness, brother. Will you bestow it?"

"The mighty Lord Meren, Friend of the King, is asking my forgiveness? I should sacrifice an ox in honor of this day. Oh, don't glower at me. I'll forgive you if you'll get me appointed captain of charioteers."

"Gods, Ra, don't you ever learn?"

Ra turned on his heel with a smirk. "I knew you didn't

feel that guilty. I'm going home, brother. Don't invite me to your next feast of rejoicing."

Retreating to his office, Meren tried not to think of the ruins into which his relationship with Ra had fallen. Since most of his men were busy elsewhere, he sent to Kasa for a scribe to take down his report for the vizier. To his surprise, the boy Nu arrived with a scribe's palette slung over his shoulder.

"What are you doing here? I need a scribe."

Nu bowed low. "Master Kasa sent me because I'm faster and more accurate than his sons, lord."

"Is that so?" Meren said. "We'll see."

Nu sat on the floor and took out his writing supplies. Meren plunged into the formal address of the report without pausing. When he reached the end of the long salutation, he stopped. Nu kept writing for a moment, then dipped his rush pen in fresh black ink and waited. Frowning, Meren walked over to gaze down at the papyrus stretched over Nu's crossed legs. The address was perfect. The cursive hieroglyphs were clear, the words accurate.

"You're talented for one so young," Meren said.

"The lord is generous."

"I must find some post for you where your skills can be honed. You're wasted in a country house."

Nu flushed with pleasure, and Meren gave him a slight smile. He intended to find a post that would keep him busy for a decade and in a place far away from his daughter. Perhaps he wouldn't care. Service to the viceroy of Kush, far to the south in Nubia, would be most appropriate for Nu.

A knock interrupted him as he began to dictate again. At his response, Bentanta came into the room alone. Meren stuttered over a phrase, then hesitated.

"Leave us, Nu."

"That isn't necessary," Bentanta said. "I came only to tell you I'm going home."

"Leave," Meren said to the boy, who was already on his feet. When they were alone, Meren offered Bentanta a chair, but she refused.

"You could have told me you'd solved Sennefer's murder instead of sending a servant to tell me I was free. And I had to get the tale of Sennefer's death from Idut," Bentanta said.

"Forgive me. I was distracted."

"You were ashamed."

He looked at her wordlessly. That familiar feeling of annoyance he often experienced in her presence was growing again.

"And I hear Wah is dead of an accident. Such a number of mishaps. One is tempted to suspect them when they come in so great a quantity."

"I ask your forgiveness," Meren said as he stooped to pick up the unfinished report. "I'm sure you can see that my conclusions were reasonable, given what we knew."

"Oh, of course. Quite reasonable, but you're a greater fool than I thought if you expect me to believe this tale of suicide."

Pretending to peruse the report, Meren said lightly, "People seldom question my judgment."

"That, my lord, has had a noxious effect on your character."

Lowering the report, Meren asked, "Are you here to take your leave or to quarrel?"

Bentanta alarmed him by closing the distance between them and taking the papyrus from his hands.

"You're in retreat," she said, tapping his arm with the papyrus. "Routed and on guard against attack. Don't you realize I didn't want you to know about Djet any more than you wished to be told? Do you think I wanted to be dragged here to expose my foolish mistake, one of which

I'm ashamed? We should find some way to measure mortification to see whose is greater."

Meren snatched the report from Bentanta and walked away from her. "I can't speak of this now."

"All I want is your assurance that you'll stop trying to find ways to be rid of me in order to save yourself pain."

"You think I'd accuse you of a crime for such a reason? Why would you need consolation from my cousin for, for . . ."

"Don't confuse the past with the present, Meren."

"Don't confuse what I do as the Eyes of Pharaoh with my private actions."

"We haven't spoken privately, not about Djet."

He waited, but she didn't continue. Keeping his back to her, he said, "Go home, Bentanta. There's nothing for us to discuss."

"Merciful gods, you really would rather face a horde of nomad bandits unarmed than—"

Turning quickly, he faced her with his courtier's impassive mask in place. "Please don't force me to be any more discourteous than I have already been."

She met his gaze with a gasp of exasperation, then stalked out of the room. The last thing he heard was her voice sailing to him from the stairwell.

"Coward!"

Kysen came in, staring over his shoulder in the direction of her voice. He didn't comment.

"Nento is hiding on the barge and refuses to return to the haunted temple."

Fighting an onslaught of confused emotions he didn't want to face, Meren finally responded. "What? Oh yes— well, we won't be using the temple much longer. I've just received word from pharaoh."

"Nento will be overjoyed. You're distracted. Is something wrong?"

"No. Nothing. Help me with these reports, Ky, and

then I must go to Memphis. I'm going to take the girls with me. They're too much for Idut."

"Too clever, you mean."

Meren collapsed in a chair and sighed. "Do you know I'm more weary now than when I arrived here for a rest? Interfering relatives are far more dangerous than ordinary murderers and spies."

"They're tolerable separately, Father, just not all at once."

Meren picked up a royal letter from a stack on the table beside his chair. His eye caught a passage mentioning his promise to take the king on a raid, and he groaned. Pinching the bridge of his nose, he thought for a few moments, then sat up and slapped the arm of his chair.

"Ky, fetch those acrobats from the feast, and we'll leave at once, before Aunt Cherit can find me and have that long talk she's been wanting."

"And what am I to do with the musicians and singers and acrobats?"

"They're coming with us." Meren swept his arm across the table piled with correspondence, sending the letters tumbling to the floor. "We're going to have a feast, a sailing feast on *Wings of Horus*. Not with the pests Idut thinks I should invite, but with those who know the true meaning of the word rejoice."

Kysen gave a loud whoop. "At last. It's been months since you gave one of your entertainments. Maya spoke to me about it before we left Thebes. Said the whole court was complaining."

"Maya has a fondness for singers. We'll send for him too," Meren said as he kicked his way through scattered papyri to find a clean sheet on which to write. "And I'll tell him to bring lots of pomegranate wine. I've acquired a taste for pomegranate wine."

"Oh?"

At Kysen's tone, Meren turned to smile at him. "Only the wine, damn you. Only the wine."

If you enjoyed this Lord Meren mystery,
you won't want to miss

EATER OF SOULS
by Lynda S. Robinson

Read on for a glimpse into
Lynda S. Robinson's latest exciting combination
of mystery and historical fiction . . .

Memphis, Year Five of the Reign of the Pharaoh
Tutankhamun

She could smell the darkness. Night in the land of the
living was a feeble imitation of the obsidian nothingness
that possessed her own lair, yet she could smell the darkness. Lifting her hard, jutting snout, she sucked in the
textured scents—waters of the Nile, mud and refuse from
the docks nearby, the faint smell of dung mixed with fish
and smoke from a thousand dying oven fires.

The snout whipped around at the sound of a flute, a
shriek of drunken laughter from the beer house. A claw
scraped over the cracked mud brick of a wall, long,
curved, with a honed blade-edge as sharp as a physician's knife. It snaked back into the shelter of the alley at
the sudden appearance of light.

Several of the living approached. Eyes with daggered
pupils observed the strangers. Rapid, guttural chattering
made her wince. Foreigners—in rank, unclean wool
robes smelling of beer and sex. Bearing the torch that had
assaulted her eyes, they stumbled past and swerved to
disappear down the street.

Snorting to rid herself of the stench, she returned her attention to the beer house across the street. One of its wooden shutters was loose and warped, allowing light from within to escape and casting rippled shadows on the packed earth of the road. A larger group burst from the interior, arguing, giggling, swaying to the beat of a sailing song. Men from the docks. Of no interest, no relevance.

She grunted with impatience, something she never experienced below. But the evil one had been in the beer house since dusk. Leaning against the chipped plaster of the wall, she rubbed her haunches against the rough surface, scraping more chips of plaster off the surface with her rough hide. All grew quiet again, and the light from the beer house began to dim as someone quenched the lamps. Far away, in the palace district, a hound howled. At an even greater distance, out in the western desert, land of the dead, hyenas yipped and squealed.

The brittle wooden door of the beer tavern swung open again. She turned a yellow eye and saw, at last, the evil one. He was a small man, as befit his place among the living. A humble farmer with cracked, sun-baked skin, splayed, dirty feet and three cracked teeth. This was the one who had offended, had transgressed in so callous a manner that she had heard the cry of injustice from below.

She sniffed the air again and caught the scent of a decayed ka, the soul of the evil one. The farmer came toward her. He would use the alley to cross this district of taverns and beer houses on his way to the skiff he'd left at the dock. As he marched unsteadily toward her, she felt the sudden burning rush of power spiced with anticipation. It boiled through her like rolling thunderclouds.

Slinking back into the deepest blackness, she crouched on her hind legs. Heavy, irregular footsteps announced the farmer's approach. And over the sound of his tread she heard that for which she'd been listening all night. The steady, dull th-thud, th-thud, th-thud. The voice of the heart. It grew louder and louder, provoking her, taunting her, invading her skull and battering its low vault. Just as the noise threatened to shatter the bones of her head, she sprang out of the blackness and landed behind the farmer.

He turned and tottered, his mouth agape, his eyelids climbing to his brows. He had time for a rattling little screech before she bashed him in the head. The man flew backward and smacked into the hard earth. The moment he lay flat, she lunged, her forearm drawn back, claws spread wide. They cut through the air, impaled flesh and sliced, severing the farmer's throat. Drawing back, she shook her claw deftly to rid it of blood and stringy tissue while the farmer gurgled and stared up into a long, rigid maw studded with yellow fangs.

She listened for that last escaping breath. Once it issued from the body, she stooped over the farmer once more—to do what had been decreed, what she existed to do, what was righteous, what this evil deserved.

EATER OF SOULS
by Lynda S. Robinson

Published by Ballantine Books.
Coming soon to your local bookstore.